# FIRST LIGHT

A LOU THORNE THRILLER

KORY M. SHRUM

This book is a work of fiction. Any references to historical events, real people, or real places have been used fictitiously. Other names, characters, places, and incidents are the product of the author's imagination. Any resemblance to actual persons, living or dead, business establishments, events, or locales is entirely coincidental.

No part of this book shall be reproduced or transmitted in any form or by any means without prior written permission of the publisher. Although every precaution has been taken in preparation of the book, the publisher and the author assume no responsibility for errors or omissions. Neither is any liability assumed for damages resulting from the use of information contained in this book or its misuse.

All rights reserved.

Copyright © 2024 by Kory M. Shrum
Cover design by Christian Bentulan
Editing by Toby Selwyn

ISBN: 978-1-949577-73-0

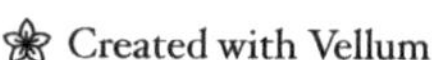 Created with Vellum

# AN EXCLUSIVE OFFER FOR YOU

Connecting with my readers is the best part of my job as a writer. One way that I like to connect is by sending 2-3 newsletters a month with a subscribers-only giveaway, free stories from your favorite series, and personal updates (read: pictures of my dog).

When you first sign up for the mailing list, I send you at least three free stories right away. If free stories and exclusive giveaways sound like something you're interested in, please look for the special offer in the back of this book.

Happy reading,

Kory M. Shrum

*For Max*
*who has taught me that love lost*
*can always be found again*

$$1$$

Piper Genereux stood in the entryway of the emergency room, heart hammering in her chest, hands fisting her pale hair. She was torn in several directions at once. King and Melandra lay on stretchers as separate teams pushed them away from the ambulance deloading zone, deeper into the hospital.

Piper watched them go, feeling helpless, frozen in place.

*Please let them be okay. Please. God. Please.*

Piper didn't know how her prayer could be answered. She'd seen the blood. Seen the way Mel and King had dropped one after the other. The screaming. The slick, clasped hands as they'd done their best to protect themselves from the onslaught that'd kept coming.

Lou's piercing cry broke through Piper's paralyzing fear and spiraling thoughts, forcing her to look away from Mel's and King's retreating forms.

Lou's bed was traveling down the adjacent hallway. Piper caught sight of her just before the bed cut a corner and was rolled out of sight, pushed by the emergency personnel flanking it.

"Come on," Dani said. She grabbed Piper's hand, now sticky with drying blood, and pulled her forward. Piper's shaking legs resisted, trembling from adrenaline and overuse.

"But Mel—"

"We can't help them, but we can help Lou," Dani said. Her eyes were as wide as saucers, the shock showing in her dilated pupils, her breath just as strained and shallow as Piper's. Blood was drying on her face too. Her collar was soaked red with it. But she was up and moving. Piper was beyond grateful for that. It had almost gone very differently for the both of them.

Lou screamed her name again.

"I'm coming!" Piper called out.

Piper and Dani pushed past the throng of bodies crowding the corridor and made their way to Louie's side. They caught up with the bed and the emergency crew, realizing as they approached that they must be heading for the elevator at the end of the corridor. There wasn't really anywhere else for Lou's bed to go.

"What's happening?" Dani demanded. "What's the plan?"

The nurse only glanced at them. "Are you family or next of kin because HIPAA—"

"Yes," Lou growled.

"Sorry," the nurse said. "We just need your permission to share medical information with—"

"*Yes.* Tell them—" Lou hissed through grit teeth as another contraction washed over her. "Tell them whatever the hell you need to tell them."

"Fourth floor," the doctor barked, and one of the attendants mashed the elevator buttons.

The bell dinged and the doors opened. Everyone piled in. Piper and Dani pressed themselves up against the far wall, doing their best to stay out of the way.

"You still haven't told us what you're planning to do,"

Dani pressed. "You must have a procedure for a woman in labor who's been shot."

Once the elevator doors closed, the nurse said, "We're taking her up to surgical. They're prepping for the C-section and—"

"No," Louie said. "I don't want a C-section. She's coming."

"You've lost a lot of blood and the delivery will only—" the emergency room doctor began, but Lou cut him off.

"*No.*" Lou pulled her gun.

*Damn she's fast. Even lookin' like a mess she's fast.* Piper marveled at how fluid the movement had been. It was terrifying, sure. Even though Lou would never point a gun at her, it was still scary as hell to see that look on her face. That look made Piper believe that Lou wouldn't hesitate to pull the trigger.

Everyone stepped back, pressing themselves against the elevator's walls. Everyone except Dani and Piper, who were too exhausted from the night they'd just survived to view this as a real threat. Still, Piper felt horrible for the medical personnel once she saw the fear in their eyes. It was real terror.

"Lou, they're just trying to help Elena," Piper said. "Take a breath, man."

"If they paralyze my legs I can't go get him." Lou kept the gun pointed at the closest doctor, but her gaze flicked to Piper. "I *need* my legs functional."

*Fuck. Not this again.* "Lou—"

"He's *dying.*"

Piper ran a hand through her hair again. What the hell could she say to talk Lou down from this suicide mission? She looked down at her in the bed, soaked in blood that was at least half her own, and knew the answer.

Absolutely nothing.

She tried anyway. "I know you want to save him but—"

"I can go back—"

"Lou—"

"I *can*. I can go back. It's *her*. I know it's her." Lou gritted her teeth again as another contraction washed over her. They were definitely closer together. What was that? Two minutes apart? Less than two minutes?

"Get her *out*," Lou moaned. "Get her out and I'm gone."

Piper turned to the doctors. "How close is she?"

"Ma'am, we can't help you with a gun in our faces."

Lou handed her gun to Dani. This gesture was for show, of course. After what Piper had seen tonight, she knew that Lou didn't need a gun to kill people.

Immediately, Lou slid into another contraction.

The nurse at Piper's arm looked concerned, her eyebrows raised high. "We should check her dilation."

"Then *check*," Lou ground out. Dani took Lou's free hand and squeezed it. "You can do this, Louie. This is nothing. What's pushing out a baby compared to what just happened?"

An ice pick of pain stabbed Piper behind the eyes.

*Don't think of that now*, she warned herself. After the night they'd just had, she had to save what little strength and will she had left to clean up this shitshow of a mess.

"We can't check how dilated she is until we get her clothes off of her." Then, as if motivated by the scowl twisting Lou's face, she added, "Sorry."

The doctor hit a button on the elevator and the doors opened. "General delivery is on this floor. If we're not going up to surgery, we have to get off here."

They pushed her bed out of the elevator first and into a dark room that lit upon entry.

"Only one of you can be in here," the doctor said. "As the support person."

Lou hissed as another contraction seized her.

"One of you step out, please," the doctor insisted. "It's regulation."

"Pretty sure guns are also against regulation," Lou said.

But Dani was already stepping out of the room.

"Don't go," Piper pleaded. "I'm not baby-welcoming material."

"I want to get updates on Mel and King. I'll be right back, I promise. You've got this. Don't let her break anyone's fingers. Including yours."

Dani came up on her toes and gave Piper a rushed kiss.

Piper let her go because she knew that Dani was as desperate to see if Mel and King would pull through this as she was. But if Lou really intended to pop this baby out and bail, Piper didn't want to be the sole adult left in charge here. She wasn't even ready to hold a baby.

"I'll be right here." Dani gave Piper's hand a reassuring squeeze, then ducked back into the elevator, the doors closing between them.

Piper turned back in time to see the nurse cut away the last of Lou's bloody clothes as a second helped get a hospital gown on her naked body.

"Please lay back and we'll see how close you are," the doctor said. Tension had visibly left his body now that the gun was no longer in Lou's hand.

"She's coming," Lou ground out as her abdomen contracted again.

"Do we got a ring of fire?" Piper asked. She'd read about the ring of fire. Absolutely terrifying.

"Yes!" Lou screamed.

"Oh, well...uh..." Piper wasn't sure what to do in her role as *support* person. Lou wasn't exactly the handholding type under the best of circumstances. She didn't think it was in her best interests to put her hand in that vise grip.

"You're doing great," Piper said weakly from the side of the bed.

Lou scowled at her.

"Really," Piper said. "We're alive, aren't we? For now, anyway."

Because there was more than one moment tonight when Piper had been certain that none of them would make it.

"Not everyone," Lou said. And of course Piper knew what she meant.

Konstantine wasn't here. And while Piper was touched that she was the one to share this moment with Lou, she did so knowing that she wasn't her first choice.

But Konstantine's absence was a problem that Piper couldn't worry about right now. Their own problems were too pressing.

"She's coming," Lou cried again, pressing her head back on the pillow, her back arching slightly. She grabbed Piper's hand and squeezed.

Pain shot up Piper's arm. "Ow, ow, ow, *owwww*."

Graciously, Lou released her, and Piper couldn't move her crushed fingers.

"Actually, she is," the doctor agreed. "She's crowning now. Tabitha?"

"Yes, Dr. Sloan." A nurse in a face mask rushed to prepare a small table off to one side. Piper didn't know what any of the instruments that Tabitha was so quickly arranging *did*, but she suspected that they would be needed for the baby once she was out.

Piper turned her gaze away at the last second so that she didn't accidentally glimpse Lou's vagina as the doctor lifted the blanket to do—whatever the hell it was that doctors did in delivery.

She loved her best friend, but that wasn't an image she needed burned into her retinas.

"Now when I say, we're going to begin pushing," the doctor said.

"Tell me what to do again and I'm going to *push you* off a bridge," Lou said through gritted teeth.

The doctor's face was losing color. Piper couldn't blame him. Even she had to find the courage to return to Lou's side and take one of her shoulders reassuringly.

"It's almost done," she said. "Let's get through this without killing anyone else, okay?"

Piper said this not because she believed that Lou actually needed encouragement but to refrain from saying anything stupid herself.

*Does having a literal human explode from your body hurt?*

*Are you going to be okay?*

These questions felt like something an amateur would ask. Besides, she already knew the answers. Of course it hurt, and of course Lou was going to pull through. When it came to Louie Thorne, there was little she couldn't endure.

At the moment, Lou seemed more pissed off than in pain, and that was actually scarier.

Then there was still the matter of what Lou had said.

Was she really going to go back into the fray so close on the heels of giving birth?

Yes. Probably.

Piper knew how she felt about losing Konstantine. Once upon a time it would have filled Piper with no small amount of jealousy, Lou's loyalty to her Italian stallion.

But it wasn't about that now. It was the fact that Lou wasn't at her best. Her body was a wreck, and her power was failing her. That seemed like the worst possible combination for going up against some mafia boss.

Piper gave Lou's shoulder another squeeze. "It's almost over. Just keep breathing and—"

Relief broke across Lou's face as she fell back against her

pillow. All the tension in the shoulder under Piper's hand released.

"Here we are," the doctor said. "Look at that. It's a girl."

"Is she all right?" Lou worked to catch her breath. "Did she get hurt?"

No one answered.

Piper turned toward the nurse to see what was wrong, but her back was to them. Whatever they were doing around the table was all-encompassing.

"Now the placenta," someone said. "We need you to give us one more big push and—"

"Is my daughter okay?" Lou screamed.

Piper's stomach twisted in on itself, her head light with fear. Then there was the smell. A musky, animalistic smell of blood and flesh had filled the room, mixing unharmoniously with the scent of antiseptics.

"Piper—"

"Hold on." Piper still couldn't see what was happening with the baby. "Just give them a minute."

Piper knew this could go either way.

At least two bullets were still lodged in Lou's body. She didn't think the belly had taken a direct hit, but she'd read somewhere that the amount of force that a body absorbs when shot could be enough to kill something as fragile as a newborn on impact.

"Piper—" Lou's voice cracked, and Piper's heart with it.

"Just wait. It could just be—" But Piper didn't know how to finish that sentence.

It could just be devastation. A total loss.

A stillbirth.

"It's—" Piper reached for something to say but the words wouldn't come.

Then Elena cried. A soft, choked whimper that gave way to a furious roar.

Lou's relief was palpable, and Piper rode it like a wave.

"She's fine," Piper said, feeling as if someone had just taken a hand off her throat. "She's fine."

The doctor laid Elena on Lou's chest. "There was a block-age. It happens sometimes."

"She didn't get hurt?" Piper asked.

"No," the nurse reassured her. "Ten fingers, ten toes, and she looks as pretty as a picture to me."

Despite her best efforts, Piper began to cry fat, ugly tears.

Here was this cone-headed, slimy raisin of a creature slick with Lou's gore, and yet Piper had never been so happy for someone in her life.

"She's beautiful," Lou said, her face the picture of pure bliss.

"She's something," Piper said, unwilling to lie. And they both barked a short spray of laughter.

"Shut up, she's perfect."

"Yeah, she is," Piper said. "I'm so glad she made it."

And to Piper's surprise, she caught sight of the tears standing out in Lou's eyes before they spilt over her lashes and down her cheeks.

"You did it," Piper said. She took Lou's bloody hand and gave it a gentle squeeze. "You got her here in one piece. Good job, Mama."

Wow, that was weird, and would take some getting used to. But it was true. Lou was a mother. She had brought an actual tiny human into the world.

Several moments passed, the bliss dissipating like mist while the medical personnel rushed about, taking away bloody sheets and doing something to the machines.

Then the moment broke. Piper felt it like a bubble bursting.

"I have to go," Lou said, the momentary happiness draining from her face.

"Come on. Don't do that." Piper didn't want this moment to end. "Don't go."

It was a miracle that Lou was holding her daughter at all. And the ordeal might still take King's and Mel's lives before the night was over. It might even take Lou's if she went back.

Lou placed a kiss on Elena's head. "I don't want to go. But I have to."

Piper sensed her imminent departure.

"Please don't—" Piper said. What could she possibly say to keep Lou here? Lying through her teeth, she went for, "He's probably fine. He's got his people and—"

But it was too late. Lou was putting Elena in her arms and pushing herself up out of the hospital bed. "Oh shit. Hey, wait. Just *wait*."

"Ma'am, we can't advise that you move just yet. You're still bleeding and—"

Their panic mirrored Piper's own. Two of the nurses tried to grab on to Lou and restrain her, but she threw them off easily. It was no use.

Even in her state, Lou was the strongest one in the room.

"I'll be back, I promise," she said.

And it took Piper a minute to realize Lou wasn't promising her.

She was promising Elena.

This was confirmed when Lou added, "I have to go get your father."

Piper didn't want the last moment she spent with her best friend to be with her holding her newborn daughter, begging her not to go get herself killed.

"Please be careful," Piper said. The words were a prayer. The words were a plea with the universe, God, whoever was in charge. "Please don't die on me. I can't do this."

Because there was a baby in her arms. A newborn baby. And she was *so* tiny, *so* fragile, and why in God's name was she in *her* arms. Piper's urge to yell at her friend, to demand that she come back and take this baby, Konstantine be damned, nearly overtook her.

"I'll be back as soon as I can be."

More nurses were running down the hallway. Someone must have paged them. If they tried to stop Lou from leaving, this was going to get ugly really quick.

"You better go before they sedate you," Piper said. "Hell, before *I* sedate you."

*I'm a good friend*, she told herself. *The best, actually. Look at me being supportive even when she's scaring the shit out of me.*

Piper didn't know if Lou had even heard her.

Lou gave her daughter one last desperate look and then bolted.

It would have been easier for Lou to duck into the room's adjacent bathroom and use the darkness collected there, but instead she crossed the hall to its mirroring twin.

Piper knew why.

Sure enough, the medical personnel followed, and Piper watched from the doorway as they turned on all the lights and searched the room only to discover that Lou was nowhere to be found. Eventually they decided that she must have gone down the hallway instead, toward the exits.

Dani still wasn't back.

Piper had hoped she could give her the baby, finding it more than a little terrifying to be holding something so precious and also so small.

Lou's gift had worked, at least. Maybe she did stand a chance of winning.

Assuming, that was, that her gift didn't fail her again.

There was nothing else for Piper to do but wait. Let the dust settle and then take stock of the damage.

"That leaves you and me, kid," Piper said, looking down at

the bundled infant in her arms. "It's *all* up to me to keep you safe until they come back. No pressure or anything."

*If they come back.*

*God, please let them come back.*

"We'll be okay. Don't worry." Piper tried to keep her tone light, in case babies could actually be affected by stress and fear in a voice. But despite her best efforts, she couldn't completely ease that feeling of dread that had clung to her since they'd climbed into the back of the ambulance, the five of them racing against the clock to the hospital.

Elena began to cry.

**2**

———

*Ten days earlier*

Louie Thorne was convinced that being heavily pregnant during the sweltering month of July was *definitely* one of the nine circles of hell. But a job was a job. And since Ettore Celesti made the mistake of crashing into their lives and threatening the people she cared about, Lou had made him her job.

So she had no choice but to ignore the throbbing headache behind her eyes, the aches in her back and the uncomfortable weight of her abdomen always pulling at her and focus on the men below as they made their rounds through the shipping yard.

Like mice in a maze, they traced the docks and cut paths between shipping containers.

Even from their hiding place, Lou could see they were tense, the tightness in their shoulders visible in those who passed just below them.

*Not that being ready for us will help you*, Lou thought.

She counted the guns she saw, measuring their capacity.

She sized each opponent up as they moved, unaware of her presence.

She enjoyed this feeling, that slight taste of their fear on her tongue and being close enough to strike whenever she wanted.

It delighted her even though killing these men wasn't personal.

It was their *capo*, Ettore, that she wanted.

The men on the docks were chess pieces she'd enjoy wiping clean from the board. And pieces are always sacrificed in every game of chance.

"How are you feeling, *amore mio?*" Konstantine asked from beside her.

He was hidden in the shadows of the container's roof, his body pressed flat in the groove between two ridges, moonlight sparking in his wet eyes.

"Fine," she said. It was what she'd said a lot these days, knowing that if she mentioned the headaches, backaches, or their daughter's constant restlessness, he would start fretting over her, something she could hardly stand.

No, she knew better than to complain to Konstantine, who would only insist that she was overdoing it. Beg her to rest. As if rest was something that they could afford in the middle of a war.

She just wished she could understand why pregnancy was the most physically miserable experience of her life. How could pregnancy possibly be worse than all the punches, kicks, stabbings, and gunshot wounds she'd endured? It was infuriatingly nonsensical.

*Karma*, she thought. *Lucy would tell me this is some sort of karma.*

Just the thought of her dead aunt was enough to make her throat tighten. A deep sense of melancholy and heartache washed over her.

Emotions. In excess, they truly were the worst thing about pregnancy. Lou was more excited to be rid of her mood swings than her physical discomfort. All this sentimentality was getting on her nerves.

"You look warm," he said. "Your temples are wet."

Her tenderness warped into fury instantly as she glared at him. How could he just lie beside her on the roof of this container, that doe-eyed look on his pretty face, and say something like that? Considering the situation, how did he *think* she was feeling?

"Do you need—" he began again.

"I'm *fine*," she said.

Stefano snorted beside them. *"Se fossi in te non le farei domande stupide."*

Konstantine reached over and began massaging the back of her neck.

Her irritation softened at its edges. His firm grasp made her corded muscles react to his touch.

"If you two keep distracting me, I'm never bringing you again," she said after several minutes had passed and Konstantine had withdrawn his hand.

"What did *I* do?" Stefano murmured. "You said look for his general, and I'm looking for him."

"You do not sense him at all?" Konstantine asked.

He really was cruising for a bruising, as her father would have said. Lou held her tongue as she cast her compass out across the dark, searching for Ettore and his general, Aldo. Ettore wasn't here. Lou searched the distance between them.

The more she softened into the darkness, the more she could hear the swell of voices and laughter. Ettore was somewhere bright. Lou could practically taste the sunshine on her tongue.

Elena stirred within her, as if in response to the light.

Lou felt her urge to go to Ettore now, a strong pull in the direction of all that warmth and sunshine.

*Sorry, kiddo*, she thought. *It's not safe for us there now.*

More and more these days she was convinced that her daughter reached for the light the way that Lou reached for the darkness. Lou recognized that pull well enough, the instinct and longing that came with it. And yet the flavor of it was different enough that she knew those particular impulses didn't belong to her.

She'd spoken about none of this with Konstantine yet. She thought it would be just one more thing for him to worry about, and she'd had more than enough of his overattentiveness.

"Ettore isn't here," she concluded, and turned her compass toward Ettore's general next. "But Aldo's close."

Her eyes flicked out over the water shining in the moonlight. The waves sparking with silver crests.

"I think that's his boat coming in," she said.

"Tell me when to give the signal," Stefano said.

"Not yet," Lou said. "Wait until he's on shore and they're distracted by his arrival. They'll be too focused on getting everything right to notice our movements."

"Good idea." Konstantine resumed his massage further down her back. "Have you done this before?"

Lou scoffed at his teasing. "Maybe once or twice."

The truth was that hunting Ettore the last few months reminded her of her early days. When she'd been consumed by her need for revenge and every waking moment had been dedicated to the eradication of the monsters who'd killed her parents. A slave to her drive to find and destroy not just Angelo, the man who'd pulled the trigger that took her father's life, but the entire Martinelli family, Fernando and all of his sons, one by one.

So much had changed in the years since.

What had developed between Lou and Konstantine, of course, had been a surprise. Losing Lucy, but also inducting Piper, King, Dani, and Melandra into her inner circle. How deeply she'd come to care for them. Even Stefano and the understanding that they shared a devotion to Konstantine's safety.

All the children in Konstantine's care.

In her mind, Lou could flip back and forth between the night she lay on a shipping container just like this one, searching the Baltimore harbor for the first signs of Angelo, and now, in nearly the same position but pregnant, with Konstantine and Stefano at her side.

Two nearly identical moments in time and yet they might as well have been alternate universes given how much her life had changed. Especially the differences she felt within herself.

She was stronger and more skilled in her hunts than ever. And yet she was more afraid than she'd ever been hunting the Martinellis. In the past, her fear—if she'd even felt fear—had been eclipsed completely by her need to be free of her pain.

Now—

*Because I have more to lose*, she thought.

*More to gain*, a voice countered. Her father's.

He might be dead, but he wasn't wrong.

It wasn't only that Lou was scared of something happening to Konstantine or her daughter. She was also afraid that the bright future she was just beginning to imagine for herself—a life filled with more love and light than she could have dreamed possible—would disintegrate before her eyes. That before it could fully materialize, another crime lord like Angelo Martinelli would step in and take everything. Again.

Just as the Martinellis had.

It seemed Ettore Celesti was hellbent on becoming that bastard.

Lou couldn't let that happen. Not only because she wanted that future for herself, for Konstantine, but because she *needed* it for their daughter, Elena.

*I can't fail.*

If Lou didn't eliminate this threat, then her daughter faced a future where she would grow up the way Lou had. She couldn't let that happen. Jack Thorne's inability to defeat the men hunting him and protect his family had left a father-sized hole in her heart.

Lou couldn't do that to Elena.

Konstantine and Stefano wanted revenge for what the Celesti had done to Stefano's family, dear Nario, and Konstantine's slain people. But Lou knew where her priorities lay—and what she was prepared to do to secure Elena's future.

Konstantine's hand stilled. "*Amore mio.* The tension in your—"

Lou held up her hand. Not because she wanted to cut off Konstantine's intrusive inquiry but because her inner compass had spun to life.

"Something's happening," she said.

The movement below intensified. The Celesti rats were running toward the water.

"He's here," Lou said, all of her musings and worries cut short.

Stefano's eyebrows rose. "You can see him in this darkness?"

"No, I can feel him," she said. "Give the first signal."

Stefano pushed himself up onto his elbows and grabbed the flashlight at his side. He pointed it east, away from the water, and flicked the light on and off twice.

There was a beat of darkness before a mirrored light

flashed twice in response, repeating the pattern Stefano had made.

That would satisfy Konstantine, Lou knew.

He had been the one to insist that they rely on the force of the Ravengers more than on Lou's prowess and skills now that she was so close to giving birth.

She'd relented, walking that fine line between her sense of obligation to their daughter's safety and her own sanity and freedom.

"You rally the troops. I'll go for Aldo," she said.

"We agreed that I would kill him," Konstantine said.

"It will be quicker and easier if I do it."

"But we don't want it to be too quick," Konstantine said. "We want Ettore to know that I am the one who killed them. We want information. And I want him furious at me, not you."

"What's that going to change?" Lou arched a brow. "He already wants to kill me."

Stefano swore under his breath. "*Sposatevi subito se dovete combattere in questo modo.*"

"We need to move," Lou said. "The two of you lead the others on the ground as we *agreed* and I will do"—she refrained from saying, rather bitterly, *Whatever the hell I want* —"what we agreed on *before* we came."

Using her compass to scan the landscape again, Lou felt Aldo at the water's edge. She could also sense the Ravengers' rapid approach in response to the signal given.

Before either Stefano or Konstantine could protest, Lou shifted through the dark, pulling them both with her.

She could've been mean.

She could've made them climb down off the containers on their own. But war wasn't the right time or place for pettiness —no matter how tempting or cathartic it may be.

When the world reformed, they were just feet away from

the Ravengers, weaving their way through the containers at the edge of the shipping yard.

The nearest started at her appearance, but no gunfire went off.

Good.

Lou had told Stefano to make sure they always knew when she would be joining them like this, lest they panic and squeeze off a shot at her sudden appearance. The last thing they needed was some skittish idiot giving their position away to the enemy.

"I'll clear a path," Lou said.

Konstantine grabbed hold of her forearm gently before she could shift through the dark again. "*Amore mio.*"

"You worry too much," she said with a smile, and put a kiss on the hard plane of flesh behind his ear. She chose this spot deliberately because she knew how it weakened him.

"*Stai barando,*" he said. "A kiss for good luck."

And Lou obliged him as Stefano muttered, "*Oh Dio, uccidimi.*"

"Don't be jealous, Stefano. You can kiss him once I'm gone." Lou gave him a look before she took a step backward and bled through the dark. The sound of Konstantine's suppressed laughter was cut short by the world dissolving and reforming around her.

As the world came into focus again, the first thing that caught her eyes was the shimmering water. She allowed herself only a moment to admire the beauty of moonlight sparking off the crests before turning her attention to the boat knocking against the pier.

She found Aldo immediately among the entourage of men arriving. Even if she hadn't known what he looked like, she would have recognized him given the five enormous guards flanking him, scanning the perimeter for trouble. Only the guy in charge would surround himself with that much muscle.

Lou decided to eliminate the guards before Konstantine and the others caught up to her. The guards were most likely the most experienced of the fighters, after all, and the best shots. The quicker Lou removed them from the equation, the safer Konstantine and his people would be.

Still cloaked in darkness, she gave the scene one more thorough appraisal, lining up her first few moves in her mind. Once ready, she stretched her neck and back for good measure and began.

The dark obliged her. Yielding to her the way it always had, allowing her to appear and disappear at will, much to her targets' horror.

Lou appreciated, especially in her current condition, that she didn't have to actually *lift* these men to move them halfway across the world. It was true that she would easily deadlift hundreds of pounds, but had been told very point-edly not to do that now unless she wanted to risk inducing labor.

The idea had been tempting.

No, these men would move if Lou simply took hold of them. That was enough for her gift to do the work of shifting them across the world.

And Lou did so now. Appearing at the sides of the closest bodyguards, snatching three at once with a simple enclosure of her arms, before bleeding through the dark with them.

Fresh pine and night air materialized around them. A light mist lingered above the lake and the roar of crickets and frogs faltered at their arrival.

Aldo's guards looked around, confusion knitting their brows as they took in the sight of the lake, the thick swell of pines, and the stars above.

Before they could fully process what was happening, Lou pulled a Beretta from her hip holster and put a bullet in each of their skulls.

It was a cleaner, more merciful kill than they deserved, but Lou needed to rely on her speed tonight. She couldn't indulge her desire for slow torture if she hoped to clear a path for the Ravengers.

Lou slipped through the dark again before the gun smoke could fully dissipate in the damp air.

Again she found herself near the water by the pier, but the scene was far less placid than it had been when she'd left. Now a tightly formed ball of protectors encased Aldo as he made his retreat to the boat rather than the shipping yard where he'd come to oversee business.

*That's all it took to scare away one of the Celesti's top dogs?* Lou thought, amused.

They were getting easier to scare.

Still Lou couldn't let Aldo escape. If they hoped to destabilize Ettore and his power, then they had to take out the men he relied on most. Aldo was one of those men.

Lou shifted through the dark again, grabbing hold of two more of Aldo's entourage. She pulled them through the dark and put bullets in their brains before returning.

Let the bodies pile up at her lake. She'd have to carry them over to her secret dumping ground later. For now, she had to focus on preventing Aldo's escape.

There was an easy solution to that, but Konstantine wouldn't like it.

Their original plan was to murder Aldo in front of the Celesti while they watched, driving their fear and panic to new heights.

That was no longer an option. Aldo was retreating too quickly, the Ravengers still too far away. If Lou didn't take a shot, they would miss this chance.

Gunshots went off at the western edge of the shipping yard, giving Lou a clearer sense of the Ravengers' current position. They were still stuck behind the first line of men.

Lou drew her own gun and began to fire, abandoning the plan.

She aimed for Aldo, but a dutiful guard took the bullet to his own throat instead. Annoying but admirable, even as blood spilt over his collar and burbled up past his lips.

It would not deter Lou in any case.

Lou kept shooting. Her bullets cleared a path between Aldo and herself. Aldo's entourage, to their credit, stood firm until she was nearly on top of them.

Then they split, darting away from her gunfire.

*Loyal, but only to a point*, she thought. *How unfortunate for you, Aldo.*

Aldo realized he was exposed just a second before Lou seized him by the lapel of his leather jacket. Before he uttered a word, she pressed her gun to his sweaty temple and pulled him through the dark.

Her lake materialized once more, the stars bright and the scent of pine strong. A cool breeze licked the sweat dampening the side of her neck just behind her ear.

"Now that I've got you alone," Lou said, riding the high that always came when she acquired the target she was hunting, "we should talk. Aldo, isn't it?"

"*Per favore, per favore!*" He dropped his gun as his knees hit the mud. The weight of him dragged Lou forward, suddenly off balance.

She almost fell thanks to her enormous belly, and was forced to release her hold on him at the last minute or risk being pulled down.

Her back twinged, but after a deep breath, she managed to compose herself. Fortunately, Aldo seemed unaware of her momentary weakness. His hands were covering his head as he begged for his life in lilting Italian.

"Whether you live or die is up to you," Lou said. And this was partially true. Of course, it would be her call whether or not to put a bullet in his head, but he did have options. If he would just stop whimpering long enough to hear them.

"Aldo, are you listening?"

He looked up, hopefully. "*Sì?*"

"I need to know what he's planning," Lou said.

His face crumpled as if Lou had asked him to sacrifice his firstborn. "No, *Strega. Per favore.*"

"Tell me what he's planning and I'll let you live. Don't tell me and I'll kill you. It's that simple. *Mi capisci?*"

"Yes, but I can't help you. He kill me if I tell you."

Lou threw up her hands, realizing in that instant that she was affecting one of Piper's mannerisms without meaning to. It was her *Are you kidding me? How dumb can you be?* expression that Piper often did automatically when encountering people trampling on her last nerve.

Lou pointed her gun at him. "Who is here right now? Me or Ettore?"

"You, *sì*, you."

"Then I'm the one you have to worry about. Tell me the plan."

"*Strega—*"

"*Uno...*" Lou began counting. "You know what happens when I get to three, right?"

"*Strega—*"

"*Due...*"

"*Lasciami parlare con lei,*" a voice said.

Lou froze. The hair on the back of her neck rose.

The voice hadn't come from Aldo, who'd devolved into terrified whimpers as she'd counted. It was muffled and mechanical, but it was a clear voice.

She looked down at the corpses of Celesti's men and confirmed that none of them were alive enough to speak. And yet—

"*Aldo,*" the voice said, "*dai, dai.*"

Lou realized what was going on only when Aldo's hand began reaching for his chest. Lou pressed the muzzle into his forehead.

He froze. "It's a phone. A phone. Take it. You take it."

Lou kept the muzzle of her gun pressed into Aldo's forehead even as she reached into his jacket pocket and found the cell phone.

After claiming it, she took two big steps backward, careful not to trip over the dead body behind her.

"*Strega*," Ettore said. "Are you there?"

"And who might this be?" Lou asked, even though she knew exactly who it was. She hoped by pretending not to know him it would only piss him off more.

"Ah, you *do* speak English. *Capisci anche tu l'italiano?*"

"*Sì, e parlo anche la lingua dei topi.* Use whichever you like."

There was a cold derision in his laugh. "I suppose a demon would need to speak multiple languages. Though the Italian doesn't sound so natural on your tongue. That's okay. We can use English."

"I've been called *Strega*, an angel of death, and now a demon. What makes you think I'm a demon, Ettore? Maybe I'm just your karma."

"No."

"Shame," she said. "What did you want to talk about? Your plan, I hope?"

She couldn't pretend that she wanted anything else. He'd already heard her threatening to kill Aldo for it. What did she stand to gain by being coy about it now?

"I want to know why you are helping him. Is it because he is the father of your child? It can't be. Because my sources tell me that you helped him defeat Nico and Dmitri and—"

"Maybe he was helping *me*," she said. "Did that occur to you?"

Of course, this was bullshit. Lou had been the one to save

Konstantine from Nico, who'd almost killed him not once but twice. Dmitri Petrov had been her mess.

Ettore seemed to consider her words for a long time. Long enough for Lou's focus to shift to the night around her. The cold air, the sound of crickets. Aldo's soft crying.

Something about it bothered her.

"Your alliance began before the baby," he said at last. "Why? Do you love him? For women it is often love. Are you a woman, *Strega?*"

Lou arched her brow. Would it serve them to share the fact that Konstantine was, by far, the loving romantic in their relationship? Probably not.

"You jealous, Ettore? Don't have a girl of your very own?"

It was easier to taunt him than share the truth.

*I actually hated him at first. I was going to kill him—just another Martinelli—until I realized who he was.*

She sure as hell wasn't going to tell him how she used to slip through the darkness into his bedroom when she was still a child, grieving the murder of her parents, and how to this day, she had no idea why her power had brought them together. Why him of all the boys in the world that it could have chosen.

"Why do you protect him?" Ettore asked again, and Lou heard that edge of desperation in his voice.

She ignored it. "Is Aldo going to tell me your plan or should I kill him now?"

"Kill him," Ettore said.

Aldo burst into sobs. "No, no!"

The utter look of betrayal that crossed his face made Lou feel sorry for him. She pulled the trigger anyway, and the crack of her gunshot split open the night.

Lou pressed a finger to her lips, indicating to Aldo that he better stay quiet if he wanted to live.

At least for a little longer.

"I can still hear him crying, *Strega*," Ettore said.

"That's someone else," she said, lying. Messing with Ettore was proving to be fun.

"It was Fernando Martinelli who first reported a creature like you. A demon who moved through shadows. He told the Celesti before me that you killed all of his sons. Then one day we heard that Fernando himself was dead. Killed by *La Strega*. Is this how you met Konstantine?"

*Yes.*

Lou remembered well her vow to destroy the men who'd killed her parents, and all those hungry years it took for her to keep that promise. How delicious it had been to be the one who'd ripped their souls from their bodies, one by one, watching the light in their eyes go out.

"What does it matter, Celesti? Fernando is old news. This is about me and you now."

"You destroyed the Martinellis but you spared Konstantine. Why?"

"Maybe I liked him."

"But *why*?"

"You're starting to sound like an old boyfriend, Ettore. Why him? Why not *me*?" Lou affected a pouty, petulant voice that she was sure would annoy the other man.

That was the point.

"There is nothing he can give you that I can't give you. More. And better. Even a child. I can fuck you twice as good as he ever did and give you strong children if that's what you want. I will prove to be the better man in every way."

*Ew, gross.* Piper's voice sprang up in Lou's head.

And Lou snorted in spite of herself.

"Does that amuse you? This is my only offer, *Strega*. You spared Konstantine, now spare me and I will pay you in kind. I won't kill the child you're carrying."

Lou's blood iced. The very idea that this asshole could

even *think* of hurting her daughter made her want to bring the world down upon him.

"Speak of her again, I will skin your dick with rusty pliers."

"Her. A daughter then. A daughter like you, perhaps. Is your gift the kind that must be passed on? Is that your desire?"

As if he could ever fathom what Lou wanted. Men like Ettore only knew power, control, and holding dominion over everything they touched.

Not one could understand the simple drive to be free.

At peace.

Lou's face was still hot with rage when she said, "I want you to stop selling people. Can you do that? Even if I crawled to you on my hands and knees and promised to *serve* you instead of him"—Celesti couldn't see her incredulous eyeroll—"would you stop? If that was my price, would you pay it?"

There was no world in which Lou would subjugate herself to such a man, but she knew what men like him wanted to hear. And she knew the rumors. The underworld thought that Lou's hunts, her kills, were in service to some higher aim, a plan crafted by Konstantine himself.

Silence filled the phone.

"Are you picturing what that might look like? Me on my knees?" she purred. "Keep dreaming, Celesti. Because I don't think you'll stop for anything. It's good business for you, isn't it? Selling people. Especially children."

"Is that really all it is, *Strega*? You disagree with my *product*? The Martinellis sold—"

"And they're dead."

"So you are the patron saint of whores?" he said, his tone dark.

"I thought you said I was a demon. Now I'm a saint?

Make up your mind." Lou thought again of the priest that had once called her the angel of death.

*God has use even for one such as you*, he'd said.

"Is that really why you spared him? Because the Ravengers aren't in the business of—" Ettore's voice was cut off by another. Lou couldn't hear the second man very well through the phone, but judging by the tone, someone was giving him news. Ettore grunted a sound of approval. "Whatever you are, whore, demon, I'll find out soon enough."

*What does he mean by that?*

Lou's compass tugged, drawing her attention to something. That's when her ears caught a faint sound.

A helicopter. Unseen blades whirred in the dark, somewhere in the distance but quickly approaching.

"Did you trace this call?" she asked him, doing her best to add amusement to her voice. "Did you think you'd find something interesting by following me out here? This is just a little place I like to come when I want to be alone with someone special. Like your Aldo."

Lou had been careful over the years never to leave evidence, even though her lake was far from civilization. But now there were the bodies of the snatched guards lying at the water's edge.

She'd have to drag those to La Loon quickly if she wanted to be gone before the helicopter came into view.

"Why don't you come and see me, *Strega*. It's time we should meet, don't you think?"

"Are you alone?" she asked. "If you're all alone, I'll come now."

"Yes," he said. "Come to me, *Strega*."

She used her compass to lock on Ettore and found that he was, in fact, surrounded by several others. "*Liar*."

She could sense at least twelve people near him. Then again, twelve wasn't so many. It was tempting, actually.

Aldo, emboldened, bolted through the trees away from her. He probably thought if he could just outrun her until the helicopter arrived, he would be saved.

Idiot.

Lou had been prepared to cut him a deal for information on Ettore. Even set him up somewhere plush and safe for his trouble.

She fired a shot into the back of Aldo's head and he dropped like a rock.

"*Strega?*" Ettore asked.

Lou caught the first glimpse of a searchlight passing through the trees a few miles off.

She estimated she had five minutes tops to get the bodies into the lake—cell phones too—and through to La Loon before she'd be seen.

"Looks like our meeting will have to wait," she told him, already starting toward Aldo's corpse. "I'm a little busy right now."

"*Strega*, wait. I have a gift for you."

"Aldo? Yes, I already have him. Thanks."

"No. It's on the pier. In the shipping containers."

Lou's stomach dropped.

"Check the containers," Ettore said, his voice darker than ever. "Now that I know how you feel about my business, I'm sure you'll *love* what you find."

3

———

No sooner did Konstantine cut around the corner of the shipping container did he see Lou disappear with Aldo. A momentary flash of irritation at her deviation from the plan folded into concern. He trusted Lou. If she'd acted impulsively, then she must have seen something he hadn't.

*Mama, proteggila.*

This wasn't the first time he'd prayed to his dead mother. Konstantine had been praying to her more and more lately. For Lou's safety. For the daughter that would share his mama's name once born. He knew that Lou didn't have the same faith that he did, but it brought him comfort to imagine that his mother, though dead, still had the power to intervene on his behalf.

*Mama, proteggila. Per favore.*

As Stefano ordered the Ravengers into position, Konstantine's attention shifted to the cargo containers around them. For a moment, he thought he'd heard a scream within.

He pressed his ear to one container and knocked.

Nothing.

He moved on to the second and repeated the motion, then the third.

Maybe he was mistaken.

The escalating commotion made it harder to hear. And once gunfire erupted between his people and the Celesti, this method proved useless.

Two of Ettore's men cut around the corner of the shipping container Konstantine had just pressed his ear against and started at the sight of him. That was when he realized they were running from the fight rather than into it.

Konstantine shot each in the head before recognition brightened in their eyes.

Not that there was any point hiding who he was. Ettore already knew he was here.

Konstantine cut through the containers, following the sound of gunfire, carving a path closer to the water's edge. There were fallen bodies between the containers, left like breadcrumbs in a children's story.

When the maze broke open again, Konstantine found the thick of it. He searched the bodies for anyone he knew, any of their own, but saw none.

The advantage to bringing Stefano was how little Konstantine had to do himself. The Ravengers were used to following Stefano's commands. They obeyed him without objection and moved well as a unit. Stefano himself was a brave fighter and a damn good shot.

He didn't waste bullets and knew how to direct their people in a way that limited casualties. It was moments like this that Konstantine couldn't help but marvel at how far they'd come since they were just boys, running around Padre Leo's courtyard after school. He hadn't known in the early years how much his friend would come to matter to him.

In fact, he'd been somewhat resentful of Stefano in the early days. The way Padre Leo had called them brothers. *You look so similar*, others had remarked, at a time when Konstantine had wanted to be singular in every way.

But now, as he watched Stefano lead the charge, Konstantine was proud of how close they'd become and was honored, rather than repulsed, by their similarities.

Stefano put a bullet in the last of the men charging him and looked up, meeting Konstantine's eyes. "What?"

*Fratello.*

"You look like you're enjoying yourself," Konstantine said.

Stefano pushed his damp hair away from his face. Then he spat on the corpse at his feet. "They deserve worse for Ilaria and my nephews. Michele. Simone."

Konstantine noted that Stefano did not mention his sister's husband. "No justice for Davide?"

Stefano gave an indifferent shrug. "Ilaria could have done better."

Konstantine suppressed a laugh. Usually he would have refrained from jokes made about the dead, but this was Stefano. He relied on humor to release tension and fear. Konstantine wouldn't deny him that.

The last of the gunfire bled out into nothing but the lapping waves on the shore. Silence swelled around them.

Stefano bent and checked the man's pockets. Once he found his wallet, he relieved the dead man of his cash.

Konstantine swore. He hated it when Stefano did that. There was something indecent about it.

"Do I not pay you enough?" Konstantine knew he did. Stefano was a very rich man.

Stefano saw him scowling. "Money is money, *fratello*. He won't need it. And don't tell me it belongs to his wife or children because we both know that whoever cleans this up will take it before they see a dollar."

The pressure between Konstantine's ears increased,

releasing with a slight pop the moment before Lou stepped toward him from the darkness.

He hadn't expected to see her so soon. The plan was to interrogate Aldo and move the bodies to La Loon, yet here she was. And dripping wet.

"You went to La Loon?" he asked.

"Quickly. Ettore traced a cell phone in Aldo's pocket," she said. "He sent a helicopter to my lake."

"How in the hell could he move that fast?" Stefano said, pulling a cigarette from his pocket.

He slipped it between his lips and struck the lighter twice before it burst to life. His face momentarily glowed orange in the reflected firelight before all that burned was the cherry of the filter.

"He has as many resources as we do," Konstantine said. "He has people everywhere. There must have been a police station or someone nearby that he could get into the air."

Stefano took another drag of his cigarette, the cherry flaring brighter. "They still must have been far away if a helicopter was their first choice."

"It's pretty remote," Lou said.

"Your lake," Konstantine said, wondering if the loss would irritate her. Undoubtedly. "I'm sorry, *amore mio*."

"I have another," she said. "And now that I know he's trying to track me, I'll be sure to relieve everyone else we take of their cell phones beforehand. No need for him to know our movements."

A disquiet settled in Konstantine's chest. Had the Celesti been tracking them all this while? And if they had, had they already mapped out all of the important places in their lives?

Did he know of the villa Lou and Konstantine shared?

Did Ettore know of Lou's friends in New Orleans?

The children they'd hidden away at boarding school?

Isabella's clinic where Lou had her prenatal appointments, and where she planned to give birth?

All of these places were vulnerable. He didn't want the Celesti to know of them.

"Let's worry about ourselves for now," Stefano said, pulling a piece of tobacco from the tip of his tongue. "He'll send reinforcements here soon, no?"

He was right. Konstantine put his gun away. "Have the others take what they can and head out. I want to check these containers though. I am sure I heard someone scream."

"The containers." Lou's expression turned serious. "Is that what he meant?"

Before Konstantine could ask what she meant, Lou pulled a glowstick from her jacket pocket and cracked it. As she shook it, neon-orange fluid lit up in the tube.

Stefano pointed at her with his cigarette. "Why do you have that?"

"You don't want to know," Lou said with a wicked grin.

And Konstantine pushed down a twinge of jealousy. He was glad that his second and Lou were getting along better. Or so he told himself at moments like this.

"For the monsters in your cave?" Konstantine ventured, wanting to remain in the conversation.

"*Sì*," she said coquettishly. "But now it'll help me see inside the containers."

Her gaze slid down and away.

He knew she was using her compass to search the area.

She started off toward an adjacent container, her orange glowstick held high like a torch, and stopped. She knocked on the outside of the container but was met with only silence.

She bled through the darkness and then reappeared a moment later.

Though her face was half hidden in darkness, Konstantine saw the furious flex of her jaw.

"What is it?" he asked cautiously.

"They're dead," she said.

Stefano swore. He threw his cigarette down and ground it out with the twist of his boot heel.

"How many?" Konstantine asked.

"I don't know," she said. "I'll—I'll need time to count."

Engines roared in the distance. Both he and Stefano turned toward the dark horizon at the same moment.

"There are the reinforcements," Stefano said. "We'll buy you time."

Then he was gone, shouting orders at the Ravengers.

Lou still hadn't moved. It wasn't like her to freeze like that. Konstantine was about to reach for her when he realized she was shaking.

"*Amore mio?*"

When she looked up, her face was a mask of fury.

"That piece of shit," she said. "This is what he meant."

"Who? Aldo?"

"It was something he'd said on the phone once I realized he was tracing the call," she said. "He said he'd left me a gift. There are *children* in there."

Konstantine's own fury burned. To say that he couldn't wait for the day that Ettore was wiped from the face of the earth was a gross understatement.

"If there are survivors, we need to move them as soon as possible," Konstantine said. "Do you sense any?"

Lou's gaze slid down and away.

"I don't—I—" Gunfire blatted in the distance. Stefano must have intercepted the approaching gang.

"Take your time," he encouraged her. "Stefano knows what he's doing."

"I'm only picking up a few," she said. "I think most of them are dead."

"Then we'll save who we can," he promised her. "How are you feeling? How's Elena?"

His own anger mirrored the cold fury in her face, but he chose to focus on what mattered.

Their daughter. Their safety. Helping who they could. And dismantling the Celesti empire brick by brick.

"We're fine," Lou said through gritted teeth, as if struggling to regain control of herself. "But we should hurry. We can't expect Stefano to hold off the calvary all night."

"*Sì*," Konstantine said, and pulled her close. He placed a soft kiss on the side of her throat. "Let's hurry."

Though everything in him wanted to do the opposite—to take Lou and Elena home, to shower, maybe have a glass of wine. To climb beneath the covers together and pull Lou into his arms and feel her bare skin under his hands.

But such dreams would have to wait.

**4**

———

Robert King gestured across the console at the glovebox facing the passenger seat. "Grab the binoculars for me."

"You can't use *binoculars*." Piper scrunched up her face and pointed at the park beyond the windshield of the Buick SUV where they hid. "How suspicious is that? Us looking like a couple of weirdos, parked under some trees, in the shadows, using *binoculars* to look at kids. They'll send someone to pick us up."

"We're not looking at the kids. I'm trying to read that sign. It's too far away." He'd been squinting at it for the last five minutes but had been unable to will the letters into focus. Moments like this, when he was forced to confront the inevitability of his encroaching age, he was more than a little insulted on his behalf.

"I'll go read it," she said.

"Go on then." He waved her on, watching as she slid out of the SUV and jogged toward the plastic play equipment.

King suspected that Piper may even have been able to see

it from where she sat beside him but didn't want to embarrass him. She was nearly forty years younger than he was.

King scanned the park and counted heads. If he'd been asked to do a profile on the park's demographics, King would have said upper-middle class, college educated, a seventy/thirty split between men and women. Parents stood near the small set of playground equipment, chatting the morning away while their children climbed on the plastic configurations. To the left was a large gated section hosting five or six dogs off leash, their owners lingering near the perimeter of the chaos.

The trail circling the playground seemed to be a favorite of runners, some of whom also had canine companions.

King and Piper had intentionally come at an off hour in hopes that the park would be mostly empty. It would have been easier to sketch the area and look for evidence that the police might have overlooked on their first pass. So much for that.

The one thing that King could appreciate about this new car, as loath as he'd been to get it, was that it was certainly convenient. The SUV did offer a higher vantage point than his previous low-rider could have ever managed. It didn't feel broken in the way his old car had. Nor did it seem as sturdy and dependable as the older model.

When he'd closed the door on his old Buick, it had sounded like he was slamming the door on existence itself, heavier than a solid slab of steel. Now, when a door closed, it practically bounced off its hinges.

But since a would-be bomber had blown his Buick to smithereens, a new car had become a reluctant necessity. And it hardly seemed like something to complain about, given how lucky he was to be able to afford a new car at all.

"You'll get used to it. It's a nice ride," he mumbled to

himself as Piper stopped in front of the sign and came up on her toes to read it. But he'd been reassuring himself of this for months now. "It's a nice ride."

He watched as she stared at the sign a moment longer, then started heading back to the parked SUV. She stopped and talked to a lady who was pushing her little boy on a swing.

There was the shy hello, the short exchange of what King suspected were pleasantries, before Piper pulled a flyer from her back pocket.

While Piper spoke to a few of the parents lingering by the playground equipment, King searched the tree line again. The county maps they'd reviewed had told them that this copse of trees was about half a mile thick on all sides. To the east, it opened up on an apartment complex where one of the two victims had lived, to the west, a shopping center. The north border was the lake and the south was a subdivision, where the second victim had lived.

King had been interested in the park as a hunting ground, given its proximity to all three attacks. But it was possible that they were unrelated.

The apartment complex mostly had graduate students who attended the closest university or young professionals who worked nearby. The subdivision was home to mostly families. In the first two incidents, a young woman had been stalked and attacked by a young man in a ski-mask who then attempted to rape her.

The third young woman disappeared.

Maybe the attacker had no connection to the area at all. Or if he did, it wasn't that he lived or worked nearby. Perhaps he had simply picked it at random as his hunting ground so that there wouldn't be an immediate connection between himself and the women. That would have been the smart thing to do.

Piper moved on from the swings, to the benches adjacent. King smiled, pleased by her initiative.

*Go on then*, he thought. *Get us some answers.*

In truth, King continued to be impressed by her growth as an investigator. She was going to make one hell of an agent one day.

Not for the first time, he imagined the moment of her graduation. King there in the audience, bursting with pride at how far she'd come from their first encounter, when she'd been a slightly lost, very love-crazy co-ed trying to overcome her trauma and difficult home life.

*I'm damn proud already*, he thought.

He'd almost lost himself in this little daydream when a woman caught his eye. She was leaving the dog park, her small gray schnauzer leashed, when a man stooped, clearly asking to pet her dog. It had been the slight recoil in her body language that had caught King's eye.

Before he could watch the pair more closely, his phone went off.

He reached over and dug his cell phone out of the cupholder where it sat, answering on the fourth ring.

"King."

"What time are you getting back?" a familiar voice asked.

King's heart lifted. "Four or five, why? You need us to pick up something?"

It was a pleasant surprise to hear from Melandra unexpectedly. He felt more than a little foolish, with his heart fluttering like a schoolboy's just because a woman—a woman he liked—called him. Part of him chastised himself. For being so silly at his age. He was in his sixties. He wasn't a teenager.

And yet, he was also thrilled to realize that he *could* still feel this way. When he'd lost Lucy, had said that heart-wrenching goodbye before the cancer took her, he'd been certain that the part of him that loved—that believed in romance and connection—had died with her.

True, he'd met Beth, and they'd had a good time. But even with Beth he could tell that he'd kept that part of himself locked up and hidden away, out of her reach despite Beth's best efforts.

His attraction to Mel felt different than what he'd felt with Lucy.

With Lucy, it had been so complicated. First, he'd fallen for her despite his better judgment. As the sister of his mentee, Jack, he should have kept his distance. And yet, he'd been drawn to her. Then there had come their brief but intense love affair, in which Lucy came in like a whirlwind, introducing King to a world so different than his own.

Lucy had been different to him in every way possible— free-spirited, wild, a borderline hippy with her pacifist world view—quite the contrast to his buttoned-up, black-and-white, and disciplined approach to life.

Then Jack died, and Lucy disappeared to take care of Lou. And King was left to pass the years filled with regret, wondering what could have been. When Lucy had turned up in those final months, King had felt like he'd been offered the second chance he'd always hoped for. More than once, King had wondered if their rekindled romance had been more about closure for the two of them than anything else. Their connection certainly hadn't had the same whirling dervish energy that it had all those years before.

With Mel, it was different. There were no complications. No roadblocks or barriers. No confusion about how he felt or why. There was simply a quiet knowing that he wanted to be by her side for what remained of his life.

He hadn't told her that, of course. He had no idea how she would take such declarations.

"You still there, Mr. King?" Melandra said.

King realized she'd been speaking and he'd missed some crucial question.

"Yes, sorry. I'm a little distracted." And this was true. It wasn't just his thoughts that kept carrying him away, or the increasing warmth collecting in the tips of his ears. It was also Piper. Now she was talking to a young man with his hands in his pockets. King recognized him as the one who'd stopped to talk to the woman with her schnauzer.

"I was asking if you could come over an hour earlier tonight."

His heart skipped a beat, worried she might cancel on him altogether. "Do you need the night off?"

"No, I want to have dinner," she said. "But I also need an early bedtime. I didn't sleep well last night with the storm. Does the new time work for you?"

It didn't. He was supposed to meet with a client thirty minutes before, but King would gladly reschedule.

"Of course it does," he said.

"Are you sure?" Melandra asked. She seemed surprised. "I thought you had to work."

"It's not anything that won't keep," he said, and that was the truth.

"In that case, bring me some sweet tea when you come over. And some garlic bread too," she said. "Goodbye, Mr. King."

And with that she was gone.

He'd be seeing Mel even earlier than he'd planned. And there would be garlic bread. His mood lifted considerably.

The passenger door flew open.

"Stop it," Piper hissed as she slid into the seat.

King frowned, confused. "Stop what?"

"Thinking about her."

"Who?"

"Don't play dumb!" Piper said, reaching across her torso to grab the seatbelt and fasten it. "I know you're thinking about Mel."

He scoffed. "How can you possibly know I'm thinking about Mel?"

"Because when you think about her you get this dopey look on your face." She screwed her face up and made her eyes bigger in a parody of a lovesick fool.

A full laugh escaped him this time. "That is not what I look like."

"Yes, it is," she said. "Pull yourself together, man. We're *professionals*."

King found Piper's obsessive fear about Mel and King's relationship status amusing. No matter how much he assured her that there was nothing to worry about, that he wasn't, in fact, going to ruin their lives with his feelings, Piper seemed hellbent on believing otherwise.

"Was it Mel who called?" Piper asked. "I saw you on the phone."

"Yes. She wants garlic bread. And tea. And for me to show up at six instead of seven. It's hardly marriage plans. You and Dani are the ones shopping for engagement rings, not me."

He knew for a fact that they'd gone to three different jewelers the week before.

Piper's face was red when she said, "You've got Paulson at five thirty. You'll be cutting it close."

"I could leave it to you," he said.

She perked up at this. "Really?"

"Really," he said, happy to have pleased her. "Why don't you take lead on it? It'll be your case. From start to finish."

"*Really*." It was no longer a question but an elated gasp. "What if they demand to see you?"

"I'll tell them that it's you or nothing," he said, turning on the SUV and putting the car in drive. "They'll change their tune."

She seemed to consider this, and the more she did, the bigger the grin spread on her face. "Don't think I've forgotten about you and Mel, sir. I still think you pursuing her is the worst idea of the year."

King wasn't interested in being told yet again all the reasons why it was in his best interests to keep all feelings and interactions between Mel and himself strictly friendly, free of any romantic entanglement.

"You know if we broke up," he said, "she and I are adult enough to remain friends, right?"

Piper shook her head. "That never works. Sleeping with your friends changes everything, and you know it."

"It doesn't have to." But even as he said it, a whisper of doubt flicked through his mind. "It's different when you're older."

She tilted her head and squinted her eyes at him suspiciously. "Really?"

"Really."

"Are you *sure?*"

"Yes, I'm *sure.*" And this was the first time that Piper seemed to reconsider her staunch stance against their potential romantic entanglement.

"We are mature enough to handle this responsibly." King was only about eighty percent confident in what he was saying, but he kept his face impassive so that Piper couldn't detect even a flicker of doubt in him.

"Just be careful, okay. I won't survive the divorce if you guys break up. I need you both."

King reached out and gave her shoulder a little squeeze. "That'll never happen. I promise. Now tell me what you learned on the playground."

He stopped short of saying that Piper also meant the

world to him. He'd been fond of the kid—everyone under thirty was a kid to King—ever since he'd met her. Once he learned about what a shitty hand she'd been dealt regarding her parents, his feelings of protectiveness had only increased.

Yet King still felt more than a little ridiculous discussing a relationship that he did not, in fact, yet have. He suspected that Mel knew what his feelings were, but if she did, she was also working hard to hide the fact that she knew.

King had no reason whatsoever to believe that Mel wanted to have a relationship, and he certainly wasn't the kind of man to push his affections on a woman unless her explicit interest was known.

Despite outlining all of this to Piper, he'd still found himself in these conversations with her whenever he made the mistake of smiling too broadly—especially if Mel was the cause of his happiness.

Piper sat up straighter in her seat, smoothing out the crumpled flyer against her bare thigh. "A few of them remembered Willa's dog. But not Willa so much. I guess that's what happens when your dog is super cute."

"No one has seen her?"

"No," Piper said, her expression sorrowful.

King hadn't had a great feeling about this case from the beginning. When Willa's sister, Caty, came to the Crescent City Detective Agency for their help, there had been something about her story that had given him pause.

Willa hadn't answered her phone for several days. Caty had gone over to her apartment—the apartment that had been adjacent to the little park—and had found it empty, but with signs of a break-in. The police were brought in, and they discovered trace amounts of blood on the mattress and a partial print near the front door that had proved useless. No matches.

Someone had scrubbed the place down clean.

Then the police connected Willa's disappearance with two attempted rapes that had happened in the months leading up to it, marking the similarities in the case.

When the police reached a dead end, Caty had been referred to King. But picking up a cold trail was harder than it looked. So far, the only information they'd gotten was out of one of Willa's neighbors in the apartment building, who had told them that Willa liked to bring her dog to this park every day before and after work.

It wasn't looking good for Willa.

King really hoped that the attacker's third attempt hadn't proven to be the charm.

"I hope she's not dead," Piper bemoaned. "Is it bad to wish that someone is locked up in a basement somewhere, but like, alive?"

"I hope she's not dead too," King said, sliding past the basement comment. He'd had a case like that when he was a DEA agent and didn't want to tell Piper that some places were actually worse than death.

Instead, he threw the car into drive and left the park. Once they were back on the main road, he asked, "So what's our next move, Genereux?"

"I think we should go by her apartment and see if we can get a full breakdown of her routine. Maybe call a few of her friends, talk to everyone again. If this park proves to be a bust, I want to have other places that we can go to get a sense of her movements leading up to her disappearance. Then maybe we can piece the story together."

He smiled, pleased by her assessment. "You're going to be an incredible agent."

Piper's smile faltered. "You're just saying that."

King balked at her insecurity. "I mean every word of it. It's been a long time since I've seen such a quick study. You're a natural."

Her cheeks and ears were red, and King suspected it wasn't just from the blistering July heat. He had the A/C on full blast.

"Thanks," she managed. She pointed at the turn coming up. "Don't miss this or we'll be stuck on the I-10 at rush hour. You'll never make it to Mel's in time if you do."

**5**

————

Melandra Durand stared at the tarot cards laid out on her glass countertop in front of her and frowned. No matter how she asked the question, the answer was the same. The Magician, The Empress. The King of Cups. The Knight of Cups.

*It's in your hands. His feelings are sincere, but it's in your hands.*

Mel didn't like that at all.

She didn't *want* this to be in her hands. It wasn't that she was incapable of making decisions about her own life. She had been on this earth for too long and had been through too much not to know her own mind.

It was only that for the first time in decades—*decades*—Mel wasn't sure what she wanted.

She liked the comfortable ease between her and King. Their friendship had grown strong in the years since he had turned up on her doorstep, answering her ad for a renter.

She remembered that day clearly.

Business had been slow. She'd wasted the earlier hours dusting shelves that were already dusted and taking inventory only to reassure herself that she was overburdened with stock and in no danger of running out of anything. She'd only put that ad in the paper because she was worried that her business would go under completely and she would default on the building's mortgage if she didn't find someone to rent the empty apartment.

Then he turned up on her doorstep.

She'd been resistant at first. He looked like a cop, a haunted one at that, and Mel hadn't had the best personal history with the police. She'd lived in fear that her worst secret would be discovered by a cop and that she'd spend the remainder of her life in prison, locked up like that good-for-nothing ex of hers.

But she'd taken out her cards, hoping for some clue to the respectability of this stranger on her doorstep, telling her that he wanted to rent her space.

King of Cups. Three of Swords.

A sincere and honest man who was dying of a broken heart.

Reassured despite the slight air of nihilism hanging about him, Mel had offered to show him the apartment.

She had no idea then of all that would happen later. Every brush with death. Every trial and tribulation. How completely he'd made her feel seen and understood for perhaps the first time in her entire life.

He had become her first real friend. Her best friend. Someone who had seen her dirty laundry but never thought less of her for it.

She trusted him. That wasn't the problem.

She didn't trust herself.

After that decades-long fiasco with Terry, a first marriage that Mel wouldn't have wished on anyone, even her worst enemy, she'd been happy just to be free.

She never imagined love for herself.

What did she even want in a partner, if she wanted one at all?

A kind man. An understanding man. Someone handsome who made her laugh. Who made her feel understood. Wanted—

When she tried to imagine what such a man might be like, King's smiling face sprang to mind.

She clucked her tongue as her cheeks heated, embarrassment welling up, and swiped her tarot cards off to one side.

"Shush," she said, as if the cards had spoken.

Thankfully the shop was empty. No one was here to witness this heated conversation with herself.

"Mr. King might be ready, but I'm not," she said to the empty room. She tapped the tarot cards into a neat little pile and returned them to their pouch, noting distantly that the jasmine incense she'd lit first thing that morning had burned out.

It was this embarrassment and uncertainty of her true feelings that had driven her to call King with her fake excuse. She'd moved their dinner plans forward by one hour hoping to force his hand. If he canceled, then she could spend the evening in her apartment, hiding her face. Pretending that she neither saw nor felt what was going on.

Instead, he'd agreed. And now he was going to be at her apartment even earlier.

"That's what I get for not being direct," she said.

Even as she said it, she wondered how in the world she could have told him the truth.

*I don't want you to come over tonight. The cards keep saying you're falling in love with me, and I need time and space to figure out how I feel about that.*

That seemed like a ridiculous thing to say.

And yet, Mel had the distinct impression that if she *had* said those very words to King, he would have understood. He might have barked one of his surprised little laughs and said, *Take all the time you need.*

He wouldn't have denied what he was feeling—and that scared her more than anything. His open admission of how he felt would be crossing a line, and Mel knew those words could never be unsaid.

The bell rang, forcing Mel to look up. A small figure crossed the threshold of Fortunes and Fixes, leaning heavily on the cane at her side.

The chandelier overhead moaned, emitting a ghostly shriek as the lights in it flickered.

The old woman looked up, penciled eyebrows arching. "Oh. *Spooky.* I like that very much."

"Hello, Ms. Genevieve. What brings you in?"

Melandra was surprised to see her. Their weekly meeting for women business owners wasn't until Thursday.

Genevieve flashed a manila folder at her. "I've got the festival flyers here for you."

"You didn't have to bring that in. I could've come and picked them up."

Genevieve waved her away. "It ain't no skin off my back. I'm driving around to e'rbody this morning. Gettin' you all in one go. I just came from Hattie and I'm headin' to Rosa next."

The woman pointed out the window at the white Cadillac parked haphazardly on the street. One of its tires was up on the sidewalk. Mel made a silent prayer for the woman to give the wheel a sharp left tug as she drove off and not to hit the gas pedal too heavily, or she might very well drive into Mel's storefront window.

"Still, you didn't have to come all this way, Ms. Genevieve."

Genevieve reached the glass countertop and rested her

weight heavily against it. Once she'd put the folder on the counter, she shifted her weight to the other leg.

"We've gotta do what we can to make the most of this opportunity. That's what gets us ahead, you know."

The opportunity in question was the upcoming BexFest. A week-long celebration of African American music, health, food, and culture. As a board member of the association, Genevieve was fully integrated in their community outreach efforts. It was no surprise to Mel then that she'd chosen to get so involved.

Yet looking at the tiny creature, Mel couldn't help but marvel that the woman was still mobile at her age. Mid-eighties and two strokes to her credit, Genevieve was a force. She'd been one of the most successful businesswomen in New Orleans, having established a popular chain of fine-dining restaurants. She'd let her kids take over the business years ago, but was still very active in the community, investing in women-owned businesses as if it were her personal mission. And maybe it was.

"Besides," Genevieve said, looking around her shop again, "I wanted to see your store. It's a nice place you've got here. I can tell you put a lot of work into it."

Mel shrank a little at that. Not only because she found praise uncomfortable but because she didn't know how in the world Ms. Genevieve could feel that way. Her little occult shop on St. Peters could hardly compare to Genevieve's two Michelin-star restaurants.

"Thank you," she said tightly.

"I mean it," Genevieve said. "You know, when I was a teenager, my uncle had a shop like this. Over in Pirates Alley."

"Really?" Mel asked. The real estate prices must have been much more affordable in those days. Her place here off St. Peters was extremely expensive.

"It was a special time of my life. Lots of good memories," Genevieve said with a fond smile. "He had me reading cards at a little table in the back, if you can believe it."

Piper sprang to mind. Mel didn't think Piper had time to read cards in Jackson Square these days, but the image was clear enough that it was easy for her to superimpose Genevieve's face onto the memory.

"Do you read cards?" Genevieve asked.

"I do," Melandra said. "Tea leaves, bones, most forms of divination. I've no talent for I-Ching, though. I gotta be honest about that. Did you want a reading?"

Mel was unable to hide her surprise.

"No, no," Genevieve laughed, waving her off. "At my age, it's risky business. I'm too close to the end to be trying to peek behind the curtain. Lord knows who I'll see."

Mel laughed obligingly despite the darkness of the joke.

"Well, I'd better scooch on out of here if I'm gonna make it home in time for my afternoon nap."

"Of course." Mel remembered what some of the other ladies had said after one of her earlier meetings with the business association, about how Genevieve had a stiff drink and a nap every afternoon like clockwork.

"And don't worry about the festival. I know everyone is working really hard to make the most of it."

"I'm not worried," she said, using the cane to push herself up. "We've got a good group. You girls sure do make me proud."

They shared one final wave at the door. Then the woman was gone. Much to Mel's relief, the car did swerve left, pulling into the street rather than going straight through her storefront window.

Unable to hide her temptation, Mel pulled out her tarot cards and did a quick three-card reading for Genevieve.

Nine of Wands. Strength. High Priestess.

"I think you've got plenty of time left, Ms. Genevieve," Melandra said, gathering the cards together again.

The unexpected visit had filled Mel's heart. It wasn't so long ago that she had felt like a stranger in this city, without a friend in the world and Terry's darkness hanging over her. And somehow her life had become so full. With King, the girls—Dani, Piper, and even Lou—and now there was even a baby on the way, which Mel was more than a little excited to meet.

Could she really bring herself to believe that her life could grow even fuller still?

Mel left her post behind the counter and crossed to the collection of incense in the middle of the store. Canisters filled two shelves, samples poking from the top of the open jars inviting shoppers to smell them.

Mel plucked a stick of Nag Champa from its canister and lit it with the lighter from her pocket. She waited as the tip burned, before blowing it out, leaving a half-inch of glowing red.

As she placed the stick in its holder, a vision flashed in Mel's mind.

King's body pressed against hers. He had enveloped her in his arms, the smell of him filling her nostrils as intensely as if he were standing here *now*, holding her *now*.

But this wasn't now. Some part of her had jumped forward in time, to a moment that had yet to come.

The vision started to fade, melting back into the black even before Mel could fully grasp what it was she was seeing.

*Wait*, she thought, trying to grasp it by its edges and pull it back into focus. *When? When?*

There was no use. It was as slick as an eel, slipping away from her.

The only remnants she had been able to hold on to were

the scent of King, the feel of his warm body against hers. And a sharp emotion cutting across her awareness.

Fear? Desire?

Then the moment was gone. The scene behind her eyelids now nothing but darkness.

*You can try to bring it back.* A bright memory of her Grandmamie on her creaking porch rose. The woman took a deep drag on her hand-rolled cigarette before blowing the gray smoke skyward away from the granddaughter, a ten-year-old Melandra, who stood in front of her.

*But I only seen part of it*, little Mel explained. Mel couldn't remember, now that there were forty years between that moment and the one she was living in now, if it was the first time she'd had a vision, or simply one of the first she'd shared with Grandmamie.

*It don't matter*, Grandmamie said. *You can still call it back. I'll show you how.*

*I could do that now*, she thought. *I could figure out what that was all about.*

Or she could even ask the cards for clarification.

"Do I even want to know?" she muttered.

Part of her found the desire to know nearly irresistible. The other part—the arguably wiser part of her—knew that there was a danger to seeing the future before its time. That these previews caused as many problems as they fixed.

Or was this hesitation representative of the lack of self-trust she had for herself, that she'd only recently begun to rebuild. After her ex-husband, Terrence, walked into her life, turned it upside down with his manipulation and lies, she'd been forced to square with a lot of things she'd sought to ignore for far too long. She was still working out, especially in the quiet hours before dawn, as she lay alone in her bed, just how much her connection to Terrence had affected her intuition. Because he'd been so good at driving a wedge between her heart and mind, she'd chronically doubted herself. She knew she couldn't do what Grandmamie had called the old magic without faith in herself. Magic was a gift, true. But it required power and faith to wield it well.

And it had been a long time since Mel had felt in possession of either.

"No," she said. "I should wait."

*I should wait.*

Even as she thought this, she knew there was a big difference between *should* and *would*.

**6**

---

Ettore Celesti ended the call and slipped his phone back into the pocket of his tailored pants. For a moment, he could only stare out over the water. The sea burned blue, brightening the homes clinging to the Amalfi Coast on either side of the vista. It was a gorgeous sight. And yet he was so furious he could barely see it, no matter how the crystalline sunlight invited him.

A little hand slipped into his. He turned to find his daughter, Martina, smiling up at him. "Papa."

"What is it, my love?"

"*La mamma dice che il tuo caffè è pronto.*"

Still holding her small hand, he turned to find his wife, Sofia, waving to him from their table in front of the café.

"So it is. Come on."

He led her back to the table, where he found his coffee and sfogliatella waiting.

"*Martina, vieni qui. Siediti,*" Sofia said. Their daughter dutifully climbed up into the seat beside her mother.

When Sofia had suggested that they go away to Ravello for the weekend, Ettore had thought it was a good idea. Not only because he needed to step away from this ugly business of war but because he was hoping the mountain air would clear his head.

But ever since they'd left, he'd received only bad news. Phone call after phone call reporting loss and destruction. Disappointments all of them, and still no sign of *La Strega*.

Worse, he had lost his port. Konstantine had paid the right people, buying the allegiances he needed to extend his realm of power. For those that had remained loyal to the Celesti, he'd killed them all, leaving their bodies strewn on the docks.

All that planning and Ettore had only managed to track *La Strega* to some remote location in Nova Scotia of all places. Once his men were on the ground, they'd uncovered almost nothing.

Even the bodies of Aldo and the guards had been missing.

His plan to track her, know her movements, and trap her had proven impossible.

He could not track her the way he did others. Wayward cargo, backstabbing subordinates. Unless he shot a tracker into her ass like some wild beast, keeping tabs on her movements would be nearly impossible. And even if he did know where she was, what did it matter? She could simply be gone again before he was able to mobilize his people—which had been proven in this latest fiasco.

Still, that place must have meant something to her. It wasn't as if his team hadn't recovered *anything*. Maybe there would still be a way to leverage his find to his advantage. If not drive her out, at least unbalance her. Test her.

"You're not eating, Papa," Martina said, her brown eyes large and bright. "You don't like it? Is it burnt?"

He looked down at the pastry. Perfectly golden brown, sugar glistening.

"It's not burnt. Papa was just thinking."

"About what?" Martina asked. His six-year-old daughter bounced slightly as she swung her legs beneath the table.

*About how badly I want to hurt him.*

What had *La Strega* said?

*I will skin your dick with rusty pliers.*

It was a great idea. No wonder she was so skilled at what she did, if in addition to her tremendous power, she had an imagination like that.

How was it that Konstantine had managed to capture such a powerful ally?

He didn't deserve her. What had he promised her?

How had he managed to seduce her?

*Konstantine.*

Ettore remembered the first time he saw Konstantine. A thin young man, no older than twenty. Nico, Padre Leo's own son, had been abandoned by then, shipped off to some work camp in Russia. It was Konstantine who stood just behind the old priest's shoulder, watching the meeting unfold with eagle-sharp eyes. Padre Leo had called Konstantine his secretary, but even then Ettore knew him to be his apprentice. Ettore knew intelligence when he saw it, too. In the Celesti, few men with considerable brains were allowed to keep them in their head.

It was easier to rule when he remained the smartest man in the room.

Ettore had achieved the rank of third general by the time he'd been sent to Florence to broker a deal with Padre Leo.

Konstantine hadn't even filled out yet, and he'd been young enough to be Ettore's own son, with thirty years stretching between them. The idea he was forced to face one so young now felt insulting.

*What does he have that I don't?*

The Florentine had a handsome face and a great empire. Ettore wasn't incapable of seeing the obvious. But Ettore had those things as well, and years of experience that Konstantine had not earned.

Yet *La Strega* had not come to him.

"My love," Sofia said, looking at him reproachfully over the rim of her cappuccino. "Your daughter is speaking to you."

"Sorry. Eat your breakfast, then we can talk," he said. *"Forza, fai colazione."*

Neither of his companions said anything else as he ate his pastry and drank his coffee, his attention split between the beauty of the day and the problems churning in his mind.

Once he sat down his empty cup, his wife reached across the table and briefly clasped his hand, sparing him a gentle smile.

It was one of the things he appreciated about Sofia. She was a woman who knew how to keep her mouth shut. She saw much but said little. As far as Ettore was concerned, that was the perfect blend of qualities in a wife. Someone who would keep his secrets, but also both eyes peeled for trouble. There were times when her temper had flared over his infidelity. When he had been less than careful in his pursuits. But for the most part, he'd managed to keep peace in their marriage.

For him, the marriage had been a political one. She came from a rich and powerful family with deep connections in the underworld. But that didn't mean she couldn't drag a knife across his throat if he wasn't careful. That was reason enough to treat her with the courtesy she was due.

"Can I feed the pigeons?" Martina asked, holding up the remaining corner of her pastry.

"Go on," Sofia said, helping her to escape her chair.

Once Martina was out of earshot, Sofia said, "It's bad, isn't it?"

"And here I was just thinking about how wonderful it was that I have a wife who minds her own business."

"If we are in danger, I deserve to know. We have Martina to think of."

His irritation spiked, heating his ears. He looked around the café, at the tourists taking pictures of their food, wearing their sloppy premade clothes. Americans, probably.

"Ettore—"

"You think I will let something happen to Martina?" he asked. He refrained from slamming a fist down on the table as he would have certainly done had they been alone.

Sofia's eyes were wide as she leaned across the table, keeping her voice low. "I know what *La Strega* is capable of. And Modesto—"

Ettore clucked his tongue at the mention of his dead brother-in-law. He'd been looking for a way to get rid of Modesto without offending his wife for years.

Ettore supposed he had *La Strega* to thank for cleaning up that mess for him.

"She will kill all of us if she gets the chance. And then Martina will be taken and—"

"Lower your voice," Ettore commanded.

Sofia quit speaking altogether.

What could he tell her? That Konstantine had slaughtered hundreds of their people in the months since he declared war against them? That casualties were unavoidable in war, but by any account, they were losing? That his so-called best attempts were, as of yet, proving as clumsy and useless as Modesto's had been?

That if she was going to wring her hands and whimper her way through it, it was better that she went to Los Angeles to stay with her sister? Would it even matter if he pointed out that *La Strega* must be close to her due date, that now was the time to find a weak spot and press it? Before the bitch was free of her burden?

Or would Sofia only sympathize with her—mother to mother?

Before Ettore could compose himself, or an answer, his phone rang again.

Sofia muttered a curse under her breath as she pushed back her chair in exasperation. He watched her cross the square to Martina, who was still chasing the pigeons in the shadow of the Chiesa di San Giovanni del Toro.

Ettore pressed the phone to his ear. "*Pronto.*"

"I think I have something." Raffaele's voice was thin over the connection.

"Regarding?" Ettore was finding it difficult to hold on to the threads of his patience. Surely Raffaele knew that he had more than one matter at hand.

"*La Strega.*"

Ettore sat up then in spite of himself. Was he really that desperate for answers that he was ready to leap at the smallest thread of hope?

"Go on."

"You asked me to search for any possible connection to the Ravengers specifically, no?"

Ettore did not humor him with a reply. Of course he remembered. It had been a detail that had haunted Ettore's mind, causing him many sleepless nights. Why had *La Strega* formed the alliance with Konstantine, of all the *capi dei crimini* in the world? There were so many powerful men vying for the top, even some women. She could have chosen any one of them.

Then one night, after a few hours of feverish dreams, he began to ask himself when it had begun. When, exactly, might the pair have crossed paths.

"I've confirmed that the first accounts of *La Strega* coincided with the demise of the Martinelli family. No one remembers her before Fernando rang the alarm."

This was not news to Ettore. He'd already risen to power by the time the great Martinelli family had fallen. It had been a shock. But no one believed in *La Strega* then. Ettore thought that the idea of an old and powerful family like the Martinellis becoming extinguished in such a short time had simply been so shocking that men with small minds had needed to create a boogeyman in order to comprehend the unexpected shift in power.

"I did as you said," Raffaele continued. "I focused on those who would have a reason to take revenge against Fernando. Americans in particular, since you said you thought her accent was American."

"Get to the point, Raffaele."

The man sped up. "All the deaths were men. We've gone back as far as twenty years, but all of Fernando's targets had been men."

Martina turned to him and waved then. The sunlight had created a ring of light on her dark curls, giving him the impression of a halo. At the sight of her innocent face, an idea sprang fresh to his mind.

"Did any of them have children? Daughters?"

Raffaele was silent for a moment. "Yes, several had daughters. It looks like the youngest daughter was four, the oldest sixteen. No. There's another that was twenty-two."

"Focus on the daughters for now," Ettore said. He thought that *La Strega* couldn't be more than thirty now. "I want names, their stories, and where they are now."

"Of course."

"And pictures," he added, as Martina showed her mother something in her cupped hand.

Ettore was certain that if he saw a picture of *La Strega*, even as a little girl, he would know her at once. Though he struggled to imagine that such a creature had ever been a child.

"How many of them are there? How many girls?" he asked.

"Thirty-three," he said. "Including a pair of sisters."

"I want all the details of each by the end of tomorrow."

"Sir—"

"Tomorrow," Ettore said again, and ended the call. He didn't want to be on the phone as Martina ran toward him, her hands cupped around something protectively.

She stopped just short of his chair. "Papa, look!"

She opened her hands and showed him a small blue stone. "Isn't it pretty?"

"Very pretty," he said, though there was nothing so special about what she held cupped like a treasure. It was a rock. She could have found any hundred like it half buried in the dirt on the hillside.

As she stood before him, he searched her face, considering.

Would Martina hunt for vengeance? If *La Strega* killed him and her mother, would Martina grow up to be a killer?

He didn't think so. Martina had a soft heart and was too much like her mother. Forgiving and diplomatic.

Watchful but obedient.

Resigned.

It begged the question of what had been different for *La Strega*. What had pushed her to evolve from a grieving child into the dark executioner they'd grown to fear?

Maybe he would find out, soon enough.

**7**

———

Lou stepped from the shadows. Before her was an Olympic-size pool, blessedly free of people. The lights from the bottom rippled through the water, throwing waves of light against the walls.

Since Ettore had followed her to Nova Scotia, she didn't want to use her lake again so soon. She suspected that he'd left his people in the area, watching and awaiting her return.

Lou's other preferred haunt was her lake in Alaska. But in July, it was too bright in that part of the world, where the midnight sun would reign until November.

She was here for another reason. To see if she could slip through the water, even in the presence of some light. Usually some dark corner was enough.

Or at least it had been in the past. These days, her gift was proving to be less predictable. And it was the unpredictability, more than Ettore's movements, that drove her to be cautious. To keep testing herself as if she expected to fail.

With an unpleasant taste in her mouth, Lou recalled how her power had glitched two weeks before. It was the first time in a long time that she could recall such disobedience.

There had been other incidents in the past, in those early days of hunting Angelo and the Martinellis, when she had to be careful when she slept. Her drive and desire had been so singular that there was the danger she would slip against her will to her target while she slept.

But this problem—if it was a problem—was quite different.

Because it was one thing for her power to work of its own accord. To take Lou where it wanted her to go without her consent.

It was an entirely different thing for her power to not take her anywhere at all.

Yet that's exactly what had happened.

Fortunately, Lou had not been on the hunt when her power failed her. She hadn't been in a compromising or dangerous situation when she'd reached for her gift and had simply found it inaccessible.

She'd been with Piper and Dani. Had spent the afternoon on the beach, soaking up the sunshine. They'd brought a picnic to eat by the water. There had been a moment—several, in fact—when Lou's heart had felt so full to bursting. Where she could imagine herself as a young woman in a very different life. Spending a day in the sun with her friends.

But once they'd finished with their snacks and their gossip, after they'd shared their thoughts and fears and long stretches of peaceful silence had settled between them, it had come time to leave.

The sun had dipped low on the horizon and there were plenty of long shadows at her disposal. But when Lou had tried to step through them, nothing had happened.

She stood there, warm sunlight collected on her skin, fixed to the spot.

Piper and Dani had been even more shocked than she was.

Lou found that her compass was still there. Her inner knowing and connection to distant points in the world. She found first Konstantine and King in turn—but no matter how she reached for them, the darkness hadn't obeyed her. Despite her best efforts, her feet had remained firmly planted on the sand, holding the cooler and a beach towel, unmoored by her confusion.

Piper immediately fell into a catastrophizing panic that would have done Konstantine proud, asking her if it had ever happened before, what did she think had caused it, and what if it happened when she was in a fight. She'd only stopped when Dani pinched her arm.

"I'm sure it's just a pregnancy thing," Dani said. "One of my cousins lost her sense of smell for two months when she was pregnant. I bet if we just wait a bit, it'll work."

Dani had been right. Once the air had grown cool, her skin chilled in the absence of sunlight, Lou had found her power obedient again.

But Dani's words shimmered through her mind now as she slid into the pool and dipped below the surface.

*Maybe it's a pregnancy thing.*

Lou had suspected that her daughter would be gifted as she was almost as soon as she learned of her pregnancy. She had even suspected that Elena's gift might materialize in a way different than her own.

After all, the power had varied between Lou and Lucy. Lucy could shift through the darkness if it was complete enough.

Lou had been able to master moving through darkness, but also through water. And she didn't need complete darkness as Lucy had.

So why shouldn't Elena have her own gifts?

It hadn't occurred to Lou that her gifts might be lost or interrupted by her pregnancy. That what she needed most to keep them safe—her ability to be anywhere at any time—might be sacrificed in order to bring her daughter into the world.

Or maybe it was an issue of age. Aunt Lucy had once told her that it had been easier to slip when she was younger, and that as she'd aged, her power had waned rather than grown stronger, as it seemed to be doing for Lou.

Lou could now do things with her gifts, with the darkness, that she'd never imagined as a child. But maybe that would change. Maybe Lou had peaked without even realizing it, and would only experience a decline from here.

Lou was relieved to see that the water around her transformed from slate gray to blood red, warming considerably, even without the necessity for full darkness.

A moment later, she broke the surface and found La Loon as she always did.

A black shore lining the blood-red lake. The hazy sky, twin moons, and mountains in the distance. She swam for shore, trying not to think of the countless corpses of men under her feet. Surely the creatures who hunted these waters had devoured most of her offerings, but she had brought too many bodies to this strange world for there not to be bones or other remnants collected on the sea floor.

The corpses below her weren't what troubled her most. Nor was the inconvenience of Ettore's tracking her, limiting her, and forcing her to be more cautious in her movements.

*What if I lose my power altogether?* Lou thought, her stomach wrenching. *What if when Elena is born, my gift is passed on?*

Aunt Lucy had never had children, so this was unknown territory. There was no one else alive to ask. No record or instruction manual for how to proceed.

Lou's mind was still churning with these dark thoughts as she swam into the shallows. She didn't immediately rise, letting the waters rush over a small cut on her upper biceps for a few moments longer.

Konstantine had been worried about what the strange microbes in this nightmare landscape might do to her. But their daughter's development, at least from a medical sense, had been smooth sailing. The Ravengers' faithful doctor, Isabella, reassured Lou and Konstantine with each prenatal check-up that as far as she could tell, Elena would be born healthy.

Lou could credit these blood-red waters to her quick healing and improved strength and immunity. And once, when she'd been poisoned and nearly paralyzed, they had even nullified its effects. More times than she could count, Lou wondered if these waters would prove as beneficial for her daughter as they had for Lou.

*Make her strong.*

This was a silent prayer that she'd murmured in each of these spa-like reprieves.

*Even stronger than me.*

Atheist as she was, Lou was willing to pray to any god in any heaven that her daughter never experienced what she had. If someone even thought to stab, cut, shoot, or strike her daughter, Lou would wipe that miserable soul from the face of the earth.

Powers or no powers.

A screech sounded in the distance, followed by another.

Lou heard the thunderous approach of the serpentine creatures before she saw them.

The black foliage thick at the water's edge split open and two black heads burst into view. It was Jabbers, Lou's long-time companion, and one of the offspring.

Six legs, and puffy white mouths that reminded Lou always of the cottonmouth snakes she'd seen as a child. The way the light shone off their scales and their bodies shifted, a mass of constricting muscles as they approached.

She smiled at the memory of Konstantine freezing, dumbstruck with horror at the sight of Jabbers.

She was a horrifying creature, to be sure. The first time Lou had seen her, at the age of ten, she'd bitten Lou's shoulder, tossing her back into the water.

Now that Lou had time and distance from the memory on her side, the more she was convinced that the first bite had not been malicious. It had simply been the same exploratory bite that large sharks sometimes gave when mistaking a human for a seal.

Not that Jabbers hadn't proven to be fond of human flesh since. The most meaningful offering Lou had made, Angelo Martinelli, had been the very man who'd put several bullets in her father's head.

But there had been hundreds of unfortunate souls since.

Lou kept her eyes on the smaller of the two creatures as they approached.

The offspring were hard to predict. Lou didn't have the long-shared intimacy with them as she did with their mother.

It approached slowly, head bent low, nostrils flaring. Its pus-colored eyes fixed on her with intense curiosity.

There was a moment of uncertainty, a tension in the air, when Lou thought it might spring forth and attack her. She moved away instinctually.

Then Jabbers barked a loud, sharp cry. The offspring whined in return. And that was the end of it.

"Thanks," Lou said, certain that Jabbers had just spared her an altercation, whether playful or menacing.

Jabbers came to her then, pressing her black snout into the side of Lou's swollen abdomen. A soft cooing followed.

"Yeah, she's almost ready," Lou said, as if she understood

this language of clicks and screeches. "Less than a month and she'll be here."

Jabbers made another sound that Lou took to suggest pleasure or perhaps even anticipation.

"Assuming we get through this," she whispered.

She had to hope that luck stayed on her side.

That when the moment came and she finally stood before Ettore Celesti, it wouldn't also be the moment her power failed her.

**8**

———

Konstantine stepped into the hot shower, letting it beat down on his broad shoulders and torso. Physically, he was tired. They'd spent a lot of time renovating the courtyard today, and the fatigue rendering his muscles weak was proof of that. Yes, he could have let the contractors do most of the work—and had—but he wanted to have a hand in this work. Konstantine wanted to make the place his own.

*Their own.*

Even now he had visions of his daughter—who he always imagined with his eyes and Lou's dark hair and a smattering of freckles across the bridge of her nose—running across the courtyard and through the narrow passageways. A safe place she could explore, a walled haven in the center of Florence.

And he thought not only of his own happiness and that of the daughter he would soon meet but of Lou's too.

The shower door slid open and Konstantine whirled, ready for anything, only to find Lou gently grasping his elbow before he could extend it.

"Just me," she breathed, sliding into the shower with him.

She stepped to the other side and turned on the second showerhead. "Unless you want to be alone."

"No." He drew her close. "How was La Loon?"

He knew she'd gone, not just because of the stench of sulfur clinging to her skin but also because her hair was already wet.

"Did you hunt?"

"No," she said. "I just wanted to check on things."

She'd been doing that a lot lately. But when Konstantine pressed her as to why she felt she had to return to La Loon more and more frequently, Lou always dodged his question.

He'd only just pressed a kiss to her shoulder when his phone rang, spinning on the bathroom counter out of sight. He moved to get it, but Lou pulled him back under the hot stream. "Five more minutes."

He laughed in the crook of her neck.

Then his phone buzzed, signaling an incoming text message. Once. Twice. Three times.

After the eighth or ninth buzz, Lou raised a brow. "Sounds urgent."

"Matteo," Konstantine breathed, with partially an air of fondness and partially an air of annoyance.

Lou's face softened as her gaze slid down and away. And Konstantine knew she was using her compass to check on the boy.

"I don't sense any danger," she concluded. "But he seems desperate."

"He's only desperate for us to visit," Konstantine said, already anticipating this answer.

"Let's go after dinner," she said. "And maybe a foot massage."

"*Qualunque cosa voglia la mia regina.*" He held her again. "How's Elena?"

"Heavy."

Konstantine suppressed a chuckle. He'd learned from experience that though he found these admissions adorable, Lou did not always find humor in his amusement. Last time, she'd struck him ferociously with a pillow while asking if he thought back pain was a joke.

He'd since learned to curb his tongue.

"Where do you want to get dinner from? Giovanni's?"

"That'll do," she said. "And we can get chocolates from that place around the corner, for the kids."

Konstantine marveled, not for the first time, at how tender Lou was becoming, compared to those long years when she'd wanted nothing more than to see him dead, his corpse on the shores of La Loon along with his brothers'.

They seemed like different creatures to him now, that boogeyman of his past and this woman in his arms.

Lou interrupted his softening thoughts by biting his shoulder.

"Ow," he cried out, laughing. "*Vampira.*"

"I'm getting hungry," she said.

"*Sì, certo*," he said.

They left the shower and dressed, with Konstantine helping her into new clean shoes, lacing them tight. He confirmed with a simple glance at his phone that yes, the texts had been from an impatient Matteo, asking when they were going to come visit them again.

He was careful to say nothing about her eating an entire pizza on her own before eating half of the second one he'd been forced to order himself.

But despite her contented expression and easy conversation as they walked the streets of Florence, he noticed the way her gaze slid over the walkways, searching the crowds and the shadows of dark alleys. She was as on guard as he was, unable to fully relax even in their stronghold.

She checked Florence daily for trouble, scanning it

intensely and reporting back to him every whisper of doubt. The Celesti had infiltrated Florence months before, had killed Stefano's sister and burned down Konstantine's church. Dozens of his people had died that night, and since.

Though he knew she kept one ear turned to the city now, making sure none of the Celesti were hiding in his streets, they both knew they couldn't afford to be lax again. The price had been too high to pay the first time.

Guilt ate at the edge of his conscious as Lou bent over the chocolate counter, ordering treats for the children: four large boxes of hazelnut-flavored chocolates, Creminos, torrone candies, and biscotti too.

At the last moment, Konstantine added a bag of Galatines to the mix, even though he suspected this was a choice based on his own nostalgia rather than the children's taste.

Lou held the large bag, bouncing it. "They're going to love these. Ready?"

She led them to a shadowed corner between two narrow streets and they sidestepped into the darkness together.

For a moment, there was a pause.

Konstantine stood close to Lou, breathing the scent of soap and food clinging to her, but they did not move.

He was about to ask what was wrong when the darkness broke open and they were pulled through. Lou was scowling when the world remade itself around them.

The singular cry then swelled into a chorus of excited voices. Konstantine saw the children running toward them, full tilt, across the grounds of the monastery.

He laughed in spite of himself.

"Someone's happy to see us," Lou said, her own smile returning.

Through the smile Konstantine thought he saw something.

Was she still thinking of the graveyard Ettore had left as

his so-called *gift*? All those poor people, crammed in the containers, like cattle left to die.

Or was something else on her mind?

When the children reached them, they descended into chaos. Everyone spoke at once as Lou handed over the treats, apologizing for their delay as if they hadn't been here just five days before.

Konstantine also showed each child affection in turn, asking if they had enough to eat, enough warm socks and clothes, given that the English climate was far cooler than the Italian sunshine they were used to. Each gave a dutiful report on their progress, their studies, and a few brave ones, particularly Matteo, tried out their uncertain English in conversation with Lou.

As he watched the exchange, Konstantine found his own mind wandering. Back to the night they'd lost Nario, one child who wasn't here but should have been.

Guilt swelled up on him as Nario's face burned in his mind.

"Why can't we come home? We be safe. We be safe. Safe! Promise!" Matteo begged.

Gabriella pressed a hand to Lou's stretched belly. "*Aiuteremo con il bambino. Proteggeremo anche il bambino.*"

"*Sì,*" Matteo readily agreed. "We will help."

"It's my fault," Konstantine said, surprising himself. The words were out of his mouth before he'd intended to say them. He'd been thinking of Nario, of the one Konstantine had not been able to save. That loss had not been Lou's fault. Her talents were not what had failed them in a crucial time of need. It had been his own miscalculations that had cost him.

The children turned to him.

"It's my fault," he said again. "You are here because of me, not *La Strega.*"

Lou gave him a curious expression, clearly waiting to see what he said next.

But Konstantine couldn't tell them the whole truth. These children were not naïve. Each had come into his care because of some tragic or terrible circumstance of fate. Yet, if he had not been so arrogant, if he had not assumed that Florence belonged to him and him alone, that no one could penetrate his stronghold and walk into his home after all the precautions he'd taken after Nico's siege—that was on him.

All of that was true, but there was another reason. He didn't want the children to see him as fallible. They put so much trust in him and Lou. They believed with their whole hearts that they had the power to keep them safe. They believed that *La Strega* moved the heavens and earth. That she could be trusted with one's whole heart.

But Konstantine knew the truth. That though the love was there, they were still human—he and Lou. Humans who made very human errors.

He had let his guard down and Nario paid the price.

He would not make the same mistake again.

When he said no more, it fell to Lou to fill the gap in the conversation that his statement had made.

"When it's safe, we'll bring you home," she promised.

"But—"

Lou planted a kiss on the top of his head, and that shut the boy up. His cheeks flushed with color and Gabriella elbowed him hard, obviously annoyed by his reaction.

Lou was smiling, a rare, contented smile that told Konstantine how fond she was of the boy. But then again, how many children had she risked her life for? It was no secret that children were her weakness. Even Gein, one of the few targets who'd managed to capture and subdue Louie, had figured that out.

It was a scene that brought out a lot of tenderness in him.

Lou there in the gray light, sea breeze playing in her hair as she handed out the gifts to the children. And the thrill with which they received these reminders of home.

His heart clenched suddenly.

*We have to win*, he thought. *This is why I must win.*

There was too much at stake. Not only their lives, or his daughter's future. But all that he held dear was at risk of being lost.

He knew that Ettore was old school *capo dei crimini* like his predecessor had been. And the old school believed that when there was war, no one was left alive.

Ettore wouldn't be satisfied with Konstantine's death. His so-called principles would demand the lives of Lou, their unborn child, Stefano, and all the other Ravengers he could find. Even the orphans in his care.

He wouldn't stop until he saw Konstantine's mark on this world erased completely, leaving no trace that he'd existed at all.

*We have to win*, he thought again, even as a whisper of doubt flickered in his heart. *We have to.*

**9**

———————

Piper took a right hook to the jaw. "Jesus!"

Bane called a time-out, pulling one glove off her hand before yanking the mouthguard out from between her teeth. "Where's your head at, Genereux?"

"Why do you always ask me that after you hit me in the head?" she asked. "You *obviously* know where it is."

"I know when you're distracted. Your punches are shit when you're distracted."

Piper had been socked in the jaw too many times to protest otherwise. When Paulson, her 5:30, had proven to be a no-show, Piper had decided to head to the gym and go a few rounds with Bane. Now she was rethinking her decision.

"Is this about the war shit?" Bane pressed. She flipped one of her two pigtails over her sweaty shoulder. The black eyeliner under her eyes had begun to smudge from the increasing dampness. Piper took some satisfaction in that—knowing that at least this was a workout for Bane, too. So often Piper felt like she was fighting with a rabid alley cat on steroids. And it was always a little insulting, considering that the girl was at least five or six years younger than her.

*She might be petite, but man does she pack a punch.*

Piper opened and closed her mouth, trying to find relief for her aching jaw.

"No, it's not that," she said finally, once her ears had stopped ringing.

It honestly hadn't been. Lou had told her and Dani that the Ravengers and the Celesti had entered into some kind of old school *capo* war, but Piper wasn't really sure what that meant, only that Lou thought it was a big deal. That and she'd been pretty busy keeping Konstantine and his people alive while they battled it out.

It was Lou she was worried about. Not only because any day now she was going to pop out a kid and Piper had no idea what that would do to their lives—or their friendship—there was also Piper's concern for Lou's safety.

Her faith in Lou's abilities had been badly shaken when Gein—that psychopath—had briefly captured her back in February, early in Lou's pregnancy. Now that faith was hanging by a thread, after the beach.

Their trip to the beach had felt like such a lucky reprieve from what seemed like an endless workload. Dani, Piper, and Lou all had a tendency of taking on more than they should, and the fact that they'd made time just to hang out felt practically sacrosanct.

That was until Lou's power glitched. The look of fear, disbelief, and panic on Lou's face in that moment was seared into Piper's mind.

She hadn't been able to stop thinking about it.

What if Lou's power failed like that again at some critical moment? Like if Celesti had his hands wrapped around her throat or a gun pressed to her head?

"There you go again, flittin' off to la la land," Bane said. "Seriously, what's going on? If you know something, spill it. I have a right to know. They're my people, too."

Given the fact that Bane was part of the New Orleans Ravengers, it made sense that she'd want to know what was going on.

"It's not about the war," Piper finally admitted, only because it looked like Bane was going to hit her again if she didn't fess up.

She managed a step back before Bane threw another double punch. Piper blocked the first and ducked beneath the second.

"Everyone around here thinks this war with the Celesti is an old-world thing. That it's just a problem for the Ravengers over *there*. But—" Here Bane raised her voice, throwing it over her shoulder at the guy sitting with his back against the full-length mirrors, texting up a storm. "I think that's *stupid* to let your guard down in a *war*."

The guy looked up from his phone and rolled his eyes.

Bane socked Piper in the gut. "There were like three openings there when I was running my mouth, and you didn't take one."

*Because you scare the shit outta me.*

Piper, now winded, wheezed, "I was being polite."

"You can be polite when you're dead," Bane said.

She tapped Piper's gloved hand with her own, signaling the end of the fight.

Piper was grateful for the reprieve.

They'd been at it for forty-five minutes, and Piper hadn't been able to keep her mind in the match for more than half of it.

Bane used her teeth to rip off the strap on her glove. "You better tell me if something is up. I don't want to be a fish in a barrel. A sitting duck. Whatever the hell the metaphor is. You get what I'm saying?"

Piper thought again of that day on the beach, when Lou

had obviously reached for her power and had not found it. The long beat of silence that had followed Lou's stunned expression.

The embarrassment coating her words as Lou admitted, *I —can't. I can't do it.*

Bane was watching her carefully, watching the emotions play across her face. Finally, she said, "I get loyalty. I really do. She's your best friend."

And Piper believed her. "It's not—"

Bane rushed on before Piper could finish. "But I'll also remind you of all the times I saved your ass."

Bane had her there. But her loyalty to Lou ran deep, and Piper didn't think she could betray the confidence of her friend no matter the price. So instead of admitting that Lou's power was glitching, she said, "It's King. I'm so scared to tell him I don't want to be an agent."

Bane rolled her eyes at that. "For fuck's sake. Just tell him. If he can't accept your decision, fuck him."

At the thought of King, of what he might say when Piper told him the truth of her decision, a decision she hadn't even found the courage to tell Dani yet, her heart sped up.

"You didn't tell your girl yet either." Bane took a drink from her water bottle. "You're hoping they just, what? Figure it out telepathically?"

Piper should be used to this by now. Bane's forcefulness and no-nonsense approach to Piper's problems.

"I'm not scared to tell her," Piper said defensively. *As scared, anyway.*

"Then tell her first." Bane took another hit off the water bottle. "Then him. She'll be a warm-up."

"Sure." But Piper's mind was already wandering again as she packed up her things and took several long draughts from her own water bottle. Then she threw a wave at Garcia, who gave only the briefest of waves back before returning to the flurry of typing happening on his phone.

"Fifty bucks says he's fighting with his GF again," Bane said, coming to a stop beside the SUV Piper shared with Dani. "They've been at it for days. I think she's got another boyfriend."

"Bummer for him." Piper checked her phone. She hated making Dani wait for her, though according to Dani it was an imaginary problem, since she was perfectly happy to keep working until Piper arrived.

Sometimes it felt like Piper needed a crowbar to pry Dani away from her desk at *The Herald*.

*It's not like I'm one to talk*, she thought, especially considering the hours she'd worked the past three weeks.

"Remember what I said," Bane said, after Piper threw her stuff in the back of the SUV and closed the hatch.

"I'll tell them both." Piper climbed into the driver's seat and rolled down the window to let the grueling heat out.

If Piper didn't know Bane was such a hardass, she would've suspected that look to be actual concern.

Bane added, "And don't worry about *La Strega*. It doesn't matter that she's pregnant. She moves like a fucking ghost. She won't let herself get killed by some Celesti fucker. Even the big guy."

They tapped fists through the open window and Piper started the car. It wasn't until she was halfway to *The Herald* that she processed what Bane had said.

*She's a hell of a fighter. She moves like a fucking ghost.*

When had Bane seen her fight?

Piper cast her mind back, trying to remember the few times that Bane and Lou had interacted. But she couldn't recall a single time that Lou had the occasion to fight in front of Bane.

Maybe she had simply meant that Lou moved like a good fighter.

Bane was often going on about how great she was at sizing up her opponent long before they ever came to blows.

As Piper pulled out onto the road, SUV pointed in the direction of *The Herald*, she really hoped that Bane was right.

**10**

———

King saw Mel before she saw him. He'd just parked his Buick SUV in the alley beside Fortunes and Fixes, intent on reaching his apartment's bathroom as quickly as physically possible. After he and Piper had split up, King met with two clients over lunch in a café near City Park.

The woman had been a smoker and had insisted on sitting outside in the sun so she could smoke. King had nearly sweated to death while she recounted the details of the fraud case she'd hired him for. By the time the interview was over, King was craving a cold shower as strongly as he'd ever craved a drink or a joint.

He'd lived in a lot of climes during his life, but this particular recipe of heat and humidity had been a uniquely NOLA experience. Even though he'd been in New Orleans for years, every summer he found it shocking how the heat descended. Like a hot wet blanket thrown over him.

His daydreams of that cold shower dried up when he saw Mel through the large picture window of Fortunes and Fixes. Her back was to him as she talked to a customer, pointing at something on one of the shelves. King couldn't see what trinket or figurine it was from where he stood, but he could guess, as much time as he'd spent in that shop.

A protection medallion, maybe. Or a gris gris bag. Maybe a little statue of Mother Mary.

She turned suddenly and looked directly at him.

He hadn't expected it. The surprise of that dark-eyed gaze clamping on his startled a wave out of him. She'd seemed engrossed in her conversation with the customer.

For a reason he couldn't comprehend, he began to pat his pockets and pretend he'd forgotten something. Without looking back at Mel, he walked past the shop and hooked a right on Royal Street, heading in the direction of the agency, as if he had a reason to be there.

His ears burned as he walked, suddenly embarrassed by his behavior.

*Why in the hell did I do that? Just because I didn't want her to see me all sweaty and red?*

He had every reason to walk into the shop, say something simple, "hello" for starters, and then go upstairs and shower. Instead he'd run.

*Run.*

King hadn't run away from a girl he liked since middle school.

Beyond embarrassed, King passed the Crescent City Detective Agency, peering in only to find it dark. Maybe Paulson had canceled, or he and Piper had met somewhere else. Perhaps over dinner.

*Dinner.*

He'd almost forgotten. He hadn't yet picked up the tea and garlic bread she'd asked for.

Two blocks from the shop, he ducked into Mami's and placed the order.

He waited off to one side of the lobby as a pimply teen

bagged his food. A minute later, he was on the street with the bread in one hand and a gallon of sweet tea in the other.

As he passed the convenience store across from Fortunes and Fixes, King spotted a display of fresh flowers in the storefront window. Cheerful daisies, fragrant lilies, and deep red roses were the flowers he recognized. The other clusters of orange, purple, pink, and white eluded him. Carnations, maybe. Mums?

He'd almost gone inside for the small bouquet of daisies when he stopped himself.

Piper's strident voice rose in his mind, begging him not to do it.

*You're going to make it weird, man.*

Was he? Was bringing Mel flowers weird? It was something he'd done before. Admittedly, it had always been for birthdays or special occasions, celebrating her induction into the Women's Business Association, for example, which she'd worked hard to achieve.

But on a weekday and for no other reason except that he'd seen them and thought of her—was that too overt?

King preferred directness. Or at least he had until very recently. He supposed that shift in preference had started when she gave him that tarot reading months ago.

He'd asked for a projection of his love life, knowing full well how he felt about her. How could he not after months of sexy dreams featuring Mel as their star.

*What does it mean?* he'd asked after she'd spread all the cards on the table in her apartment.

After a pause, she'd said, *In this case, unrequited love...No one wants a heart that belongs to someone else. Even if the woman is dead.*

King took this explanation for what it was: an indirect refusal. And for months he'd been respectful, letting nothing change between them.

Until he got to thinking, of course.

It was the last statement he kept coming back to. *No one wants a heart that belongs to someone else. Even if the woman is dead.*

Mel's words had suggested that it wasn't a matter of unrequited love at all, but rather that she wasn't sure that King had truly moved on from the death of Lucy.

Ever since that night, he'd turned her words over in his mind, asking himself again and again if he was ready, if it was really Mel he loved, or the idea of her.

*Is it about Mel specifically? Or is it about finding what I had with Lucy again, and Mel just seems like the best prospect?*

No amount of obsessive self-reflection had brought him closer to clarity.

All his thinking had made him certain of only two things. That he and Mel were—and always would be—best friends. No matter what did or didn't happen between them. Nothing would change that.

Secondly, that she'd refused him.

However indirectly or gently, it had been a refusal. That was reason enough to leave the daisy bouquet in its tub of water and walk on. So that's what he did.

When he reached the shop this time, Mel was nowhere in sight.

His heart sank with disappointment.

*Make up your mind*, he chided himself. *You want to see her or you're hiding because you're sweaty. Which is it?*

As he crossed the threshold, the chandelier moaned and the lights flickered, and the sound effects gave the impression that the shop was haunted.

A furry head with erect ears popped out of the storeroom at the announcement of his arrival. It was Lady, the Belgian Malinois he shared with Mel. The pup trotted over, tail swishing and dark eyes bright.

"Hey ya, girl." He placed the tea on the floor to free his hand so he could give the dog a vigorous scratch behind her ears. "Did you have a good day?"

Lady responded by turning, pressing the weight of her hip against King's leg. King wondered if the dog was more inter-ested in the bread than him. If she was, he could hardly blame her.

Mel's bangles rang out, alerting him to her approach. It was the soft musical sound he'd come to associate with Mel's movements, the tinkling of her bracelets clanking softly against one another.

After a steadying breath, King looked up into her face. She was on the stairs, descending. Her long skirts flowed around her, her tank top hugging her torso closely. The bangles matched the long gold ankh earrings that hung from her ears. As on most days, her eyes were lined black, and her headscarf matched the color of her long skirt.

She was gorgeous. King had always thought so. It was only recently, however, that he'd begun to look at such thoughts a little more closely, seeing them for what they really were.

"You look a mess," she said.

A surprised laugh escaped him.

"I'm sure I do. It's hot out there. Just let me rinse off and I'll be over," he said, standing. His knees protested even more than the dog, who was unhappy to have her stream of affec-tion cut short.

Mel opened her arms and King's heart dropped into his stomach.

There was a moment when he wanted nothing more than to walk into those arms and press his face into the crook of her neck, feel her long nails rake across his scalp deliciously.

"I'll take those," she said. "Though I can't promise you there will be any left by the time you come over. It smells so good."

King came back to his senses, wondering if he'd seen, even for the briefest of moments, something flicker behind Mel's eyes before she'd looked away.

"I'll trust you to leave me at least one," he said, striving to match her light tone. "I'll be quick."

Once he was in his apartment, with the door shut firmly between them, he felt his face cool. He was unhappy to see that there was still a redness in his cheeks when he caught sight of himself in the bathroom mirror, but he decided, almost as quickly, that the redness could have easily been blamed on the heat of the day rather than on any attraction he was struggling to suppress.

He turned the water to cold, hissing as he stepped into the freezing stream. But it took him only a moment to adjust to the frigid temperature, grateful to feel his body cool to a more tolerable level.

Ten minutes later he was dressed, hair combed, even taking a moment to trim and clean his nails. On his dresser was a bottle of cologne that Mel had given him the Christmas before.

*I didn't know what to get you. You're so hard to shop for*, she'd said.

The idea that she'd seen the cologne and thought of him had been a memory he'd often replayed, searching for meaning by turning it this way and that. She'd looked apologetic when handing it over, as if it were a gift she hadn't really wanted to give him.

King removed the top and smelled it. It was nice. Not one of those cheap colognes which had more alcohol than scent. This one was a mix of oils including cedar and sandalwood.

He went back and forth, trying to decide if their usual dinner and TV date was an appropriate venue for cologne.

*It lets her know you appreciate the gift. Or maybe she's waiting for a reason to lean in and get close, under the pretense of smelling you.*

It was this last thought rather than the former that made him uncap the cologne and spray it on his chest.

"There." He gave himself one final appraising look in the mirror. "Now let's not cause any trouble."

**11**

___

Lou lay on the exam table, her shirt lifted to expose her belly. The doctor adjusted herself on the stool, leaning forward to apply another pump of antiseptic onto her hands before reaching for the transducer.

"It will be cold," Isabella warned, as she always did before she squeezed gel onto Lou's stretched belly. "You are the only woman who never flinches when I do this. You don't mind the cold?"

"No," Lou said. That was an easier response than, *What is cold compared to bullets or a good knife in the back?*

Lou waited with bated breath as the wand moved over her stomach, creating the image of her sleeping daughter inside her. Before Isabella could provide the update, the door opened and Konstantine strode in with a coffee in his hand.

"Your coffee, *amore mio*." He handed her the steaming cup before settling into the empty chair beside Lou's exam table.

After several quiet moments of probing, Isabella declared, "It all looks good to me. She's growing as she should, and she's in position. You may very well give birth early."

Lou was relieved to hear this. Apart from a scare in the

second trimester, when for two weeks Elena had fallen below the ideal growth rate, the pregnancy had been an easy one— the assaults to Lou's organs notwithstanding.

"I don't suppose you can tell me how close I am?" she asked.

"I cannot predict the exact moment, no, but it looks like she is ready," the doctor said with the emphatic Italian hand gestures that Lou had come to expect from the Florentines in her life. "Your due date is August twenty-sixth, no? Perhaps we will meet her in two or three weeks."

"Will it be okay if she comes early?" Konstantine asked, a hint of concern in his voice.

"*Sì, sì.* She's developed enough that she will be fine if she comes early. But I will say what I always say. Avoid stress, keep eating well, relax. Do this and you will get through this last bit without problems. If you are still feeling impatient closer to the due date, we can do a trans-vaginal ultrasound to see if there are any changes in the cervix."

"I can't wait to meet her," Konstantine said, before placing a kiss on Lou's shoulder.

Lou never tired of that—seeing his enthusiasm for Elena's arrival.

"You'll be outnumbered," she said. "Two to one."

"That is when the real fun will begin," the doctor laughed, pushing the ultrasound cart away from the bed. "Do you have any questions for me?"

"No." They spoke at the same time.

"Then I will see you next week. Be careful until then."

She pushed her cart from the room as Konstantine handed Lou a towel. She used it to wipe the gel off her stomach before sitting up with her coffee.

"How do you feel?" Konstantine asked her.

He'd been asking her that a lot lately. Every third or

fourth question it felt like, as if he expected her water to break and their daughter to spring forth at any second.

"Fine," she said. "How do you feel?"

"Nervous. Stressed. Excited," he said as he came up onto his toes. "I want her to be here. But I do not feel ready at the same time."

Lou thought Konstantine's feelings were a little more oriented toward their unborn child when it came to feeling unprepared. Lou's main desire was to see Ettore dead at her feet first, rather than making sure they had enough diapers.

Konstantine cleared his throat. "*Amore mio*, I've been thinking."

Lou took a sip of coffee, eyebrow arching. "About?"

She already had the distinct impression that she wouldn't like whatever it was he was about to say.

"I was wondering—"

"You're making it worse by hesitating."

He exhaled. "How do you feel about running away to an island with me?"

"Sounds romantic. Bad timing though, considering how busy we are."

He took her hand. "We could *not* be busy. Just for a little while."

*Ah. There it is.*

"I just think it might be better for us if we are somewhere safe until you have Elena. Until after you heal."

"You're asking for me to hide with you, rather than fight," she said, unable to keep the cold out of her voice.

"It would only be for two or three months," he said. "Enough time for you to give birth and heal and then—"

"And where is Stefano during these three months? Fighting, I assume. Because the war won't stop just because we run away."

"*Amore mio.*"

"You're going to leave your people to fend for themselves?"

"Stefano's already agreed," Konstantine said, too quickly, as if he'd known she would ask. "He understands."

"I'm sure he does. I'm sure he'll understand perfectly when he's lying in a coffin too. We can bury him next to his sister and her dead kids."

This was unfair and Lou knew it. She wasn't even sure why she was so mad.

Was it because he was asking her to run away from a fight instead of into it? A possibility that Lou could never have conceived.

Or was it because she knew he was right?

With Lou's power glitching the way it was, it wasn't safe to fight.

Granted, it had only happened one time.

True, also, that it hadn't been a matter of not being able to use her gift at all, only that she'd required more darkness than usual to move the world around her. There had been a delay. Not a total loss.

*Or so I keep telling myself.*

"I don't want to bring her into a world where we're at war," Lou said at last. "And Ettore doesn't deserve to even share a planet with her."

Konstantine took her hand. His deep green eyes searched hers. As he held her gaze, Lou pressed the tip of her finger into the scar running along his cheek. It was faded now but still a reminder of Nico, another fool who'd done all he could to wipe Konstantine from this earth. "I want the same thing that you want, *amore mio*. But it is possible we will not have it in three months, and I do not want to risk your life or Elena's. I'm willing to be as patient as I have to be if it means keeping you both safe."

"His existence is the risk," Lou said.

When Konstantine sighed, it was with the weariness of a man who knew he wouldn't win this one.

"Just think on it," he said. "Stefano is strong enough to lead in my absence. The only real risk of being alone on an island with me is that you will get sick of me. That's a long time to spend alone together."

"I do get pretty restless."

"And there is only so much I can do to entertain you," he said. His grin was wicked. When he looked at her up through his lashes like that, Lou could see a hint of the boy she'd met all those years before. "But I would certainly try my best."

She kissed him.

As she hoped, this tabled the conversation. Even after they left the clinic and reentered the streets of Florence, heading in the direction of the church near the city center, he spoke of other things. Their next meal, preparations for the baby, the ongoing renovations at the church.

If he noticed how distracted she was, he didn't press her on it.

More than once, Lou turned her compass toward Ettore, gaining a sense of where the man was, what he was doing. She was unsurprised to find he was surrounded by others, somewhere bright and sunny. She was beginning to believe that was his intention, to stay beyond reach.

Konstantine bought her two scoops of *nocciola* gelato and held her hand as they moved through the narrow streets. Lou tried to pay attention to the updates on the renovations, but her mind kept returning to his proposal.

She tried to picture herself on an island with him. Some elegant home in a secluded place with views of the water. It was a gorgeous image, him stretched out on white sheets, sunlight on his cheeks, as a sea breeze rolled over their skin from an open window.

*All that sunlight.*

Elena would love it.

She would not.

It wasn't just that such a place didn't instinctually feel like the safest place for her. It was also that she couldn't stop thinking about the last time she'd been on the beach. How her gift had failed her.

And there was the other matter weighing on her mind.

She couldn't call it her compass exactly. What she called her *compass* was always tied to the present moment. A directional point that allowed her to move through the world on her power alone.

Whatever this was, it felt more aligned to the future. An instinctual feeling, yes, but foreboding in its nature. Worse, it was stronger when she reached for Ettore.

*Something's about to happen,* Lou thought. Though she couldn't have explained how she knew this, or what reason she had for the feeling stirring within her. Was she sensing his mood, maybe? His pleasure, which certainly spelled only bad news for her.

*Something terrible is on its way.*


Ettore looked over his shoulder before accelerating his motorcycle. The Amalfi cliffside loomed formidable and gray in his left field of vision, with the sea stretching out as far as the eye could see on his right.

The wind blowing off the sea cut through his hair as he pulled to the front of the pack and motioned for the others to ease off the road half a kilometer ahead. One by one their group slid into the pull-out taking up the remaining space at the vista's edge despite the cluster of tourists standing near the railings for pictures.

He smiled to himself as a tour guide pulled a bottle of limoncello and glasses from his trunk and poured each tourist a glass. They laughed and cheered, before turning back to admire the sea.

Ettore envied them. To be on vacation, to be somewhere far away, enjoying its beauty, with no thoughts to the cares or concerns that he had waiting for him at home.

He'd thought this ride would make him feel better. It usually did. There had been no shortage of Celesti willing to join him. But even as they'd ridden through arguably some of the most beautiful parts of his glorious country, he hadn't been able to shake thoughts of *La Strega* and the Florentine from his mind.

He'd almost driven himself insane with the thought that he could *feel* her, reaching into his brain with that power of hers. As if she were lingering in some phantomic, half-existing state at the edge of his presence.

But she had not come. After several hyperaware moments in which his heart had pounded incessantly, certain she was about to appear, the feeling dissipated.

Yet this coastline, the abundance of company and sunshine, the fresh air—none of it was enough to completely drive her from his mind. He was surrounded by men who would obey his commands at the barest flick of his fingers. He had more money than God.

His small loss of all that cargo was nothing compared to all that he had gained in his years ruling the Celesti. He'd expanded the empire in ways his predecessor had never even considered.

How could he let a man like Konstantine steal his happiness from him?

What did Konstantine know of sacrifice?

Ettore knew all about Konstantine's smooth rise to power. He'd heard the stories about how Padre Leo, father of the Ravengers, protected the boy from a young age, giving him every advantage and opportunity that he denied even his own son, Nico. How his own birth had been blessed simply for the fact that he'd been born a Martinelli. Bastard though he was, he was still a son of one of the most powerful men in Italy—until *La Strega* destroyed him.

Then Konstantine consolidated all that power—of both the Martinelli and Ravenger empires—for himself, and had had *La Strega* at his back ever since. A privileged birth, a blessed life, and then a powerful ally.

What had Konstantine done to earn any of it?

Nothing.

Ettore had been born in the slums of Naples. Born and bred in the streets to an addicted whore and her dealer. Neither planned nor wanted. For every opportunity Ettore had managed to secure for himself, he'd been kicked in the teeth at least one hundred times.

Nothing had been handed to him.

Everything he'd achieved was paid for with Ettore's own blood, sweat, and tears.

A hand clamped his shoulder, and Ettore turned to find Raffaele at his arm.

"I have some news for you."

"Tell me." Ettore placed his helmet on the seat of his Ducati.

"You told me to focus on the daughters of men targeted by Fernando."

"*Sì.*" He hoped Raffaele would get to the point. The man had the most tedious way of sharing information. "Go on."

Ettore looked out over the blue waters. He found it calmed him.

"We have the photos of the daughters." Raffaele handed over his phone.

He took a deep breath and then began to swipe through the pictures.

"We eliminated the women that were too old or too young to be *La Strega*," Raffaele went on.

Ettore paused. "Then who the hell is this?"

He pointed at the photo of the child looking up at him. She couldn't be more than ten years old at the time the picture was taken.

"There were a few of the women we couldn't find current photos for, so we had to use what we could find. The photos immediately following—yes, that one there, with the little mark—that is an age progression."

Ettore kept scrolling. It was hard to believe that any of these women could possibly be *La Strega*. Too many of them had bright smiles. They looked like accountants and schoolteachers. Not a single one seemed like the kind of woman to wear a leather jacket patched with duct tape, mirrored shades, and packing enough iron to storm the Vatican.

Ettore hesitated on a photo.

The girl was young. Eleven or twelve years old. The photo itself was grainy. It hadn't been digital whenever it was printed.

Ettore swiped again to see the age progression, his heart speeding up.

It wasn't an exact match for *La Strega*. There was something off about the eyes. These eyes looked far brighter than the twin flames of hell he'd so briefly looked into.

Because he'd been there that night, in Konstantine's church. He'd pretended to be safely hidden away in Naples, of course, while the war waged on. But the truth was that he'd hidden himself in the raid amongst Modesto's entourage, wanting to see Konstantine's power for himself.

He hadn't been able to resist the temptation.

Only he hadn't expected to see *La Strega*. He'd half believed her to be a rumor, spread by Konstantine to strike fear in his enemies. Or perhaps invented by his enemies themselves to explain their humiliating defeats.

But there she'd been, stepping from the flames as if she'd been born of them. As if Hell itself had opened for her and she had only to walk through.

He scrolled through the remaining candidates, only to return to the phone again. "I want the names of these two."

Raffaele scanned his notes. "Tamara Lincoln and Louie Thorne."

"Who are they?" he asked.

"Tamara Lincoln lives in Asheville, North Carolina." Raffaele tripped over the American words, which clearly felt foreign on his tongue. It was no matter. Ettore knew enough English to understand what the man meant to say. "She teaches pottery classes and yoga, lives alone, and has three cats. Her father was a cop in Raleigh-Durham until the Martinellis put a hit on him. He'd been stealing product from the Martinellis and reselling it."

"And the other," Ettore said. He'd gone back to the grainy photo of the little girl. Even at this age, there was something dark in her eyes. Something the age progression had been unable to reproduce in its rendering. He pointed at her, turning the phone so Raffaele could see. "This one."

"Louie Thorne. A funny name for a girl," he said.

Ettore's impatience flared. "Tell me about her father."

"He was a DEA agent based in St. Louis. He arrested Benito Martinelli and sent him to prison even though Fernando threatened him. Angelo went to the house, killed him and the wife."

"But not the girl."

"In the report it says they found her later. I hear Angelo got into trouble for that. For lying."

"Lying?"

"Yes, he told his father that he'd killed them all. Then the girl was found alive." Raffaele shrugged. "It happens. He probably didn't want to look for her if she was hiding."

*Had she been hiding or missing?* Ettore wondered.

Maybe even at this young age, she'd been able to use her gifts. If *La Strega* had her gifts even as a child, it would be nothing for her to escape Angelo Martinelli.

"What does she do now?" Ettore felt that strange pressure again. The doubling, a sudden second presence in the air around him that made him feel as though *La Strega* would appear at any moment.

"We don't know."

Ettore looked up from the phone. "You don't *know?*"

"We couldn't find anything on her. She has an address in St. Louis, but it is only a PO box. There is nothing else."

Ettore resisted the urge to reach out and wrap a hand around Raffaele's throat. Instead he looked out over the blue water, letting the sight of the cheerful white crests wash over him.

Raffaele seemed to sense his darkening mood. "She was twelve when her parents died. Then she lived with her aunt near Chicago. She graduated from high school, but after that, nothing. She didn't go to a university, she didn't get a job, vote. She never married or had a baby. She has no driver's license or credit card. There's nothing."

"A strange life indeed," Ettore muttered.

Louie Thorne.

Could it be her? *La Strega?*

*Only one way to find out.*

Ettore took a screenshot of the twelve-year-old Louie Thorne and texted it to himself before handing the phone back to Raffaele.

"Find out everything you can on those two," Ettore said. His gut said Louie was the one he wanted, but there was still a chance that the other woman was *La Strega*. For all he knew, all those cats were a cover for her secret life.

"But there isn't—"

"Do whatever you have to do, but I want information on them both."

"Understood." Raffaele shuffled away without further comment, leaving Ettore alone with his thoughts and the vast blue sea.

*Louie Thorne.*

*Are you the one I'm looking for?*

**12**

King played a game with himself as he walked from the Crescent City Detective Agency to Café du Monde. Winding his way through the French Quarter, he moved as if he were a vampire and direct sunlight was to be avoided at all costs. If anyone had been watching, they would have thought his path erratic as he moved from one shaded patch to another, hugging the shadows of buildings, looming trees, and hedges. He'd had his nose buried in case files since eight that morning, and now, in need of a coffee as the afternoon slump of fatigue pressed against his mind, he'd decided to walk to Café du Monde.

No sooner had he stepped out of the agency's door did he realize that the heat of the day was already unbearable. The direct sun on his bare skin felt like a hot skillet, and this sensation was only made worse by the humidity that gave the air a damp quality. It was only this vampiric game of his that helped him to arrive at Café du Monde with some semblance of decency rather than with his clothes soaked right through.

Fortunately, the line was thin this time of year. Few

tourists spent their summers in New Orleans. It was too miserable and there were no real beaches to be had.

King ordered two coffees and beignets and caught up with Suze, the friendly woman behind the counter. She told him all about an upcoming vacation, week after next, where they hoped to pass a week in Jamaica eating fried plantains. King told her the break was well deserved and wished her a pleasant time while collecting his beignets and coffees.

Now that his task was complete, and the promise of relief from the heat was quickly approaching, King's mind wandered away from the task at hand to the night he'd spent with Mel. He'd been doing that more and more lately, reviewing their encounters after the fact, as if he were giving each experience a postmortem.

In this case, King was transfixed on the fact that Mel had worn no bra under her silk pajamas. She was usually in her PJs, her hair in its satin bonnet, when King came over to binge several episodes of *RuPaul's Drag Race* over dinner. He'd never seen her do so without her bra on.

He'd been a gentleman, of course. King wasn't some sixteen-year-old boy who couldn't control his wandering eyes.

*Maybe it didn't mean anything. Maybe she just wanted to be more comfortable.*

He'd half convinced himself of the latter before his mind wandered off to other key moments. It had helped that King had enough self-awareness to hear himself. If one of his friends, Dick White, for example, had said that a woman had decided not to wear a bra around him and surely that meant something, King would've been inclined to believe that the man was seeing what he wanted. He couldn't deny that it was the same with Mel, that there was plenty he was hoping to see, her interest in him being at the top of the list.

Thinking of Dick, King pulled out his cell with his free

hand and called his old friend. It rang four times before going to voicemail.

"I was just thinking about you," King said to the recording. "Call when you have a chance."

King's guts soured the way they always did when failing to reach White. They'd been quite close for a time. But ever since their near-death experience, the man was irrevocably changed. The bomb blast had permanently scarred White's face and part of his body, causing enough nerve damage to his firing hand that White would never hold a service pistol in that grip again.

But still, King thought he could have retrained his hands, gotten physical therapy if he wanted. Instead, he'd left the city with his family, and every attempt that King made to reconnect was met with stony silence at worst, or short, noncommittal texts at best.

King's phone buzzed in his hand.

*Thanks for calling. We're at Disney with the girls today. I'll call back later.*

King was glad to get the message, knowing that White was unlikely to actually call since he had not done as promised at least half a dozen times before.

King recognized shame when he saw it.

It wasn't only the disfigurement, or the forced leave from the NOLA PD. It was also what King had learned from the bomber kid.

The misguided boy had painted a very different picture when they'd been at his mercy, unsure if he was going to pull the trigger or explode the bomb and end their lives.

He'd told King about a Detective Dick White who had beguiled and betrayed him.

King could forgive any man an honest mistake. He'd tried to say as much to White more than once, but the man was closed off to him now. It would be best to give White time and space to work this out on his own. All King could do was keep reaching out, keep leaving the door open.

Mention of Disney World drove King to think of the other surprising departure from his life this year. Not only had he watched White leave the city, but his ex, Beth, was now living in an Orlando condo ten minutes from her son and daughter-in-law's place.

Unlike White, who left the city to escape something, Beth had left *for* something. With the arrival of her first grandchild, Beth was living the dream life she'd hoped and prayed for. She and King had kept in touch for the first couple of months, texting often. King received more baby photos than he could count. But eventually those texts petered out too. No matter how passionate the affair may have been—for her—it had run its course. Since they no longer worked in the same ecosystem or could join each other for a meal, the substance of their conversations dried up.

*Unlike with Mel,* he thought suddenly.

He and Mel could talk about anything for hours.

Just the night before, while they'd eaten their garlic bread and drunk their sweet tea, they'd covered tremendous ground. Not just about the contents of the *Drag Race* episode, but also about a few of King's cases, about Lou's pregnancy, about the upcoming parade for the festival, and changes that Mel had intended to make to the shop, stating that the layout was overdue for a redesign. They ended by exchanging reports of Lady, their shared Belgian Malinois. She was due for her annual shots, and King promised to call tomorrow with his schedule, so Mel could make the appointment.

Their conversation had been easy, and comfortable, even with the presence of Mel's nipples increasing his awareness of her body and the undercurrent of his own desire. It brought him great comfort that if nothing else, they were definitely still friends. If Mel knew he wanted more, that she was the object of his inquiry all those months ago, she hadn't let it dampen their friendship, for which he was grateful.

Even if it had created a strong urge for him to ask, *You know I'm talking about you, right?*

He imagined it in his head. The look on her face when he walked up to her and said, *You know the woman I was asking about is you, don't you?*

The door to the Crescent City Detective Agency was unlocked when King reached it. With a bump of his hip, he was able to pop it open despite its tendency to swell in its frame when the heat warped it.

Piper was on the phone with someone, an apartment manager by the sound of it, so King only put her coffee and bag of beignets on her desk before taking his seat at his own desk across from her.

*Thank you*, she mouthed dramatically as she held the receiver away from her face.

King returned with his own *You're welcome*, before turning his attention to his planner. It took a bit of back and forth with Mel to get a fix on an appointment for Lady, but once it was all settled, King was able to turn his attention to his own case work.

The walk, as hot as it had been, had been a good choice. It had cleared the cobwebs from his thoughts which had kept him from progressing with the identity theft case he'd spent the morning on. He'd hoped one of his leads would uncover who might have catfished Ms. Dixon and opened a Facebook account for the sole purpose of tormenting her ex-husband. But they had all been dead ends. The walk shook a couple of ideas loose, and King's optimism was sputtering back to life.

Back in the office, he submerged himself in the work again as the afternoon light shone through the large front windows, falling across the polished floor. The only sound was their fingers flying across the keys of their computers, and pens scratching out notes.

He would have been greatly pleased by this, the peace and beauty of it, if not for the micro-glances being shot in his direction. He grabbed a paper off his desk, opened it, and held it up as if reading it. Instead, his eyes were fixed on the upper-right corner, bringing Piper's face into sharp focus where she sat at the opposite desk.

Sure enough, more than once, Piper looked in his direction, her mouth opening and closing like a fish's.

"What is it?" he said finally, closing the paper.

She went rigid. "Nothing. I was—I'm just thinking."

"About—"

"About this case," she blurted.

"You can ask me questions if you've got them," he said. "Just because it's your case doesn't mean we can't talk about it."

"No questions," she said. "I'm just—I'm just putting it all together."

King knew women well enough to know when one wanted to tell him something. But he'd also learned over the years when not to push.

Whatever Piper wanted to tell him, she wasn't ready.

"Okay, well if something comes to you, you know where to find me," he said.

Then, just as King suspected would happen, Piper rose suddenly, putting her laptop and notebook into her bag. "I think I'll call it a day. I need a nap after looking at all these numbers. My eyes are going cross."

"Sure. Rest up," he said.

Piper walked out the front door instead of up the stairs to her apartment, forgetting the coffee he'd brought her on the desk.

"Definitely," he said to the empty office. "She's definitely got something to say."

**13**

———

Piper's face burned as she hurried away from Royal Street, down St. Peters in the direction of the streetcar stop. It was way too hot to be running, but Piper wanted to put as much distance between herself and King as she could.

Why'd she have to go and make it weird?

She'd just wanted to tell him and get it over with. She'd worked herself up to the conversation the whole time he'd been gone. She knew exactly how long it took King to walk to the café and back, and while he was away, she rehearsed what she would say. How she would tell him that she didn't want to be an agent.

Not for the DEA. Not for the FBI. That she had decided, with finality, that it wasn't the right path for her.

Her doubts had formed when they'd encountered two FBI agents during the bomber case. Agent Smith had made the job glamorous enough in her own penal code sort of way, but once, just as she was leaving the agency, she'd said to Piper, *I don't think you have what it takes to be an agent.* The words had felt like a punch to the gut until the agent elaborated. *If you were a federal agent, you'd be expected to put the case above your part-ner. Whether that be your professional partner or your life partner. Obstructing justice in order to protect the people you care about would only get you fired, arrested, or killed.*

Piper couldn't argue with her. She would know the job far better than Piper did, better even, Piper suspected, than King. Because Piper had no illusions that her experience on the force would be far different than King's, given that she was a woman.

She'd tried to jokingly tell him how she really felt, trying to appeal to his own newfound revulsion for the failings of the system, but Piper wasn't confident that the words were landing.

Now each time that she imagined declaring her inten-tions, insisting instead that the agent life wasn't for her, she couldn't help but also imagine that flicker of disappointment on his face.

It made her heart drop every time.

She didn't know why his opinion mattered so much to her. Why in the world did she need his approval? They'd been through a lot together and he was her mentor, but it wasn't like he was her dad or grandfather or something. Why in the world did she feel like his disapproval would be the worst thing in the world?

*What if he's disappointed?* she thought as she pulled herself up onto the streetcar and paid the fare before taking her seat. It was still possible that with time he would forgive her for not aspiring to more.

*That's it*, she realized. *That would be the part that hurt.*

The idea that King would think less of her because she wasn't ambitious. That she instead wanted to do what made her happy rather than work her way up the ranks of a job that felt far more limiting than aspiring. What the hell could the FBI offer her that would be better than what she already had with Dani and Lou? With her PI work with King?

When she asked herself that, it always felt like becoming an agent would be taking a step back rather than forward. She couldn't do it.

She just couldn't.

Her phone went off and it was a text from Bane.

*You do it yet or you still being a pussy about it?*

"How does she know?" Piper muttered. Was the girl psychic or something?

When Piper didn't answer right away, the little typing bubble popped up on her phone.

*You are what you eat*, Bane's next text said, followed by three chicken emojis.

Because there was no emoji for what Piper really wanted to say, she settled for a thumbs down.

*Lame*, was her reply.

If Bane wrote anything else, it would have to wait because the streetcar was rolling up to Piper's stop. She thanked the driver as she climbed down, heading east in the direction of the apartment complex where Willa had lived.

Again Piper's embarrassment swelled as she replayed telling King that she was going to take a nap and then promptly walking out the front door.

She swore under her breath, trying to focus instead on the task at hand.

A breeze kicked up, but it didn't help. The air only felt like hot breath on her face and neck rather than a welcome relief from the heat of the day.

The Spanish moss hanging from the old trees lining the street swayed in the breeze, sounding to Piper like tiny hands clapping.

By the time she reached Willa's apartment, sweat had

broken out along her hairline and the back of her neck. She was about to knock when a hand clamped on her shoulder.

Piper jumped, swallowing a scream in her throat.

She turned to find Lou standing behind her. For a moment all she saw was the twin expression of her terrified face before Lou pushed her mirrored sunglasses up onto her head.

"Geezus, Lou-blue. I almost shit myself. Don't do that."

"You were sending distress signals." Lou gave the building a once-over as if she were unimpressed by the salmon-colored exterior, no matter how cheery and freshly painted it may be. "I see no danger."

"I was freaking out about something else, and if that's your current response time, I hope I'm not in danger anytime soon. That was like ten minutes ago."

"I was eating. And I knew you weren't really in danger."

Piper huffed. "Who am I to get between a pregnant woman and her meals."

Piper just remembered the coffee she'd forgotten on her desk.

"Ah shit," she muttered, her embarrassment renewed.

"What?"

"Nothing."

Not for the first time, she noticed how round Lou's face had become while pregnant, making her look far cuter and more angelic than she could ever be. And Piper would take a bullet before admitting that. *Your face is puffy* ranked even higher on the list of things she didn't want to say aloud than telling King that all of his investment in her skills as a future agent might be for naught.

"Okay, *nothing*. Tell me what we're doing here," Lou said.

"A girl is missing. I want to interview her neighbors and look through her apartment. If I can reconstruct her routine, I might be able to figure out what happened to her."

Piper knew by the look on Lou's face that something was up.

"Don't tell me," Piper said, before Lou could speak. "I'm supposed to figure it out. Figuring it out is the exact thing that makes me the detective."

Lou shrugged. "I didn't say anything."

Piper opened and closed her mouth several times. Then, when she could hold herself back no longer, she said, "She's dead, isn't she?"

"Yes. She's dead," Lou confirmed.

"Damn it, Louie. We *talked* about this. I told you that you can't cheat and ask your compass thingy unless I ask you too."

Lou only looked at her without pointing out the obvious, that Piper had in fact just asked.

"If I don't practice these skills, I won't get great at them. Then what happens if I can't crime-fight with you? If you're home with Elena, or fighting some gangsters or something? I'll be useless. I need to get at least as good as King. Preferably better. That way I can do this work on my own."

Lou's lips were pressed in a thin line.

Piper's irritation was swiftly swallowed by her deep disappointment. "Seriously though? She's dead."

"Yeah."

"Bummer." Piper's heart sank. She'd really hoped to find the girl alive. Piper would always wonder now if she'd been too slow. That if she'd acted faster, maybe she could have changed the outcome.

"You couldn't have saved her," Lou said, as if reading her mind.

"We might have it wrong then." Because the other two incidents hadn't ended in murder. That meant their profile on the perp might be off track and that the connections between the three women were nonexistent. Or things were escalating. "I'll have to start over."

A door buzzed and a woman came out of the building with two friends, laughing loudly. Lou's boot shot forward, stopping the door from closing.

"You still want to go up?" Lou asked her.

"*Yes*," Piper whined. "I still gotta solve this. Nothing's changed except that now I'm looking for the truth of what happened. And a dead body. *Don't*—"

She pointed an accusing finger at Lou.

"*Don't* tell me where the body is."

Lou held her hands up, palms out in surrender. "I won't."

"Thank you."

Piper still wanted to give the girl's family answers and capture a killer before he could hurt anyone else. It just would've been nicer if a happy ending was a possibility. If she could have been the one to return the girl safely to her family, a reward for her hard work, and the feeling that what she did was important, no matter how unflashy and unambitious it might be.

*What are we talking about here?* her mind chided. *We still talking about the girl or King?*

Lou stopped at the base of the stairs. Piper turned toward her. "What is it?"

"I'm not walking up all those," she said, her hand on her stretched belly.

Piper was going to argue, but one look from Lou and she let it go. She supposed it was unfair to ask her super-pregnant friend to climb a bunch of stairs, especially when there was a giant *Out of Order* sign pinned over the elevator and Lou had a far faster and easier means of travel at her disposal.

"I'll race you." Piper bolted up the stairs, taking them two at a time, hoping the burst of exertion would clear her mind of the dark thoughts trying to accumulate there.

She wasn't surprised when Lou opened the apartment

door for her, leaning against the frame with a triumphant grin.

"You get an A for effort," she said, stepping aside so that Piper could enter. "Where do you want to start?"

Piper's eyes swept over the apartment. It was a cute but compact place. The furniture was colorful, if on the small size. The living room and kitchen were at the front of the apartment, by the door. To the left, the kitchen, where Lou stood, was little more than a nook. A fridge, countertops and sinks, and the island that overlooked the living room. The living room had enough room for a sofa on one wall and an entertainment center against the other. The only remaining wall opened up on a balcony.

Piper slid her backpack off her shoulder and sat it on one of the barstools at the kitchen island.

She went to the balcony first, pushing past the venetian blinds to look out.

The balcony overlooked a courtyard. The uppermost levels of the building all had balconies, while the first-floor apartments had walkout patios.

"Someone could've crawled up from the courtyard," Piper thought aloud. "But they'd run a huge risk of being seen. And it wouldn't be an easy climb. We're still on the third floor."

"They could've dropped down from the roof," Lou offered.

"Can you check?" she asked.

Lou smirked. "I thought I wasn't supposed to impede your developing PI skills."

"Climbing up on a roof is not the kind of skill-building I'm interested in. I just need to know if there's a way to access the roof that might have given our killer easy access to her balcony."

Lou gave her a little salute, sidestepped into a darker corner of the room, and disappeared.

Piper was relieved to see that. She had done her best not to seem anxious about Lou's abilities since the mishap on the beach, but sometimes it was hard. Her friend was far too reckless to not have her full power at her disposal.

With Lou gone, Piper turned her attention to inspecting the apartment again.

The police had already combed the place when they opened the case, but given that two months had passed since, there was a certain staleness to the room. She went to the balcony and opened it, letting fresh air in. The curtains lifted, ghostly on the breeze.

Piper had read the police report several times over when King first took the case. There had been signs of forced entry on the apartment door and a busted lock. King had told her that busting a deadbolt could be done quietly if the assailant bumped the lock, which was a possibility. The deadbolts on the apartments in this building were older, but the technique needed to open this lock in this way would cause some noise, which the neighbors hadn't reported.

Piper knew that the only reason the rental company hadn't moved a new tenant in was the fact that the sister had stepped in to pay the rent, hoping to preserve her sister's place when she came home.

Piper's heart sank again at Lou's reveal that the girl was dead. She was never going to come home again, to this place with its cute, overstuffed sofa and cherry-red stand mixer. Her momentary sadness was replaced by a new conviction to find the fucker who did this and make him pay.

After checking the doors and windows and reinspecting the front lock for herself, Piper moved on to the bedroom. She took video of the current placement of everything even though she knew that the police had likely altered the scene considerably. The bed, for example, had been stripped, the sheets taken and tested for evidence of rape.

Piper took a picture of the claw marks on the bedroom door frame, trying not to imagine the victim grabbing on to it as she resisted being dragged away. There was an unusual smell that Piper couldn't place, so she took a voice note on her phone, doing her best to describe it.

"Fruity but acidic, possibly moldy. Something chemical too. I don't know if it's one scent or a mixture of several. It's weird. I almost feel it in the back of my throat," she said, before sliding her cell phone back into her pocket.

After taking pictures of the bedroom, bathroom, living area, and kitchen, Piper went through each room slowly. She looked through the bathroom for medications and toiletries left behind. She reviewed the mail and bills piled up on the kitchen counter, presumably brought in by the sister.

She felt more than a little silly gathering this data when she knew she could ask Lou where the killer was and the girl's body, too. Together they could interrogate him for the details. But Piper also knew that much of PI work was like high school math. If she couldn't show her work to the authorities, the killer could get away on a technicality. Lou could kill and dump him, sure. But that hardly helped her build her credibility and skills as a PI.

If she planned to devote herself to this investigative work, she would have to build a reputation and skillset that could be seen by others. Otherwise, opportunities to help would be limited to what she read in a paper or heard in the news. She'd be forever reliant on Dani's investigative skills and Lou's power. She'd forever be the helper and never the hero.

And if she was being honest with herself, she wanted to be the hero.

She wanted people to come to *her* for help. To trust her for what she could do.

It wasn't until Piper had finished going through the girl's personal items, a shoebox full of letters and notes, a USB of unknown contents, and a half-finished journal that had been in a locked desk drawer, that Lou returned.

Piper wondered if she'd stayed away so long to give Piper space to do her thing.

She stepped through the balcony's sliding-glass door and into the living room.

"It wouldn't have been hard for someone to go up to the roof and drop down onto the balcony," she declared. "How do you know they didn't come through the front door?"

"There was damage to the lock, but the sister said she thought Willa might have done that herself. She'd lost her keys like a month before she disappeared, and the neighbor boy tried to help her break into her apartment."

"Why not call the landlord?" Lou asked.

"Apparently he's a really lazy fucker who doesn't return calls. If you look up the reviews for this place, it has about a hundred two-star reviews complaining about how poor the maintenance team is. This place looks pretty good though."

"Do we know if the balcony was unlocked?" Lou asked.

"King said it's hella easy to open a locked sliding-glass door. Any idiot with the internet can watch a few video tutorials and get it open. So, no, we don't know which way the attacker—" Here she reluctantly corrected herself. "The killer broke in. Wait. You said she was dead, but do we know if she was killed by him? Do we know if it's a *him*?"

Lou grinned mischievously. "That's for you to find out, isn't it?"

**14**

———

Melandra was struggling to keep her eyes open. It was the stuffiness of the room, the heat of it pressing against her mind until it grew heavy. Her thoughts went soft at their edges, her lids nearly impossible to keep open. She'd brought a little hand fan. It was a simple thing, given to her on the street that very morning with the name, logo, and contact information of a local real estate agent printed on its wooden handle.

But the fan had only been able to keep her awake for so long. As the committee members in charge of coordinating the Women's Business Association's collective efforts for the upcoming festival droned on about objectives and KPIs, visibility, and awareness, driving traffic and returns, Mel found their voices had a soporific effect.

More than once her head lolled, touching her shoulder then chest before she jerked awake again.

She'd caught sight of Genevieve smiling at her across the aisle twice now, clearly amused by her struggle. It was that smile more than anything that compelled Mel to pull herself together. She'd only just resolved to dig her nails into her palm hard enough to keep her eyes open when she found a far more effective means of consciousness.

The sound was faint at first. She barely registered the croaking trill at the edge of her awareness until it grew loud enough to interrupt her concentration.

Terror.

*Click click. Click click.*

She sat up straight in her seat, no longer tired. The exhaustion threatening to take her under was chased away by her thumping heart.

*Click click. Click click. Click click.*

She twisted in her seat to find the source of the sound, only to realize the little creature was on the floor, marching toward her through the chair legs that lay between them.

*Not a deathwatch beetle*, her mind begged. *Maybe it's a wood-boring beetle or, hell, just a bug.*

As it approached, the clicks grew louder, and Mel felt the vision coming at her, the way one feels the rain in the air before the first drop touches the skin.

It crashed over her like a wave. The hot, stuffy room where the members planned and strategized, bent over the papers and plans, fell away altogether.

Darkness washed over Mel, transporting her to King's arms again.

In this glimpse, King's face was bruised on its right side and swelling. Blood crusted at his hairline, darkening at his temple. A disembodied arm emerged from the darkness, pistol raised.

It seemed to Mel that all that existed was that pistol and its large, watchful eye fixed at the end of the muzzle.

The gun, trained on her, went off, and Mel screamed.

The vision was gone.

In its place were at least fifty shocked and concerned faces turned toward her. Mel turned in every direction, twisting in her seat, but there was no gunman. King wasn't throwing himself over her protectively before the gun went off.

None of it had happened.

Not yet.

Mel couldn't even be sure there'd been a beetle, given that a cursory glance at the carpet beneath her feet was bare.

"Melandra, honey, you all right?" Genevieve asked, her earlier amusement gone.

"I'm so sorry," Mel said, rising. Her face burned as heat flooded her cheeks. "I saw a bug."

At least she wasn't lying about that.

"Why don't you step out for some air," the older woman added. "Your cheeks are pink."

"Yes. That's—that's a good idea. Thank you." Mel didn't feel the need to confess that her face was red due to her embarrassment. "I'll get some air and come back in a few minutes."

She grabbed her purse, and as unobtrusively as one can when the entire room has eyes on you, Mel walked down the aisle toward the exit.

She wasn't sure she'd even taken a breath until she was on the sidewalk outside, the half-empty lot stretched out before her. The air above the pavement shimmered in the midday heat.

She swore, covering her face for a moment with her hands.

"What the hell was that?" she groaned.

She wasn't sure who she was speaking to. Herself? Grandmamie?

She had one answer though. Though the vision had been

brief in its flash, Mel had noticed its similarity to the half-formed vision that had visited her before. Of King taking her in his arms.

She knew now, at least, that it hadn't been sexual as she'd first thought. In this second, clearer vision, when he'd drawn her close, cradling her against his chest, it had been to protect her from the bullet.

In moments like this, Mel wished she smoked.

It would give her something to do with her shaky hands as she stood there in the blistering heat, trying to draw enough air into her lungs to breathe.

It had been so real. Not only the scent of King's body as it had pressed against hers. Or the metallic taste of blood, telling her that she'd already had it on her face or lips before her would-be assassin raised his gun. The burn of gunsmoke in the air, stinging her eyes.

She had heard someone crying nearby. Had heard the thump of a fist connecting with flesh and Lady growling. For a moment, if in spirit only, she had been completely and fully in the moment, experiencing it as if it were her present.

Now she was forced to acknowledge something else: the disappointment.

As she stood outside the community center, wondering whether or not she would be able to bring herself to walk back into that meeting given the embarrassment still clinging to her, she realized she felt, above any other emotion, disappointment.

Disappointment over what?

When she'd first had the vision in her shop the day before, she'd been convinced that when King had taken her into his arms, it had been romantic. Perhaps even sexual.

Was that the source of her disappointment, this sad tugging at her heart?

Was it that she was about to—Lord knew when—find herself at the end of yet another gun? And who was it that was trying to kill them this time?

No, that wasn't it. When Mel let her mind wander in that direction, she felt only annoyance and aggravation. First it had been Brasso who'd tried to kill them. Then Dmitri Petrov. She had to hope, at least for now, that they would somehow escape this peril too.

After all, why would the vision come?

When she was a little girl, Grandmamie told her it was their ancestors who sent visions. Those souls who watched over them on the physical plane as they themselves stood outside of the flow of time.

*They send 'em when we need a warning.*

As the fiery old bat had lain in her sick bed, the end rapidly approaching, Mel had asked her if she'd seen her death coming.

*No vision. It was in the cards. They don't send no vision if nothing can be done. They only wanted me to prepare my mind—and my heart—for the transition.*

When Mel had then asked if she felt prepared to die, the woman had only laughed until falling into a coughing fit.

These old memories and the nostalgia couldn't stand up to the heat of the day. They dissolved into the afternoon like the heat rising from the concrete.

"What am I supposed to do then, if something can be changed?" she asked the empty parking lot.

*Tell the others. At least Robert.* That was her first thought.

He'd helped her once before. When she'd had the prophetic dreams about Zoey Peterson, he'd helped her reach the girl in time. Their teamwork had prevented something terrible from happening. Maybe they could find a positive result this time as well.

*Don't get ahead of yourself. Imagine telling him what you saw.*

She sure as hell wouldn't say she'd mistaken their embrace for a sexual one. He didn't need to know any such details to know that she thought they were in trouble and should take precautions if they could.

There was also the possibility that more of the vision would come. This emanation had certainly been stronger than the last.

*We can do this. We can save ourselves.*

Even as she encouraged herself, she couldn't completely keep the doubt away.

*If we're going to beat this, then why do I have such a terrible feeling?*

The fear that had gripped her spine upon seeing the beetle crawling up the aisle toward her was still there, an itchy presence resting at the back of her neck.

Mel caught the trace of voices approaching from the other side of the door. The meeting must have adjourned while she stood out here in the heat trying to decide what her next move was. To avoid reliving her embarrassment all over again, Mel took off down the adjacent walkway, heading swiftly in the direction of the bus stop near the edge of the lot.

Once she was in her seat, the community center growing smaller in the window beside her as the bus drove away, she pulled out her phone. After a moment's consideration, she typed a text out to King.

*Can we have dinner again tonight?*

Less than ten seconds later, the little bubble with the three dots appeared on the screen, indicating that he was writing back.

*Not sick of me yet?* he asked.

*It would be hard to get sick of you*, she thought. But she wrote, *Not yet.*

*Come to my place after the shop closes.*

*It doesn't close until ten tonight.*

*I'll be up late anyway,* he promised. *I've got some files to go through.*

Mel's bangles jingled softly as she finished with *See you then,* before slipping her cell phone back into her bag.

**15**

———

At the same moment Melandra Durand took a window seat on the bus, Ettore Celesti slid into the back seat of an Audi parked at the corner of Via Broggia and Via Enrico Pessina. His driver closed the door behind him before returning to the driver's seat. Ettore opened his suit jacket, allowing air to pass over the pearl buttons of his shirt, ridding him of the clinging heat.

He had three missed messages.

The first two were from his wife. While he'd been in the meeting she'd sent two photos. The first was of Martina smiling at the camera, holding up a drawing of bright colors but otherwise indiscernible shapes. The second was a closeup of the drawing she held. The closer framing did nothing to improve the quality of the photo, so its subject remained undiscernible. He texted empty, encouraging words.

The third missed message was from Raffaele, asking Ettore to call him back when he was free.

Ettore hesitated.

An unease had settled in his guts during the meeting and

had followed him from the hotel's warm lobby out into the heat of the day.

He needed to look more closely, if only in his own mind, at what had just transpired in the meeting. It should have been routine, and yet—

Had it been his imagination, or were the officials more evasive and unhelpful than usual? Idiotic city officials were usually happy to accept his money to look the other way. Today, however, they asked a surprising number of questions. He'd entered the meeting expecting a quick agreement and little discussion. When all was said and done, they'd asked him for more time.

*More time!* He laughed bitterly, running a hand down his face.

Not one of them had mentioned Konstantine by name, and yet Ettore had felt the man's presence in the room. Was he pumping money into Naples in an attempt to poison it against him?

His *own* city?

Ettore watched the streets of Naples pass by his window, his lingering anger making his ears burn. A man on a scooter balanced a baby on his leg with one hand, steering the moto with the other. A woman stood at a café window, drinking an espresso at the bar. A crowd of youths huddled around a stall of shoes while a Nigerian immigrant tried to interest them in the high-top sneakers he held.

Finally, when the heat of his fury had subsided and he felt like himself again, he picked up his phone and returned Raffaele's call.

"Ciao, Ettore."

Ettore didn't humor this with a reply. "Do you have what I asked for?"

"*Sì.* I took several videos from Tamara Lincoln's social media. I am sending you one now."

Ettore's phone pinged as a text arrived from Raffaele, a video attachment opening on his phone automatically. He watched as Tamara, wearing tight pants and a tank top, walked a small group of practitioners through a yoga class. Puppies were running around the room, tackling and colliding with the attendees trying to twist their bodies into the positions that Ms. Lincoln called out.

"Yes! Let the laughter out!" she said, laughing herself. "Connect with your joy and your purpose."

Ettore closed the video. "This is not *La Strega*."

"No, I didn't think so," Raffaele agreed. "That leaves Louie Thorne."

"What did you find?"

"Not much more than what I gave you before," Raffaele said, his nervousness apparent. Ettore had stabbed him in the hand once out of anger. Perhaps that was why. "There is an article about her parents' murder that was published at that time. She is mentioned again more recently when the story about Jack Thorne was republished."

"What do you mean?"

"When he died, they thought he had personal ties to the mafia. That he was a…What do you call it? When they play both teams?"

"Double agent."

"Yes. The opinion of Jack Thorne when he died was not good. New articles were released in the last few years proving that Jack had been innocent and betrayed by his…his… person."

*Partner*, Ettore thought, but didn't say it.

"The articles focus almost entirely on the father, Jack Thorne. There is only a mention of the girl. 'Jack and Courtney Thorne are survived by their daughter, Louie.' That sort of thing. Nothing about who she is now or where she lives. What she does for work. *Nothing*."

"No social media videos either, I presume."

"None."

"Did you search videos online, surveillance footage, posts?"

"Nothing comes up when I do a basic search, but something interesting did happen."

Raffaele proceeded to tell him about uploading the image of Louie Thorne to do a reverse-image search for more stories, only to find that his request didn't go through. That it seemed to have been *eaten* by the programming, disappearing almost as soon as he'd entered it each time.

Eaten.

"Interesting. Is that something that usually happens?"

"No," Raffaele said. "It would post for a minute at most before it was removed."

"Did you try to upload it in several places?"

"Yes, on social media. On public message boards where you can ask questions. In a search engine. In all cases, it results in nothing. If the image was uploaded or saved to the internet in any way, it was removed almost as quickly."

Ettore knew that Konstantine had a reputation for being extremely tech-savvy. Apparently, it was the one area where he'd shown any aptitude. Could he have made something that erased Louie from the world? A code, maybe? A program?

He'd read an article once about how a starlet had done that to help protect her identity. What had it been? All her contact information erased? Her address? Compromising photos?

Was it possible that Konstantine was capable of the same?

An idea sparked in his mind, and his fingers tingled with excitement at the thought of it.

"If we can't search for her on the internet, then let's make the world search for her," Ettore said as his driver pulled up to the curb again. He made to get out and open the door, but

Ettore waved him off and let himself out of the vehicle. He tipped the driver and stepped into the shadow of a restaurant before saying, "Use our contacts."

He knew already that Raffaele had no idea what the plan was. "Who? Who do we contact?"

Inwardly, Ettore lamented how hard it was to get good help and vowed to patiently tolerate the man.

"First, get me the contact information for the authorities near that lake where we found Aldo's phone. We can work outward from there."

"*Va bene.* I'll reach out to them. *Poi ti richiamerò.*"

Ettore ended the call and slid the phone back into his pocket.

*You like to meddle in my business, do you, Konstantine? Let's see how you like it when I meddle in yours.*

## 16

————

Konstantine closed his phone and slipped it back into his pocket.

"What are you smiling about?" Stefano cupped his hand over the end of his cigarette before lighting it.

"They took my offer," Konstantine said.

"Who?" he asked, cigarette bobbing between his lips.

A fair question. Konstantine had several offers rolling at any given time.

"The Neapolitans," he said. "They've agreed to drag their feet and make bullshit excuses to slow him down. I asked them only for time, and they'll give it."

"*Drag their feet,*" Stefano said, after inhaling on the filter until the cherry burned bright. "*Parli sempre più come un americano ogni giorno.*"

Konstantine was used to this gentle ribbing. He went on, barely noting it. "We want Ettore destabilized. The Japanese continue to bar him from the trading in the east, and the authorities controlling the docks in Jakarta will not let him dock. Now his own port is against him."

Konstantine was deeply gratified that the Neapolitans had accepted his offer. Ever since Ettore ordered his brother-in-law to attack his stronghold in Florence, Konstantine's desire to return the blow had been great.

Konstantine wanted to strike harder still. Ettore had infiltrated Konstantine's church, killed his people including the sweet Nario, and had sown chaos in his own streets. Konstantine wouldn't be satisfied until he landed an equal or greater blow on the other man.

"What does *La Strega* say? She doesn't have your patience."

It was true that Konstantine and Louie did not wage war in the same way. For Konstantine, he targeted the Celesti's financial holdings. If he wanted to truly undo the man's empire, then it must have no financial legs to stand on. The best way to achieve that was to approach his allies with bigger offers or threats. To block his movements and disrupt his progress. Leave him with nowhere to turn and no one to rely on.

Lou's approach was more...direct.

Stefano misread his concern. "I told you we will be fine if you need to leave. *Ti preoccupi troppo.*"

"I worry for her. And for Elena," Konstantine said, realizing his concern must have been plain on his face.

"Did she give you an answer about the island?"

"I don't think she'll agree to go."

"But you want her to."

"They would be safer." Konstantine stopped short of saying yes. Lou wouldn't believe him if he said so, but Konstantine did feel the same urgency that she did—to end all of this as soon as possible. And it was that urgency that made him feel as if it would be better to stay and fight than hide themselves away for several months.

Stefano said nothing while his mind wandered. Stefano wasn't one to speak about lovers.

Stefano himself had never sought a wife or dated a woman long term, preferring instead to visit prostitutes to have his needs satisfied. He did have his favorites. But they were never on his arm in the streets of Florence, nor did he bring one of them home to Konstantine or the Ravengers.

For all of these reasons, Konstantine wouldn't have sought relationship advice from Stefano anyway.

Stefano's cigarette had only just burned down to the filter when his phone went off. He removed it from the pocket of his Armani suit and read the message.

"Ah, the shipment you sent the children arrived."

"You had a notification set up?" Konstantine was surprised.

"No, that was Matteo. He texted me to let me know."

Konstantine's own phone pinged a moment later, and he knew it was Matteo even before he checked the number.

With a little laugh, Konstantine returned his effusive thanks, telling him to remain a good boy and look out for the others, and more gifts would come soon.

More than once, Matteo asked when they could come home.

*Appena possibile. Sii paziente per favore*, he wrote back.

"Your face," Stefano said. "No one would know that you once cut off a man's entire hand."

Konstantine ignored his chiding, though he knew his friend was only trying to take his mind off the problems. More than once they tried to turn the conversation toward business. Stefano had news about two shipments sitting off the coast of Tijuana that were running into trouble with customs, since the tension at the US–Mexico border was intensifying.

They were working through their options for handling

this problem when his phone started pinging again. Konstantine was certain it was Matteo, and ignored it. He'd already sent the boy plenty of reassurances. He would have to wait.

Only thirty seconds passed before the phone went off again.

Konstantine's irritation folded into unease when his computer started pinging next. Then his phone began to ring.

"That's not Matteo," Stefano said, his brow creasing. "Something's happened."

**17**

———

Lou felt a slight tug in her guts. It directed her attention to Konstantine, to his—not fear. Not urgency. Deep and troubling concern? Something close to alarm, perhaps? Yet whatever emotion it was that had set off bells inside her, it was fading as quickly as it had arisen.

If he was really in danger, she would know. Her compass, that internal sense of direction intimately connected to her power, had never led her astray in that regard.

It wasn't as if he'd been knocked unconscious or killed either. If that had happened, Lou wouldn't feel the lingering residue of his strong emotion. She'd been in tune with Piper once, the moment she'd gone unconscious, and it had been as if someone had turned off the lights.

*Or he knows your power well enough to mask an emotion he doesn't want you to detect.*

She didn't care for that thought.

But who was she to be upset at that idea? Wasn't she keeping her own secrets?

The man Lou was stalking stepped away from the newsstand where he'd been perusing a rack of tabloids. He pulled his hands from his pockets, straightening the collar on his jacket as if it weren't scalding hot outside.

She followed him out of the bowels of the train station, onto the platform. She kept to the shadows for nearly fifteen minutes, until a train bound for Sorrento pulled in. Lou wanted to board and follow him, but the car was too crowded. It wasn't simply that the idea of boarding a hot Italian train while very pregnant didn't appeal to her. It was also the light. Lou was very aware that this open platform meant that the train wasn't like a subway. There would be no traveling through the darkness with the shadows on her side. She'd be in a crowded space, too visible, with a power that had recently proved its unreliability.

Reluctantly, Lou was forced to watch her prey leave the station without her.

Before her disappointment could settle fully on her shoulders, Konstantine tugged at her compass again. This time it felt more intentional.

He wanted her to come.

Retracing her steps from the platform, up to the world above, Lou found a shadow between two buildings and stepped through.

She found Konstantine in his new office. This office was by far the brightest. The little room was turned into one corner of a bright courtyard, and instead of stone walls, the windows allowed Konstantine to watch whoever might approach him from the only possible access point—a long hallway leading deeper into the compound.

It was as if he was in a glass box in the corner of a maze, with only one route to him.

She knew that he'd chosen the church and its grounds for this exact reason. For the fact that its enormity, its confounding twist of hallways and walls, would make it far harder to navigate, let alone overtake, by whatever enemy dared to challenge them.

She always thought he was sexy when he was working, those green eyes fixed in concentration. That sharp cut of his jaw and the way his shirt hung open, offering a glimpse of his tattooed chest. But she had no time to savor the view or her hungry thoughts.

She knew something was wrong as soon as she saw him.

"What is it?" she asked in lieu of hello. She'd come because he'd called. There must be a reason.

Whatever was so terrible, it hadn't registered on her compass. That meant no one she loved was dead, no one in peril.

"*Amore mio*," he breathed as she watched the indecision play across his face. His desire for her and whatever news he was struggling to hold on to warred with each other.

Lou was about to relent, unwilling to share his attention when it came to her pleasure, when her phone went off.

It was a text from Piper.

*Holy shit, man. You're in the news.*

Lou's heart dropped. She looked up, meeting Konstantine's eyes, and knew at once that this was what he'd been trying to protect her from.

"What's happened?" she asked.

PIPER WAS TIRED AND FOOTSORE. SHE'D SPENT THE morning walking all over the city. She'd visited the party store where Willa worked and interviewed all her colleagues. All that she learned was that Willa was obsessed with joining the Saints cheer squad. That she'd been training for her audition for months and had forced nearly everyone in the store to critique her moves. Apart from this passion, Willa was a normal girl, based on her coworkers' reports. She was always on time, cheerful—and here Piper suspected to the point of obnoxiousness—and always ready to lend a hand. Piper began to wonder if this over-friendliness might have been the very thing that got the girl killed.

No one had seen a customer lurking around, or anyone too fixated on Willa. Apart from this snapshot of her personality, Piper didn't feel like she had much to show for her hours of strenuous effort.

"It will shake out like that more often than not," King told her once she'd returned to the agency and recounted her morning to him. "A lot of what happens in investigative work is ruling things out. It's never a waste of time."

Piper tried to take this peptalk on the chin without feeling like every delay was a reflection of her ineptitude as a PI.

"Once you find her alive, you'll know every minute was worth it," he added, squeezing his stress penguin at the desk across from her.

*Alive.*

Piper hadn't told him about Lou's assistance the day before, or that she'd thought the girl dead. But it might as well have been written on her forehead because King's face fell.

"How did you find out?"

"Lou told me. I told her not to," she added quickly. "It's cheating."

"It's never cheating when someone's life is at stake," he said. "We use whatever means we can when it comes to bringing people home."

She should've been relieved by this encouragement, but instead a tremor of shame ran through her. Had she really been so self-centered, so desperate to prove her skills, that she'd been willing to risk a girl's life and safety?

"That means the clock's restarted," King said. "Now the race is to find him before he hurts someone else."

She didn't point out that they didn't know if they were looking for a *him*. King was working from statistics, but Piper knew plenty of women were just as crazy as the nuttiest of men out there.

"What's your next steps?" King asked.

"More tedium," she said. "I got her phone from the police, and now I get to read the three thousand text messages on there to see if there's any mention of a stranger hanging around or someone watching her. And before you ask, *yes*, I tried the search feature. But looking for phrases like 'guy,' 'weirdo,' 'stranger,' 'watching me' has turned up a whole lot of nothing. I even let Dani take a crack at it"—this was true, but Piper had only felt compelled to share it for fear that King would think her too prideful to ask for help—"and she's really good at that stuff, but nothing came up. So either there's nothing, or it's such a small, passing comment that I'm not going to catch it unless I go through them one by one."

"Did you finish constructing the final-day timeline?"

Piper put Willa's phone on the charger, hoping to increase the battery life before she began her epic-level scrolling. Then she took out her notepad and shared her findings with King.

"Presumably she got up at seven, when her alarm went off. Got dressed, did her hair and makeup—which was still all over her sink when the police went over her apartment. She had a breakfast of Special K and raspberries. She put the half-empty bowl in the sink and took the dog out at 7:44."

"How do you know?"

"The camera in the parking lot catches her arriving at the trailhead that connects with the park at 7:47. I did that walk myself several times and clocked it as a three-minute crossing. That's the max amount of time the killer had to grab her if he took her from the parking lot. I walked from one edge to the other several times, and it never took more than two minutes. And I can't imagine that lot is ever full, nor would she want to park in the farthest space unless she was forced to."

"You think it's more likely that he took her from the apartment."

"Her coworkers were really adamant about how friendly and cheerful she is. I think if someone knocked on her door and said they were a scout for the Saints, she would have let them right in. But Lou also pointed out that it wouldn't have been too hard for someone to drop down from the roof of the building onto her balcony and get the sliding door open that way."

"My vote is that he got her in the apartment and took her to the car in the lot. Assuming he could carry her, it means he only had to be unseen for two or three minutes. Five tops, assuming she was hard to carry for some reason."

"She couldn't have been," Piper said. "She had that starving-myself-to-be-a-cheerleader thing going on. Her sister was really worried about her, actually."

King seemed to consider this, his gaze fixed on the pen he held. After a moment he said, "A quick getaway. And if anyone saw anything, he could've just said, 'She had too much to drink.'"

"None of the neighbors saw anything," Piper confirmed. "I asked them all. One woman who was letting her dog out to pee at three in the morning thought she heard a dog bark, but then it was silent after, so she didn't investigate."

"Go on."

Piper glanced at her notes.

"They—Willa and the dog—walked from the apartment building down to that park we went to. She passes the trailhead cam at the edge of the parking lot again at 8:26, so we can assume she got back to her apartment at about 8:29. She got dressed for her shift at the party store—she's wearing different clothes when she's clocked on the work cams. Presumably, she left her apartment building at about 8:48, because she parked in the party store lot at 8:57, did something in her car for two minutes—the camera's got her just sitting there, probably scrolling—and then walked into the store right at nine o'clock for her shift. She was in the store until she took a thirty-ish-minute break at 1:12 to run across the street and get tacos. She's seen walking up to the food truck at 1:18 and leaving at 1:47. She reenters the party store at 1:53 and stays inside until she walks out at 5:03."

Piper turned the page on her notes. "The parking lot cam clocks her car passing by at 7:07, so assuming the killer didn't snatch her from the parking lot then, she was in her apartment for the rest of the night—well until whoever got her got her."

"Nothing to confirm her whereabouts after seven?" King asked.

"No. And no idea where she spent those two hours between leaving work and coming home either. Her sister said they talked around nine and she made a post about bed rot on her social media at 10:10. You can tell in the video that she's in her apartment, lying in her bed. So I think we can safely assume she was in bed for the night at that point, probably scrolling."

"When did they realize she was missing again?"

"The next morning. She was a no-call, no-show at work, and another girl who works there texted her sister. They knew each other from high school. Her sister went over to check on her on her lunch break, thinking maybe she was sick, and found her apartment the way it was and called the police. That creates a total window of ten at night to seven the next morning. Because I assume the killer got her before she took the dog out."

"Why didn't the dog bark if the killer entered the apartment?" King asked. "It suggests that the assailant was someone Willa knew."

"Or the dog the neighbor heard *was* Miss Bella Beans."

King stopped squeezing the penguin. "The dog's name is Miss Bella Beans."

"Yeah, that was like, her whole government name."

"No known enemies? Ex-boyfriends, girlfriends, anyone who had a reason to hurt her?"

"Her sister said she had a bully in high school, but also was convinced that the girl had moved to California their senior year and Willa hadn't mentioned her since. She seemed convinced that Willa would have said something if the girl had started hanging around again. No exes of note. A couple, but the breakups seemed amicable enough. No drama."

King scratched at his chin, clearly lost in thought. "It leads to the idea that our guy must be picking the women some other way."

Piper had been leaning toward the same conclusion. She had a feeling—though no concrete evidence yet—that there was a connection between Willa's abduction and the first two failed attacks. She couldn't be sure how their bad guy was picking his victims, but there had to be a connection between them.

She shared her suspicion with King, concluding, "I think I need to reach out to the other two women and talk to them. Maybe they can give me some details or even a description. It would also be nice to know what their movements were leading up to the attack, so I can look for a pattern. Right now, all I know is that they are all pretty, all single, all living with a dog, in the same area of town, within just a few minutes of each other. Maybe they shop at the same place?

Or go to the same gym? Get gas at the same station? Hell, I don't know."

King was smiling at her.

Piper's face flushed. "What? What is it?"

"You remind me of Jack."

"Lou's dad?" Piper had no idea where this was going.

King's face was soft with nostalgia. "You're inquisitive like he was. You'll be an amazing agent one day. You're gonna do a lot of good in their world."

Piper's heart was racing.

*This is it*, she thought. *I should say something. I should say something before this goes any farther.*

But her heart was pounding so hard that she felt sick to her stomach, and her mouth had gone dry as if all the spit had been vacuumed out of it. The office floor tilted.

*Why am I so scared to tell him?* She wiped her sweaty palms on her pants under the desk. *I haven't been this scared since I told my dad I was gay.*

And why should she be scared to tell him? It wasn't like King was going to hit her or even yell at her. He wasn't that kind of guy. Yet for some reason she was absolutely terrified that he would think less of her.

Why? Just because she didn't want to work for the FBI or DEA?

"What's wrong?" he asked her.

Of course he could see the fear on her face. It was so big that hiding it was a joke.

"I—I wanted to tell you something."

She started bouncing her knee without realizing it.

His face had gone cautiously blank. Damnit. She hated it when he did that. It meant he was trying to hide his feelings. That was the opposite of what Piper wanted right now. She wanted to know what he felt. It would be terrible if he was disappointed in her, but even worse if he tried to hide it from her.

"I've thought a lot about being an agent," she said. "But something that Agent Smith said has really stuck with me. She said that if I was an agent, I would be expected to put the job first. Above what I wanted and above the people I care about. She didn't think I had what it takes to do that."

Piper stopped short of saying, *And I don't think I could do that either.*

"She was pretty pissed at us for impeding her investigation," King said, picking up the penguin again. "I wouldn't let one miserable person deter you. I hate to be pessimistic, but you'll likely encounter a lot of dickheads in this line of work."

*All the more reason to carve my own path.*

"Yeah, I know, but—but I think that it really just got me thinking about what I really want and—" She looked up, hoping to see anything on his face that would encourage her. She was so close. She should just rip the Band-Aid off and tell him the truth about her decision. Was it really so shameless to look for a little bit of encouragement on that inscrutable face before she did?

Only she found no encouragement. In fact, what she saw etched into those deep features was far worse.

He looked genuinely concerned. "Shit."

"I'm not saying that—" Piper quickly backtracked, abandoning her plan to tell him the truth.

King didn't let her finish. "Did you know about this?"

King turned his computer around to face her. On his laptop screen, Piper saw a news report playing out in real time, the scrolling banner flashing at the bottom. The banner read, *Louie Thorne, a person of interest, wanted for questioning.*

Above that was a photo of Lou—or at least a photo of someone trying to look like Louie.

Piper had seen enough AI-generated photos lately to

know an age-progression shot when she saw one. What really gave it away, though, were the smile and the eyes.

Never in Piper's life had she seen Lou smile like that, nor had her eyes ever been so bright or...optimistic?

The Lou Piper knew was full of darkness. Whatever artist had created this replica had clearly never laid eyes on Lou.

"What are they saying?" Piper asked. She saw the captions flashing across the top of the screen, but they were too far away to read across the room.

Unable to stop herself, Piper rose and went to his side.

King read the text aloud.

"They found human remains at a lake in Nova Scotia. Teeth, bullet casings. A hunter said that he saw *this* woman"—King pointed at the photo—"leaving the area. The authorities want to question her."

"Holy shit."

King added, "Someone else reported seeing a pregnant woman of similar appearance getting on a plane in Halifax. They're saying she could be anywhere, and if anyone sees her, to call the authorities."

"Bullshit. She wasn't getting on any plane," Piper said. "And no one is going to look at Lou and think *that's* her. Her vibe is totally different. That woman, whoever the hell she is, teaches kindergarten or something."

She gestured at the photo.

King rubbed his chin, lost in thought. "But someone must have seen her to know she's pregnant."

*So much for telling him the truth.*

At least for now, she would keep the secret of her decision a little longer. Bane had been right though. She would have to tell him eventually, the sooner the better. But now was obviously not the time. Not with this monumental shit show arriving on their doorsteps.

"I think it's really unlikely that she would have been in an airport in Halifax, so why would they say that?" King asked, squeezing his stress penguin harder. "Unless they knew about her power and that she could be anywhere. Then how else would they get everyone outside of Nova Scotia to be on the lookout for her, unless they had a reason to believe she could be anywhere."

"You're telling me that someone who knows what Lou can do, and with enough authority and clout to get Lou's name in the press, is publicly hunting her? Holy shit. Who could even do that?"

"Konstantine," King said at once.

"Or that other mafia boss. I know whoever they're tracking down is also a bigwig. Maybe he's behind this."

A chill ran down Piper's spine. She pulled out her phone.

"What are you doing?" King asked.

"Texting Lou. If she's out hunting, it's possible she hasn't even seen this yet. Gotta warn her."

"She's not the only one in danger," King said.

"Elena, too, I know."

"No, not just the baby. If they can find Lou's name and dumping ground, who's to say they can't draw a connection to us. Petrov managed it."

"Awesome," Piper said. She decided to compose a text to Bane while she was at it.

*La Strega compromised. Bad guys probably heading our way.*

Bane returned her text immediately with a slew of emojis.

Eyes open. A punch. A bomb. Fireworks and guns. Piper had no idea how to interpret all that.

She returned with a single thumbs up of her own before slipping her phone back into her pocket.

No sooner did this text go off than Piper's cell phone rang. It was Dani.

"Did you—" she began.

"I saw it," Piper said before she could even ask.

"Holy shit," Dani said. "What's she going to do?"

"I don't know. We'll have to wait and see how she wants to play it."

"Tell her to be careful," King said.

"She knows," Piper said. Not only because Dani could surely hear him, as close as he was to the phone, but because Dani was well aware of what the mafia did to people they were hunting. She'd had a finger cut off by that Petrov fucker. That wasn't something someone forgot.

"I'm serious," King said, mistaking her tone for flippant rather than dread. "We have to be careful. Be on the lookout for anyone watching us, following us. They might not make the connection, but if they do, let's not make it easy for them."

Piper couldn't decide if she was relieved to have a temporary reprieve from her difficult conversation with King or disappointed that she didn't yet see it in her rearview mirror.

With a knot in her stomach, she said, "Awesome. I can't wait to be hunted down. Again."

**18**

———————

onstantine had insisted they return to his office before he explained what he thought had happened, and what he was doing to counter Ettore's bold move. Lou had reluctantly agreed. Of course Konstantine wanted to have a perfectly rational response to this blow, whereas Lou wanted to wrap her hands around Ettore's throat and squeeze until his face was bloated and purple, every vessel beneath the skin burst.

She followed Konstantine in silence instead. In his office, she eased herself down onto the leather sofa. Her back ached and she was pretty sure that if she tried to pull off her boots now, they would resist. Her feet were swollen and tender.

"I thought you had a program that kept my face and name out of the press. Off the internet, at least." She tried to keep her tone even. It was unfair to blame Konstantine for this.

He'd worked tirelessly over the years to protect her anonymity. She was the one who'd been careless. She went where she wanted, took or killed who she wanted. She'd done so with little fear that anyone or anything could touch her. Anyone in the world with her body count would have been arrested years ago. Lou could recognize her own privileged advantage not just in her power but in her allies.

She also wondered if she'd been a bit naïve. Did she really think they would come up against Ettore, one of the most powerful *capi* in the world, and not take damage?

Ettore's move had brought a stark problem to light, however.

Lou had always had mobility and flexibility on her side. The fact that she could be anywhere anytime. If her gift really was failing her, now would be a terrible time to be taken in for questioning, or worse, arrested, charged, imprisoned.

Even if her power remained strong and kept her out of reach of anyone who would capture her, something was becoming more and more clear to her. Lying on top of the shipping container, realizing how her life had come full circle, beginning with Martinelli, ending with Ettore, had made it more and more impossible to ignore the obvious.

She was no longer the vagabond she'd been all those years ago.

The hurt, angry teen who threw herself carelessly into danger in order to destroy the men who'd destroyed her childhood had transformed.

Now Lou had friends. She had a home.

She had Elena and Konstantine.

She had a *family*.

She had never set out to build this life for herself. She'd sought only to destroy what had hurt her. But that life had grown up around her. And Lou was going to be damned if she let another asshole take that from her.

Konstantine pulled a tablet from his desk drawer and began tapping on its screen while he talked. "Ettore didn't look for you on the internet. If he had so much as typed your name into the search bar, I would have known. There were a few hits on the article about your father's death lately, but there always are. One came through a masked VPN. I was unable to trace it to an original location. This happens sometimes, so I was not too worried about one search. The masked VPN and the minimal use of the internet lead me to believe that he knows about my efforts to conceal your identity online. If I were him, I would have asked my contacts directly to find me everything I could. I also have my suspicions that it was the lack of information that gave you away."

When she was sure she could ask the question without sounding cross, she said, "What do you mean, the lack of information?"

"Vittoria told me that someone was asking about when *La Strega* appeared in the underworld. When did anyone remember first seeing her?"

Louie wasn't surprised to hear that Vittoria would come by this news first, though she hated that the woman was still alive. Lou had refrained from ripping her throat out for Konstantine's sake, since the bitch was his half-sister. As the other bastard child of Fernando Martinelli, she was as entrenched in the mafia game as he was. Lou's hatred of the woman had to do with the fact that she'd dare lay hands on sweet Matteo and for no other reason than to provoke a response from Konstantine.

"If that was his line of inquiry, it wouldn't have been hard for him to look at all of Martinelli's connections to you. If he, say, wanted to know who might want Fernando dead or prosecuted, it would lead him to Jack. If he wanted to know which children of his adversaries were still alive, it would lead to you, except there isn't anything to find, is there?"

Lou understood now. It wasn't what Konstantine had done that had made her a target. It was what she herself *hadn't* done.

She'd never bought property in her name. Never voted, went to school. Never had an email or social media account.

Never had a job. Lou had intentionally left no trace of her existence, because once upon a time she'd been afraid that the men she hunted might come looking for Lucy if they ever figured out who she was. When she'd made those decisions, she couldn't ever have guessed that Lucy would be long dead before a real threat arrived and that the trail was the one created by the void she'd left in her wake.

"This might also be a bluff," Konstantine went on. "He may not know if Louie Thorne is really the one he is looking for. He might simply be making a guess to see how we react. The fact they are using that terrible picture tells me he only had a childhood photo. Perhaps the very one from the article about your parents' murder."

"If you rush to get my name out of the press, then he will have his answer, won't he?" Elena stirred inside her, and a swell of protectiveness rose up in Lou. Her desire to kill Ettore was stronger than ever. "Don't do it then. Let him wonder if he's made a mistake."

A smile tugged at his lips. "I already have. Sorry."

When she said nothing, he went on.

"He might have your name and know why you initially began hunting the mafia, but he can do little with that information if he isn't allowed to use it. And I can prevent him from doing so."

Lou was certain he'd stopped short of saying, *I can prevent him from destroying your anonymity with a lot of cash.*

Money was something he had. Fine. Let him spend it. Not for Lou's sake but because the more visible she became, the more vulnerable their daughter would be. If not now, while she slept safely inside her, in a year. Five. Ten. Whenever the next Ettore Celesti decided he'd had enough of *La Strega* looming over his shoulder.

"What did they find at the lake?" Lou asked. She was still pissed that he'd traced Aldo's call, but there had to be other remote lakes in the world. Lou would find another, even though she was loath to do it.

"Teeth, bullet casings. An incomplete boot print that could belong to either a man or a woman. Not much. I was worried that perhaps they would find your blood or hair, but it doesn't look like any has been submitted."

"Would there be anything in the system for them to match my DNA to?"

Because Lou knew that she'd had several near misses in the past. Though she never left a body or weapon behind, it wasn't like all of her kills had been perfectly clean. It was true that she tried to snatch her victims and take them to the lake first, but there were occasions when she'd taken bullets or blades at the scene before managing it, which meant it was very possible that her DNA had been collected from some other crime scene. The last thing she needed was her DNA pinging a slew of unsolved cases across the country.

"No. The DNA that was collected in the past just"—he made a little poof motion with his hand—"disappeared."

She scoffed. "Convenient."

"All he stands to gain from this is confirmation of your identity, and the possibility of limiting your movements."

"Someone might recognize me."

He looked ready to laugh.

Lou didn't understand. This situation seemed far too serious for him to be amused.

"What's so funny?"

"Would you like to see the image they've released of you? The photo that they have was generated based on the photo from your father's obituary. I'm sure of it. Or maybe the post-mortem piece they did on him. In either case, they didn't have much to work with."

Konstantine pulled his tablet toward him. After several

moments of furious tapping, he came around his desk and handed it to her.

Lou took the tablet, looking into the face of the woman staring back at her.

She arched a brow. "Who the hell is this?"

She could see the similarities. Even in this stranger's face, which was a clear mixture of Jack's and Courtney's features, harmonizing. They'd managed to get the coloring correct, at least, for her hair, eyes, and skin.

That was where the recognizability ended.

There was the absence of Lou's hard jaw, for starters. This woman was also far less muscular than Lou—when she wasn't pregnant, of course. This not-Lou looked soft and feminine. Her teeth were perfectly straight. Her gaze benevolent and kind.

She felt like she was looking into the face of some alternate universe Louie Thorne. Some version of her whose parents hadn't died, who'd never been terrorized by her unexplainable power. And because her parents hadn't died and she'd never had to contend with either the literal or metaphorical darkness, she'd remained soft.

"Look at that photo and tell me someone will recognize you on the street, *amore mio*."

"Then the only danger is leaving my name in the media."

"Through my connections, I am circulating a second story. Because you were named only as a person of interest, wanted for questioning, I have room to manipulate the situation. It was already known that the mafia killed your parents. I am leveraging that to make it seem like these kills might also be mafia-related. That the authorities are looking for you because you may have information. I've also made mention of witness protection, in case a journalist starts looking for your contact information and realizes you are a ghost. I have reasonable explanations for all of this that do not point to guilt."

Lou hoped that Konstantine's misdirection would be enough to deter anyone hunting for a story. "I can ask Dani how hot it is. She should be able to let me know if your efforts are working or not."

He looked a little incensed at that.

She added, "I'm not saying that you're not doing a great job. Or that you can't handle it. But you'd like to know if it's working, right?"

"Yes," he conceded.

"What can I do in the meantime? Besides staying out of sight?"

"You can come away with me," he said. "You can lay on the warm sand, and I will rub your feet while we listen to ocean waves."

She went to him. He leaned back in his chair, looking up at her. She pushed her fingers into his hair, staring into those green eyes. "Tempting."

And it was. She could easily imagine how gorgeous he would be, sand clinging to his skin, his eyes bright in the sunlight.

Thinking of the beach reminded her of her recent day in the sun with Piper and Dani. Of the terrible moment that her power failed her. If she spent the remainder of her pregnancy lying on some beach with him, Elena would love it, undoubtedly.

But what if Ettore came for her friends and Lou couldn't go to them?

"What is it?" he asked.

She'd let her fears play across her face, and he'd seen it.

*I should tell him.*

But Lou knew that if she confessed this newfound vulnerability, it would only scare him more.

His eyes were wider now. "What is it, *amore mio?* Tell me."

She bent and kissed him. "Nothing."

"You lie to me."

"Only a little."

His face remained solemn. "You hate the idea of being isolated from the others? We could visit. It would be nothing for you to take us to New Orleans and back."

She looked away from him. The urge to start a fight, to distract him from his offer, pressed against her.

*There's no need for that*, she told herself. *Don't hurt him just because you don't want to tell him your secret.*

"Forgive me." He gripped her hip and pulled her closer. "I'm not telling you what to do. You kept yourself safe for many years before we met. I only want to protect you. Both of you."

He placed a kiss on her stomach.

*And I want to protect you.* Which was why she wouldn't tell him. He had enough on his mind, trying to outmaneuver Ettore in the game of chess unfolding between them. Lou knew her place on the board, as the queen waiting to checkmate the opposing king the moment the opportunity presented itself. That opportunity would be of Konstantine's making, so there was no need for her to tell him something that would only compromise his concentration when he needed it the most.

"We're safe," she lied, and pulled him close.

**19**

———

King tried to make sense of the mess of paper surrounding him. This week had proven to be one of those fortunate weeks when several cases resolved at once. Running an agency required that he be a master of patience. For months, revolving cases could hang in the air, waiting for a break, and that was the limbo that he'd been operating in since May.

More and more cases had come in, but a stubbornness surrounded them. Witnesses remained elusive. Evidence insubstantial. But this week their work had finally paid off. The Crescent City Detective Agency confirmed two cases of infidelity, found a missing vehicle, solved a workplace injury case, three identity theft cases, and even finished a profile on a man whose fiancée wanted to make sure that her fiancé was a good man before agreeing to marry him.

With all these cases resolving at once, it meant the agency remained committed only to the handful of background checks they'd agreed to, and Piper's missing persons case.

Since there was room to take on new cases, King had brought home several files from the office to survey his options. The cases that had been on the waitlist longest seemed like the most obvious choices, but there were more than a few with more pressing deadlines, and still others that, frankly, were far more interesting to him.

Two child custody cases looked promising. A father was trying to get custody of his kids, but given the court's tendency to defer to the mother, he was worried that he had little chance. There were many notes in the file about the mother's history of reckless behavior, drug and alcohol use, and general neglect of the kids. The potential client wanted King's help in confirming evidence of these behaviors ahead of his rapidly approaching custody battle.

King read Piper's diligent notes on the case—it was clear she had done the intake interview given her bubbly handwriting, and he could also tell that she'd felt great sympathy for the man. By proxy, King was also moved by his story, and added his case file to the *yes* pile. He'd give the man a call in the morning to confirm that he still wanted their help and proceed accordingly.

"What do you think, Lucy?" he asked the urn at the corner of his coffee table. "You think we can help him get his kids back?"

He liked to speak to her like this. Obviously, only when he was alone, but it brought him great comfort. What he never did was ask her advice about Mel. It felt strange to ask her advice about another woman. As if, not cheating exactly, it was at least disrespectful of her memory.

*Don't be silly, Robert. Why do I care if you're in love with her? I'm dead.*

The inner voice was such a perfect mimicry of her humor, he laughed to himself as he returned his attention to his remaining choices.

King had just moved on to a corporate investigation file—

a boss wanted proof that her secretary was embezzling funds —when a knock came at his door.

He knew it was Mel even before she spoke. Lady pressed her nose to the crack in the door and sniffed deeply.

"Mr. King, are you in there?"

"Coming," he called out.

Only a distant part of his mind registered that he'd checked the security of his belt, his fly, and smoothed his hair all before he reached the apartment door.

"Hey," he said. "I thought you weren't coming over until the shop closed."

Not that she needed a reason to visit him.

"It's slow. I closed early." She swept into the apartment smelling strongly of incense. Her bangles jingled and skirts swished. "I saw the news."

Right. He'd forgotten to call her after the story about Louie broke.

"I'm sorry I didn't call you earlier."

Lady trotted over to her food dish first to check if anything had been left for her. Disappointed, she went to the living room and settled down in her large, overstuffed bed.

But King only distantly registered the dog's movements. All of his attention was on Mel. Not just the way she smelled, the warmth of her body in proximity to his, or his own desire to greet her more intimately. With a kiss. By embracing her. By taking her hand at the very least. Or how delicious it might be if she reached out of her own accord and slid her arms around him.

This indulgent train of thought evaporated almost as quickly as it arose as soon as he realized the tense set of her shoulders. The hard line of her mouth, and the little crease between her brows.

"What's wrong?" he asked.

She finally met his eyes, a hint of surprise in her gaze. "Am I that easy to read?"

"What's wrong?" he said again.

"I need to tell you something. Can we sit down?" She moved toward his sofa before waiting for his response.

At the last minute, he remembered his manners. "Can I get you anything to drink? A snack?"

"No, come sit down here."

Now his heart was picking up its pace. As he took a seat beside her on the red leather sofa, his mind ran through a quick list of possible offenses that he may have committed. When he could think of no suitable possibility, his thoughts turned to doomsday scenarios.

*She's gotten a bad test result. It's cancer. She's going to get sick and die like Lucy did.*

*She wants some distance. I've made her uncomfortable.*

*She wants me to move out. She's dating someone else.*

"I had a vision," she said.

These words stopped his mind from its frantic inventory and scenario-making. "What?"

"I had a vision," she said again. She was watching his face carefully, almost defiantly, as if daring him to contradict her.

It was true that difference in their world views was often at odds with the other. King was a man of logic and evidence. Mel followed her intuition, things she felt, saw, but could not explain.

Had King known her ten or twenty years ago, he was sure he'd have treated her with more disbelief—possibly disdain—than he did now.

Knowing Lucy—Lou—had created that first rift between him and his ironclad rationality. Their powers couldn't be explained. They made no sense. Mel's gifts also didn't make a lot of sense to him. But the more he'd gotten to know her, to love and appreciate her, the more he came to accept that her experiences were real and valid, at least to her.

"Like the dreams you had about Zoey Peterson?" he asked.

Because that had been the closest thing to proof that King had experienced directly of Melandra's gifts.

"A vision isn't a dream. It comes when you're awake. But they can be as vague and nonsensical as dreams."

"Okay." He wasn't sure what the proper response was, so he fell back on his old interrogation tactics. An *okay* that was nonintrusive and didn't disrupt the story. A confirmation that he was listening.

As he'd hoped, Mel went on. "I had them more when I was a child. To tell you the truth, I didn't even know I *could* still have them. It's been decades."

"Then how do you know what you saw was a vision?" He thought this was the most polite way of asking if maybe it wasn't a daydream, or depending on when this so-called vision came, maybe even a dream that happened quickly in a moment of nodding off.

If she was insulted by this inquiry, she didn't show it. "It's hard to describe why they feel so different. It's the vision itself. I mean, how the eyes see. A darkness presses in on the sides. It...it washes over you like a wave and then you're in it. It's a brief glimpse into a future moment of time. You can hear everything, smell everything. It's like you're really there. But then it fades into nothing."

"I assume you're telling me about this vision because it involves us—or the girls."

A silence grew between them and a hint of color filled Mel's cheeks. King was about to ask what the hell she had seen in this vision when she finally spoke up.

"I think we were being attacked. You and me. But there were others nearby."

That was the vaguest description King had ever heard. His reticence must have shown on her face.

"I know it isn't much. I kept going back and forth on whether to tell you until I saw the news report. Things are getting dangerous for her, and we both know that means things are getting dangerous for us."

He couldn't argue with her there. They'd learned their lesson with Petrov and Diana. If this war with the Naples crime lord was escalating, and if the enemy knew enough to call her out on public media by name, it wasn't hard to believe he'd figure out her connection to King at the very least. He and Jack had been too close for too many years.

"I was going to let it lie," Mel said, wringing her hands now. "But I think I need to call it back. If the vision was a warning, rather than—well, rather than meaningless—then it might be helpful to know."

King had the impression that she'd been about to say something other than "meaningless."

Lady came to his side and placed a heavy head on his leg. He began to scratch her ear. "How do you call it back?"

"There are a couple of ways. One my Grandmamie taught me, but it's been so long I'm not sure if I remember all the steps. Then there's the simpler, more direct way."

Her face was definitely turning pink.

"We recreate it."

"*We?*"

She licked her lips before saying, "The brief glimpse of what I saw involved you."

A slow smile spread across King's face before he could stop himself. It was dawning on him that perhaps Mel had found herself in the position he'd struggled with months before, when every night he'd dreamed of her. Sometimes the theme was soft, romantic. Other times the sex explicit and realistic enough to leave him spent upon waking, his heart racing.

Cautiously he said, "What did you see?"

"You had your arms around me," she said.

She bent down and petted the dog, suddenly very interested in the Belgian Malinois. Lady didn't object to the attention.

King tried to match her attempted nonchalance. "My arms around you how?"

"I'll show you. I have to show you, actually. There's a direct method. To recreate it."

He only arched a brow to this.

"One of the easiest ways to call it back is to mimic it. If we place our bodies in the same position, if we try to recreate an atmosphere that is as close as possible to the original, it may come back to me. Are you willing to—"

"I'm willing," he answered too quickly. "Show me what to do."

Willing was an understatement. He cared less about whether or not the vision was real and more about the request that Mel put her arms around him.

Mel rose, pushing a nonexistent strand of hair away from her face. "I think we were in your apartment. The arch looked the same as mine, but the door was slightly off."

King understood what she meant. Their apartments were mirror images of each other.

"Does it need to be in the exact same place to work?" he asked. He resisted the urge to touch her too eagerly.

"When Grandmamie taught me this, we used my bed because I'd been looking at a ceiling in the vision, though later I'd learn it hadn't been my bed at all."

"Got it." His voice hitched because Mel had taken hold of his forearm.

She was leading him away from the couch, toward the

edge of the room. One of his feet was in the living room, one in the kitchen. Mel laid herself against the wall.

"I was holding you up against a wall?" he asked. He repressed the urge to laugh. First and foremost because it wasn't really funny. He was only nervous, and he refused to let it show.

"You turned and covered me."

"Walk me through this," he said, managing a controlled tone.

"I'm here and you were there."

He had the distinct impression that she was giving a very basic version of this story, but he didn't care.

She motioned him forward, and he took a step toward her.

"Closer," she said.

"Are you—"

"*Closer.*"

Obediently, he inched forward until he was truly almost on top of her, less than an inch between their bodies.

"Now," she said, her voice dry. He heard her voice click as she swallowed. "Put your arms around me."

He hesitated.

"Put your arms around me," she said again, looking up into his face.

He was trying to figure out if this was a trick, or a joke. "I'm not sure how to get any closer than this."

That was the truth. He couldn't get closer without pressing his entire body against hers.

"Pretend you're shielding me from something. I think that's what you were doing."

King tried to visualize it. If Mel had been standing in his room here and there had been a threat, an assailant from the balcony perhaps, one with a gun, what would his move be?

He shifted his weight, covering her body with his own,

pressing her against the wall beneath him. Only after he'd done so did he realize just how completely he'd pressed himself against her.

He began to pull back. "Sorry, I—"

"Wait!" she hissed. Her hand shot out and gripped his waist, pinning him in place.

Desire tightened his muscles, warming him. Their bodies were so close he could feel the top of his thigh rubbing against hers. And the grip she had on him was iron.

"Mel—"

"Shush."

He did as he was told, staying where he was, his arms protectively on either side of her. He was able to turn his chin just enough to catch a glimpse of her face.

Her eyes were pinched closed, her brow furrowed in concentration. He was so close that he could see two of her lashes were gray, not black like the others.

It would be so easy to kiss her.

Her breath was hot on his face. He kept waiting for the lines in her face to smooth out and her grip on him to soften. But instead, her nails began to dig into the flesh of his arm hard enough to hurt. And her mouth had begun parting in an unformed gasp or cry.

Then he saw the tears standing out in the corners of her eyes.

The embrace became real then. He stopped holding himself off of her, his forearms braced on the wall, and pulled her away from the wall into a hug.

Her shoulders shook, but she made no sound.

"What is it?" he asked. "What did you see?"

When she only buried her face deeper into his neck, he held her tighter.

Finally she did pull back, wiping her eyes with her sleeve.

"Did it work?" he asked. He thought that this might be a safe question.

"I didn't see everything, but I saw more. There was a gunfight, and we were all there. Me, you, Piper, and Lou. I think Dani was there too. I heard her call out, but I didn't see her. You—you were blocking my view."

Mel had chosen the word "gunfight." That suggested there was more than one gunman.

"How many?" he asked. "Did you see how many there were?"

"There were bodies on the floor. I think—I think Lou was handling a lot of it, but she—My god, King. She took at least two bullets. I saw them. I saw them go in and heard her scream and—"

"It's okay," he said. He resisted the urge to kiss the top of her head. "It hasn't happened. It'll be okay."

"But when I see—"

"You saw Zoey Peterson fall into the Mississippi River and drown, didn't you?" King couldn't remember if that was what had happened exactly, only that Mel's dreams of the girl hadn't been perfectly right. Had Zoey been in danger? Yes. Had she almost gotten seriously hurt? Definitely. But Mel's very actions had prevented the girl's death.

"Why would you have this vision if you couldn't do anything about it?" he asked, pulling back to see her face.

She looked up at him with those big golden-brown eyes. Again, the urge to kiss her rose to the surface of his thoughts, his body leaning toward her of its own accord.

What stopped him wasn't politeness or gentlemanly concern. It was the look on Mel's face. She was searching his eyes for something. And the sadness.

What the hell had she seen? By the looks of it, it had scared the hell out of her. Or had broken her heart. Because in all the years he'd known her, Mel had never been easily rattled. Even in moments when she should have been terrified, she had remained calm.

"Were you hurt in the vision?" he asked.

"I was in pain," she said. "I could feel it."

Pain wasn't dead, but it was still more than King wanted to happen to her. If anyone put his hands on Mel in this or any possible future, that would be the last thing they ever did.

Mel's gaze was distant. "I tasted blood on my mouth. I don't even know if it was mine. I have no context for any of it. It was a few seconds of complete chaos. That was it. That's the thing about entering a vision. You're really there. Or at least you are for a moment. I could smell the gunsmoke. I heard everyone screaming. The pain was real. But I don't know what happened up until that moment. I can't be sure who attacked us or why we were here. I saw—"

She pinched her eyes shut again, and fresh tears spilled over her cheeks.

"You're not there now," he said, a steady hand on her back. "You're here. With me."

She let herself be held for several moments. Then the heat of the moment dissipated and Mel's body relaxed. Whatever part of her had lingered in the future had returned to her.

"We'll prepare," he said. "Now that we know this is coming, we can do something about it."

"Sleep in bulletproof vests?" she asked with a sharp, humorless laugh.

"If we have to," he said. "Get better locks and security in our apartments. Hire bodyguards to watch the outside of the building. There's a lot we can do."

Just this short list seemed to ease some of the tension from her face, and he was glad to see it go.

"We aren't helpless." He pulled some tissues from the box

on the end table and passed them to her. "We have a lot more experience with this kind of bullshit."

"Oh, Robert," she said, sniffing. "You make it sound so easy."

"Because everything is easier with you," he said. "Even mafia showdowns."

He thought she would laugh. Thought she would maybe even slap his shoulder playfully or scold him.

Instead, a look passed over her face, and King got the sense that there was something she wasn't telling him. He wasn't sure if it was about the vision or if there were other troubles on her mind. Before he could ask, his cell phone went off, vibrating a tune on the coffee table.

He stepped away from the circle of her warmth and retrieved it, irritated at someone's terrible timing. Once he saw the number, his own stomach clenched.

*This can't be good. He wouldn't call if something wasn't up.*

Mel was dabbing at her damp face and nose with the tissues he'd given her.

"I'm sorry, but I really should take this," he said, before pressing the button on his screen. "King."

Sampson's deep baritone greeted him. "Robbie. How've you been? I haven't spoken to you since that bomber blew up your car."

This would be the third time that King had spoken to Sampson in about as many years. The first time it was to deliver a warning that King's unauthorized use of the DEA's systems had not gone unnoticed. He'd had little reason since to contact King, or at least that had been true until his flaming Buick had made the national news.

"Nothing as exciting as that going on," King said, switching the phone to the other ear. "To what do I owe the pleasure?"

"Are you still in contact with Louie?" he asked in a low voice.

King's heartrate sped up. "I haven't spoken to her in a minute, no."

Sampson didn't need to know that a minute translated to roughly two days.

"Someone is here in the office, sniffing around. Asking questions."

King noted Sampson's hushed tone. He tried to remember what the news report had said about Lou that morning. Not much, which was what had led King to believe there wasn't much to find.

"A journalist?" King ventured. "Feds?"

"I don't think so," Sampson said. "They don't look friendly, if you know what I mean."

*They.*

If it was the mafia that was hunting Louie Thorne, it made sense that they'd go to the St. Louis office. That was where Jack and King had been working when Angelo Martinelli murdered Courtney and Jack.

"First, they had a meeting with the director. Clarice in filing said they pulled every file they had on Jack Thorne. Two agents were pulled in for questioning after and were asked not about Jack but about Louie."

King's concern deepened. So it wasn't just a matter of putting Lou's name in the press and trying to force her out into the open. Whoever was searching for her was doing their best to get real, concrete information. That didn't feel like an empty power move to King.

Who had the power to walk into the DEA and ask questions? King knew about the corruption. His own ex-partner Brasso had proven to be in the pockets of a politician before he'd tried to kill King.

That was one of the many reasons King didn't regret leaving the agency.

Coupled with the fact that Mel was now sitting on his leather sofa, her eyes still red from crying, it made King wonder exactly what was heading their way.

*Nothing good, Robert.* That was Lucy's voice, soft in his mind.

"If they want information on Jack or Louie, it's only a matter of time before they turn up on your doorstep, Robbie. I wanted to give you both a heads up."

King did know. He'd been invested in every step of Jack's career from the moment he arrived in Quantico with the other new recruits. If someone wanted information on Jack Thorne's career, King would be the most obvious choice.

"I appreciate that. Hey, if you think you can get a picture of these *admirers* without putting yourself at risk, text it to me. It would help to know who I'm looking for," King said. Though he suspected that if it really was the mafia, they had plenty of lackeys to spare.

He ended the call.

Mel rubbed at the end of her nose. "Who was that?"

"Sampson."

"The agent who climbed up your fire escape that time I told him to leave you alone?"

King laughed. "Yes. I'd forgotten about that."

She waited, looking at him over the tissue she held pressed to her nose. Clearly she wanted him to go on.

"He said that someone is at the St. Louis office, digging up old files on Jack and asking about Lou."

"Legit agents?"

"Probably not," King said. "Sampson wouldn't have warned me if he'd thought it was a legit investigation. Above all he is a man of the law. No matter how friendly we've been in the past or how much guilt he felt over Jack—we all did—if he actually thought Lou was facing legitimate charges, he wouldn't have done anything to compromise the investigation."

"But he did call you."

"That tells us that something feels off to him, even if he isn't sure what."

Mel rose then. Lady rolled out of her bed, falling into line behind her without having to be called.

*Good dog*, King thought. *Keep our girl safe.*

As he watched Mel head for the door, he searched for some reason to call her back. More questions about her vision, just so he could keep her here and talking?

Before he could decide, she turned to him and said, "Thanks for your help. I'll let you know if anything else comes to me."

"And I'll let you know if I hear anything too," he replied lamely.

She took his hand and squeezed. It took considerable will to resist the urge to keep hold of it, or better yet, to pull her back.

Then she was gone, and he found himself alone on the sofa again, the files of his potential cases spread before him, waiting.

It wasn't until long after Mel had left and he had replayed that strange exercise in his mind that he realized she'd called him Robert, when he'd only ever heard her say "Mr. King."

*Robert.*

He wasn't sure if that was a wonderful or terrible sign.

## 20

With their half-eaten po-boys spread before them, the tang of vinegar hanging in the air, Piper and Dani sat at the island counter in their kitchen above the Crescent City Detective Agency. As Piper moved on from her sandwich to her chips. Dani turned her attention to the neat stack of photographs at her elbow. She wiped her fingers with a paper napkin then lifted the first one from the pile.

"Is it me or is there something manic about the eyes?" Dani was frowning at the age-progression photo of Louie. She'd printed it at work, using *The Herald*'s color photo printers.

"It definitely doesn't look like her," Piper said, the words squeezing past her second handful of chips.

Some distant part of her brain recognized this for what it was, stress eating.

Not the best response to a difficult situation, but she was struggling to find other ways to self-soothe as their problems began to escalate that didn't tip into the realm of self-destruction.

At least she had a plan. That counted for something. And the plan was to tell Dani the truth tonight. Her attempt to come clean with King and face the fallout may have been interrupted by Lou's television debut, but this—this she could manage.

Though her nerves were still getting the best of her. Dani had once shared her own view of their future. One in which they got married, got a house, lived happily ever after. But Piper wasn't sure if she was just a PI in this vision. Given how ambitious Dani was, maybe she had grander aspirations for her partner as a decorated federal agent.

What if she was disappointed in Piper's choice to follow her heart?

Her anxiety spiked at the thought of it, and rather than biting her nails, she shoved a third beignet in her mouth instead.

"Where's Lou now?" Dani asked, looking up from the photograph.

"I don't know. I haven't heard from her. I texted her to say she was on the news, and she just wrote back, 'I'm aware.'"

"If she's not worried, it's pointless for us to be." Dani put the photographs on the counter and turned her full attention to Piper. "I reached out to my contacts to see if I can get any more details on Lou's story. I haven't heard back yet."

Piper wasn't sure what use it would be to know the details considering that the story was bullshit anyway. She and King were convinced it was too.

"In the meantime, we should focus on your case. You said you needed help going through the footage."

Piper repressed a groan. Reviewing hours of footage wasn't her favorite PI task. It still beat fraud cases though, when her eyes practically bled from hours of combing transactions and cross-referencing them against receipts.

"I've got the trailhead cam footage and the park footage left to go through. I did the rest of it earlier today."

"What are we looking for? Just anything suspicious?" Dani asked.

"Repeat characters? Anyone that we see more than once. Since all the victims used this park, I just want to see if there's someone who hangs around. Anyone who looks like they are on a hunt."

"That might be everyone," Dani said, resting a hand on Piper's leg. "People tend to repeatedly visit the places they like, right? How far back did you go?"

"Just two weeks." Piper would have to go further if this returned nothing, but at least it was a place to start.

Dani stood, slipping off the barstool, and went to the sofa. "Shall we start then?"

They brought their laptops to the low coffee table so they could sit side by side on the floor, in the space between the couch and table, using the couch as a chairback.

Dani took the USB with the copy of the footage on it that Piper had made for her and slid it into her computer.

"Wait." Piper hadn't intended to blurt it.

Dani didn't look alarmed, she looked amused.

"You have salt on your lips."

Instead of wiping it off, Dani leaned forward with a mischievous smile and kissed the corner of Piper's mouth. She pulled back, licking her own lips.

"Yum," she said, still smiling.

Piper wiped her mouth with the napkin.

As she did, the flirtatiousness slid off Dani's face. "What's wrong? Was that gross?"

"No, it's not that." When Dani's frown only deepened, she said, "Seriously, it's not about that. It's just that I have something I want to tell you."

*No **turning back now**, Piper thought. *You swore you'd stop being so dramatic.*

Which was proving to be a harder promise to keep than she'd expected.

Dani sat up straighter. Piper recognized this movement as one of Dani's own anxiety tells. Whenever she was confronted with something, she straightened up as if preparing herself for battle.

"I made a decision that might affect our future."

God, when she said it like that, it sounded so big.

"Okay," Dani said, her face carefully neutral. "Is this about the ring shopping?"

"God. No. That's fine. We're fine. We're *amazing*. It's not about you and me."

"Good." Dani visibly relaxed. "Then what's going on? What did you decide?"

"I've decided I don't want to be a federal agent."

The relief on Dani's face was palpable. "Oh, okay. What do you want to do instead?"

"I know that the FBI has a reputation and it would be cool if I were an agent, but I just don't think it'll make me happy. You have to work the cases they make you work and you can't just go where you want you have to go where they tell you and—"

Dani cupped her cheeks, cutting off her outpouring. "You don't have to justify your choices to me, baby. I was on board the minute you said, 'I don't think it'll make me happy.' That's enough for me."

Piper's heart expanded in her chest. For some reason, she felt close to crying. "You won't think less of me?"

Dani tilted her head, her smile a little sad. She released Piper's cheeks and pulled her close instead. "I know that you feel like you have to prove yourself. I *get* it. I'm the same way, and I just want you to be happy. And with me, preferably. But believe me when I tell you that there's not a job in the world you could have which I wouldn't love you and support you in. I believe in you, Piper Genereux."

Piper did cry then. She tried not to be dramatic about it, but the tears pooled in the corners of her eyes before spilling over her cheeks.

"I'm so scared to tell King."

"Why?" Dani wiped her tears with her cuffs.

"What if he's disappointed in me? What if he feels like he spent all this time and energy investing in me and then I don't even go to Quantico."

Dani kissed the top of her head, still holding her close. "I don't think he will see it that way."

"I hope not. But I'm still scared shitless."

"When are you going to tell him?" Dani asked.

"I almost did today, but Lou popped up in the news and the moment was gone."

"Do it soon," Dani said, pulling a pack of tissues from her purse and using them to wipe Piper's tears. "You're just going to obsess about this until you do. Get it over with so you don't keep torturing yourself."

It was sound advice, as usual. Dani had never given her anything else.

"You never told me what you wanted to do instead," Dani said, after Piper had wiped her tears, gone to the counter, and stuffed another chip in her mouth.

"I love the PI work I'm doing now."

"Then keep doing it. You can be a PI anywhere," Dani said.

"But if we never leave New Orleans, are you okay with that?"

"It's hard to say what our lives will look like in five, ten, or twenty years," Dani said, "but I do know that as long as I'm with you and we're doing what we love, how could we possibly be off track?"

It was Piper's turn to pull her close and squeeze her. After kissing her deeply, one hand on the back of Dani's neck, she said, "Thank you, Daniella Allendale, for being so amazing."

"And you, Piper Genereux, are magic," Dani said, looking up into Piper's face. "And you'll be magic anywhere you go."

"Tell that to your mother," Piper grumbled, releasing her.

"Oh, that reminds me. Don't forget that we've got dinner with Dad on Friday. Seven sharp. Don't worry, she won't be there."

Dani's mother had yet to accept any of these standing dinner invitations, but Piper hadn't minded. She loved Dani's dad, Señor Allendale. He was warm and funny and incredibly kind toward her. He did keep giving her expensive cigarettes which Piper didn't smoke, but that was far from a deal-breaker. Her friend Henry loved them.

"I won't forget. It's in the books. Shall we?" She pointed at their laptops. If they didn't start now, they ran the risk of staying up late into the night.

"Only if you're one hundred percent aware of how much I love you," Dani said, batting her lashes.

"I'm one hundred percent aware. Are *you* one hundred percent aware?" She kissed the tip of Dani's nose.

"*I am aware, yes.*"

"Then let's begin."

**21**

———

Ettore stood on his balcony, his arms braced on the railing as he surveyed the scene below. To his right was the city. The lights were kaleidoscopic and the chaos of bodies moving through the streets echoed up to him. To his left was the water. Dark and endless. He wondered how many men had stood here, at the water's edge, and wondered about their destiny, and what might be lying just beyond the horizon.

Behind him, Martina's laughter echoed through the penthouse. The smell of dinner was escaping through the open door into the warm night around him and his stomach turned hungrily. He could give credit to his wife for her cooking. Sofia's mother had taught her well.

Instead of going inside to help with the preparations, he remained devoted to the task at hand. He'd spent hours watching Lou Thorne's name rise on the American news channels, only to see it dissipate almost as quickly. He had his answer then. It had come more easily than he'd expected, and for some reason it unsettled him rather than provided him the solace he'd expected.

At first he'd believed that confirming she was—as he suspected—just human would strengthen his resolve. After all, she would be far from the first adversary, or even woman, that he'd had to destroy on his path to greatness. He thought he'd be comforted to break apart the ironclad illusion of *La Strega*, the all-knowing, all-seeing boogeyman that held so many of his men in fear. But his unease grew as he contemplated that who he stood against wasn't a ghost.

A woman committed to her cause. Devoted, as he was devoted, to enacting her vengeance. It would be a matter of will then. Hers versus his.

Ettore pulled his cell phone from his pocket and set out to do what he'd come out on the balcony to achieve.

Konstantine answered on the fourth ring. "*Sì.*"

Ettore hated how smug the bastard sounded even in that single syllable. *Sì.* What he wouldn't pay to kick the man's teeth in.

"I wanted to thank you for confirming *La Strega's* identity for me." When Konstantine said nothing, he added, "You certainly did nothing to protect poor Tamara Lincoln. She's been arrested for fraud."

"I don't know what you're talking about," Konstantine said. "Is this all you called to say? Nonsense?"

Irritation heated the back of Ettore's neck. "Give my regards to *Louie*. Tell her I'll be seeing her soon."

And before his anger could goad him into saying something he would regret, Ettore hung up, returning his gaze to the dark water once more.

He finished his drink between deep, slow breaths. He let the pulsing of the city wash over him, centering him, bringing him back to himself. He let it remind him who he was and what he was capable of. Half the money that flowed through these streets was money that had passed through his own hands. He said where it went. He had the power to tear down buildings and end lives.

He was Ettore fucking Celesti.

His ease was nearly complete when a bell rang through the penthouse and he heard Sofia call out. In a panicked moment, he whirled, half expecting to see *La Strega* walk through the front door and into his home, guns raised.

But that was ridiculous. His place was surrounded by guards on every block. There were twenty men on the balconies above and beside him. No fewer than a hundred eyes watched him at all times.

He recognized Raffaele's voice at once before Sofia told him where Ettore could be found. He listened to Raffaele's steps echo across the tiled floor as he approached.

"Signore." Raffaele stepped out into the dark a moment later.

"What is it?" He didn't try to hide his irritation. Raffaele may not have been the cause of it, but Ettore felt no need to put the other man at ease. Let everyone around him treat him with the care he deserved.

"I came to tell you what we found."

Ettore finished off his drink before looking at the other man.

When Raffaele didn't speak, Ettore said, "Are you going to tell me or do I need to blow your brains out and read them on the ground?"

"No, signore. We sent our people to the DEA headquarters in St. Louis as you asked. We were able to get more information on Jack Thorne from the files we found there and also by asking some of the older agents who had known him when he was alive. The younger agents weren't much help. They only knew the stories that had been in the press. That he had arrested Benito Martinelli. That he and his wife were killed by the Martinellis for it. Also, some of them knew that he had been framed as working with the mafia when the hit came and that for many years after his death he was considered a disgrace. It wasn't until more recently that the story changed when new information was found."

Raffaele handed him a USB that Ettore presumed held all the information and files they had been able to gather from the DEA office.

"Nothing on her?" Ettore asked, pocketing the USB. He would look at it in his office later, after he had dinner with his girls.

"There was a report that she was kidnapped when she was ten years old. Though the person was never found."

Ettore's interest piqued. "*Veramente?*"

"She disappeared from the home and was found far away. A man claimed she walked out of his swimming pool and she had a very bad bite on her shoulder."

*A swimming pool.* How strange.

Perhaps Lou had her gifts even as a child. It would support his theory that she'd used them to escape Angelo.

"Before we could finish our questioning, we were forced out by other agents. I don't think it was the fault of our people."

"No, I don't think it was," Ettore agreed. He suspected that the same people who were able to remove Louie's name from the public news reports would have no problem sending someone to the DEA. Now he knew that he was smart to send someone ahead as soon as he realized who she was. Had he waited, perhaps all the information would have been lost.

Raffaele seemed slightly encouraged by this affirmation, as if he'd expected to bear the brunt of Ettore's anger at the interrupted investigation.

"What we did find was an address for an apartment in St. Louis. We sent someone there, but it was empty. The owner said no one had lived in it for years, and confirmed that a young woman had lived there in the past."

"What about any friends? Family that she might still be connected to?"

"She had an aunt who died nearly four years ago. No other family is listed. Most of the people who knew Jack Thorne are dead or moved away from St. Louis a long time ago."

"Who had he been closest to when he was alive?"

"A man named Robert King. He's in New Orleans now."

Raffaele gestured at the USB in Ettore's hand. "There was a company picnic at which Jack and Robert are seen together. Louie is in the photo too, as a little girl." Ettore looked forward to seeing it.

He turned to the skyline again, his gaze sliding up to the moon above. "Who do we have in New Orleans?"

**22**

───────

Lou couldn't have explained her unease. More than once Konstantine had eyed her over the rim of his cappuccino at their dining room table, his eyes full of questioning. First he asked her if there was anything wrong, and she said no. Then when that answer seemed dissatisfactory, he began offering her vague reassurances that her name would not appear in the press again. When Lou had been unable to handle another second of those soulful, apologetic eyes, she rose from her half-finished plate and strode to the dark closet, offering only a vague, *I need fresh air*, to assuage his concerns.

*If fresh air is what I needed, then what am I doing here?*

She stood in the moonlit street across from Ettore Celesti's apartment building. She knew that he lived in the penthouse, which by American standards wasn't all that high. But the balcony had a view of the water, which she was sure the prick enjoyed.

Why she had come, and why she was hovering here in the dark so close to the man she wanted dead most in the world, she couldn't say. Vaguely, she was aware of the fact that she was too close. That the men loitering near the building's entrance were likely his men. That any one of them might recognize her if they peered into the thick shadows where she hid.

A light fell across the balcony, and then Ettore himself stepped out into the open air.

Her heart hitched. Without thinking, she pulled a Browning pistol and pointed it pitifully at the balcony. The shot would never make it. She was too far away.

She'd asked her compass to carry her to the balcony if it was safe, and it did not. She had only to suspect that it must be rigged in some way. That there was a sniper on the roof, or some booby trap. In all cases, here she was, so close and yet so far away.

She realized then why she'd come.

She was pissed and wanted payback.

She almost laughed at the realization. It shouldn't have been a realization at all. One need only look at all the bodies in her wake to know that Lou Thorne wasn't above vengeance.

But she'd been surprised to find that she'd been more annoyed than she realized by his intrusions. First he took her lake from her. Then he tried to take her anonymity by blasting her name and that stupid photo all over the internet. Both attacks had felt personal.

*Two can play at that game.*

It might be true that her compass didn't want her to come closer than this—and whether that was because of her fluctuating power or because of some hidden measure that Ettore had in place, she was still here.

And this was close enough.

Louie scanned the area for Celesti, for any people that surely belonged to Ettore.

Her compass drew her to two men to her right. They

leaned against a building, smoking. Every so often they cast nervous looks around the street and the entrance to Ettore's building before resuming their conversation.

Lou's Italian was improving, but she still missed much of their conversation. She did recognize the word *Ravengers*. If she wasn't mistaken, *se ci uniamo a lei non importerà più di noi* was part of a joke about them joining the Ravengers instead.

*Too late for that.*

One asked for a cigarette, and before the other could reach into his jacket pocket, Lou had already pulled them both through the dark. Because she had not planned this impromptu hunt, she had to ask her compass for help on the fly, unsure if it would be able to deliver a safe location on such short notice.

The words that flitted through her mind were short and useless in any other context.

*Remote. No one for miles. Water. Dark.*

She half expected her gift to falter, but was relieved when the world opened for her.

The first thing that struck her was the blast of cold. Wind cut through her like a knife, burning. Falling snow made bright by moonlight reduced her visibility greatly, leaving her with only the vaguest sense of the landscape. Tall trees. A black monolith, looming. The jutting structure could have been a mountain or a cliff face of some kind. A plateau?

She put a bullet through each man's head. The blood splashed red across the white snow.

At least six inches of it climbed up her boots, spilling over the tops and sliding into the space between her calf and the leather. Even before their spilt blood stopped steaming, Lou was gone again.

*More*, she thought. *Give me everyone I can take closest to him.*

One man was bent over, trying to relace his leather shoes.

Another had turned his head away at the last moment to yell at a passing car.

Lou took them both with ease, delighting in the way her heartbeat rose eagerly before each pull of the trigger. She didn't savor the moment. Didn't indulge in the frightened look in their widening eyes the second before she pressed the gun to their heads.

That wasn't the point of this hunt.

She'd managed eight kills before something changed.

When she returned to Naples for the fifth time, hoping to grab at least a ninth victim, the energy had shifted. The borderline bored guards were circling the exterior of the apartment building like vultures scattered from their kill, waiting only for the opportunity to land again and recommence the feasting.

What forced Lou into retreat wasn't the increase of manpower, or their flashing guns. If anything, that felt like an invitation. *A dare.*

It was the men coming toward her. They paused at the mouth of each alleyway to shine light into the darkness, while shouting their findings into the cell phones pressed against their ears.

Lou didn't want to take her chances with the light.

This small rebuke would have to be enough.

Reluctantly, she threw one last look at Ettore's balcony, her guts full of longing.

But he was not there.

**23**

———

Lady pressed her cool snout into the palm of Mel's hand, bringing her attention back to the present. Mel's focus sharpened. It took a moment to orient herself. Sunlight from St. Peters poured cheerfully through the large shopfront windows of Fortunes and Fixes. Sleepy passersby with cheeks reddened by the sun slinked on, heads down as if bracing against a strong wind rather than the relentless heat.

Her mind had always been the wandering sort, but since leaving King's apartment, after he'd had his arms around her, it had seemed especially unreliable.

True, she had been the one who had wanted to call the vision back. She'd been the one, after Lou's identity had been blasted across the news for all to see, who had thought it would be better to know what they were up against rather than hide from what was coming.

But part of her had believed that her vision would prove innocuous. That she would reenter it only to find that King had embraced her. Perhaps kissed her.

What had been waiting for her had been quite different.

She'd told King the truth of it—mostly.

She had *not* told him about the blood on her hands. How it had poured out of him, spilling warmth over her hands as she'd tried to hold up his sagging body. How the weight of him had brought her to her knees.

Or that the last thing that she saw was a man raising his pistol and pointing it at her before everything went black.

*It hasn't happened.*

*It hasn't happened.*

*It might never happen.*

She repeated these words like a prayer as if they would protect her. Protect all of them. But Mel knew the truth. It would take more than wishing and praying to change their fate.

*Prayer only takes you so far, baby girl. God helps those who get up and do something.*

But what could she do? She wished Grandmamie was still alive so she could ask her.

No clear option had presented itself to her. And whenever she tried to consider her choices, her anxiety rose to such heights she could barely keep her skin on.

The chandelier moaned, and Mel looked up from the blank notepad that she hadn't even really seen, to find Piper crossing the threshold.

"Hey," she called out. "I came to see if you needed help prepping for tomorrow."

For a moment, Mel couldn't remember what tomorrow was. Her mind saw the scene again, the gunman upon them, the smell of gunsmoke thick enough to burn her nostrils, her ears ringing.

Piper's open, friendly face hardened into something like concern. "You're still going to set up a booth for BexFest, right?"

The festival. Right. "Yes," she said, her wits returning. "I'm sorry, my mind's all over today."

Piper's brow arched at that. "Tell me about it. My eyes are bleeding from this case I'm working. That's why I thought I'd take a break and see if you need help. King says that when you fixate too much on something, you can get stuck. That sometimes the best thing you can do is walk away for a minute. This is me walking away."

Mel welcomed the distraction. "Help me move these boxes from the storeroom out into this little alcove here by the register." She could still give instructions as if she meant them, even if she didn't feel all that sure of herself. And by carrying the boxes from the storeroom, they had something to do.

"Good job," Piper cooed to Lady as she placed her third box in the alcove. "You sniffing for bombs? You keeping us safe?"

Lady's tail swished, the dog obviously pleased to be acknowledged for her efforts, while she continued to press her long snout to the crease of the latest box.

"Is that it?" Piper asked, looking up from where she'd bent to scratch Lady's rump.

Mel did a count. "Two more."

Once all the boxes were piled in the corner where the large window met the glass case, Mel said, "One of these should have the branded goody bags, and the others the Fortunes and Fixes freebies. I got enough to stuff five hundred, give or take."

"Let's get to stuffing then."

Together, they sorted each item in a pile: the branded bags, business cards, the tumbled crystal stone, the incense cones, oracle card samples, and branded lighters.

Piper held one up. "Oh, this is cool! Can I have one? I'll buy it."

Mel shook her head. "No need. I bought extras to sell on the counter. They're a good impulse buy."

"Hell yeah they are," Piper said, pocketing the lighter. "The Quarter is crawling with smokers, and spooky-woo people need lighters even if they don't smoke."

Mel was pleased to have her choice affirmed. "I'm glad you like it."

They worked in relative silence, filling the bags from the assembly line they'd created. They'd pick up a bag, one of each item, put them in the bag, and fold the top down before setting it inside one of the empty boxes.

Mel's mind began wandering again.

But there was something sweet about the moment. It reminded her of the early days after she'd hired Piper. How her energy and attitude had been a welcome change to the shop. It was true that in the beginning Mel had been just as likely to be soothed by Piper's presence as annoyed by it. She had spent so long on her own, hermiting in her own life, that inviting the bright and bubbly twenty-something into her life had felt like breathing new air into her days.

Overwhelming but welcome.

"Do you know it's supposed to be over a hundred tomorrow? Can you imagine that direct sun beating down on us? My *god*, it's going to be brutal. We gotta be there early to set up the umbrella under a tree or we'll *die*. And do you still have those mini fans that—What?"

Mel's hands had slowed as she'd listened to Piper talk. She'd only been half listening at first, warring with the distractions fighting for her attention. But then, gradually, Piper's face had come more and more into focus.

Until then, quite suddenly, Mel's vision blurred.

"Mel," Piper said, her surprise morphing into fear. "Oh my god, is it what I said about the tent? You don't have to do it. I'll go early and set it up myself and—"

"No," Mel said. Her bangles clanged musically as she dabbed at the tears in the corners of her eyes. "No, that's fine."

"*Is it?*" Piper said, leaning toward her. "Because I don't want to make a big deal here, it's totally natural to feel your feelings, but I've, like, never seen you cry before."

When Mel's fingers weren't enough to make the tears stop, she tried using the end of her scarf. "It's nothing."

"Okay, but if you need me to get you something," Piper prattled on, unaware of the silent war waging within her, "I would totally—"

The chandelier moaned and Piper broke off midsentence.

"Oh *hey*," she said, perhaps too cheerfully.

Mel didn't need to look up to know that it was King who'd crossed the threshold. An entrance by anyone else would not have solicited such a positive response from Lady. The dog had risen from where she'd sat, one hip pressed into Mel's, tail swishing.

Mel also didn't think it was a coincidence that Piper had pulled herself up straighter, as if using her body to block King's view of her.

*She's doing you a favor*, Mel thought, and took the chance to turn her tear-stained face away and pretend to search for something in one of the inventory boxes.

She hoped he didn't look too closely. Otherwise, surely he would realize that this box was full of lighters and nothing else. There was no reason for her to search it so vigorously.

"I needed a cold shower," King said. "It's not even noon and I've already sweat through my clothes. It's disgusting."

His voice shivered over her skin and a stone in her stomach hardened, nervously.

"That's what you get for wearing clothes," Piper said, a strained laugh escaping her.

King slipped his hands into his pockets. "I suppose so."

Mel heard his footfall on the stairs, followed by the solid thump of his apartment door sliding into place a moment later.

She loosed a breath she hadn't realized she was holding.

Likely King had known that she was upset, or at the very least that he had walked in on a conversation. In either case, he'd chosen to go upstairs without comment. Either he didn't want to interrupt or he wasn't sure if she was upset about the vision. Maybe he was trying to gauge whether or not she'd told Piper anything about it. It would have been easy to discern from her reaction that she hadn't, and so he had decided to remain quiet too.

"That's what you get for wearing *clothes?*" Piper muttered under her breath. "What a stupid thing to say. I panic and *that's* the first thing that comes out of my mouth?"

Mel's breath was slowing, but she could still feel her pulse in her temples.

"I was just so focused on hiding you so he wouldn't ask what's wrong that I think I made it *super* obvious. Way to go, Genereux."

She turned then and seemed to realize that Mel was still in the grip of her emotions.

A strange expression played across Piper's features. In a low voice she said, "Mel, can I ask you something?"

Mel looked up, surprised by her tone. "What?"

"Do you like him? I know it's not my business," Piper said, "but I've spent all this energy, worried about him making a move on you and ruining everything, but like, you're blushing, and so if I'm wrong you should just tell me to mind my own business and I will."

Mel almost laughed at that. It wasn't only the girl's endearing tone, or how obvious it was that she was worried for Mel, but the ridiculousness of this conversation struck her again, giving the moment a strange, dream-like quality.

She felt as if she were outside her body watching the scene unfold.

"I'm not blushing," she said. "That's ridiculous."

"Fair enough. It's on me for prying."

Piper returned her attention to the goody bags, stuffing them without further commentary. She'd moved five completed bags to the new pile before Mel whispered, "I don't know how I feel."

Piper's hand hovered over the box of cone incense, her fingers smudged dark blue from their residue. Mel thought she might even be holding her breath, waiting for something.

"The only man I loved for a long time was Terrence, and he had such a hold on me. For more than half of that, it wasn't love that bound me to that man, it was fear. Fear of what would happen if I stopped him from trying to control me. Fear of what my life might look like if I was really free. I've only ever known a man like that. What they want from you, what they can get from you. I guess you don't know about that since you're a lesbian."

Piper snorted. "Oh, you'd be surprised. Girls are just as crazy. But go on."

Mel took a handful of lighters from the pack in front of her and said, "I don't feel the way about him that I did for Terrence. But I think this is a good thing."

"Like *love* love. Or..." Piper was transfixed on their conversation now, the goody bags in her hands forgotten.

"I don't know."

"This might sound stupid," Piper said, realizing she still held her bags. She dropped them into the box. "But do you think he's handsome?"

"Any idiot with eyes can see he's handsome." Mel bit back her irritation. "It doesn't take a genius to see that."

"Yeah, but do you think he's handsome in *that* way? Do you like the way he smells, do you feel something when he touches you or says your name? God, the name thing is huge for me. It tears me up when Dani says my name. I *melt*."

Mel did like the way he said her name, and she had certainly felt something in those brief moments in his apartment when he'd wrapped his arms around her. As she'd waited for the vision to return, she'd been nothing but aware of the heat of him and how her skin had reacted to his proximity.

Then the vision came, and now romance was so far from Mel's mind that whatever she felt or didn't feel for King was under a wall of anxiety and fear.

"You don't have to have any answers now," Piper said. "I was just wondering if I should stop lecturing him to leave you alone. And it looks like I don't need to do that, so I've got my answer."

Mel dropped a lighter into a bag before picking up another.

"There's no rush anyway," Piper said. "You've got plenty of time to figure out how you feel."

Mel felt King's hot blood washing over her hands again, felt his weight sag in her arms, pulling her to her knees.

*I'm not so sure about that.*

24

No matter what he tried, King couldn't stop replaying the image of Mel, her face turned away from him as she pretended to busy herself with something in the box. That was hours ago, and the relief he'd felt from his cold shower was already gone. Even his short walk back to the agency after lunch had been enough to heat the back of his neck and make his head feel swimmy again.

Leaning back in his desk chair, his hand furiously clenching and releasing his stress penguin, King had begun to worry he might waste the rest of the afternoon thinking about her.

That was until two shadows darkened the agency door.

King looked up as a man and woman crossed the threshold of the Crescent City Detective Agency.

He had only seconds to school his features before the woman spoke.

"Are you Robert King?"

"That's me," he said, suddenly glad that Piper wasn't there.

He reached across the desk and accepted the hand the

woman offered. The man kept his hands in his pockets and only offered King a nod.

"What can I do for you today?" he asked.

"We are looking for my friend," she said.

*I bet you are.*

"She is not answering her phone." The woman's face was a parody of concern. It was the eyes that were giving her away. She looked far too excited to be there. King had worked a lot of missing persons cases. He knew from his experience with grieving friends and family that the reactions to a loved one's disappearance greatly varied. Some reacted as if they were locked in a dream, disbelief shrouding their features. Others reacted with desperation, each word a passionate demand for King to take action.

This woman seemed like she was having a good time, as if this entire conversation was only a dress rehearsal.

*Because it's all a show*, he thought.

The man wasn't so good at pretending either. His eyes were roving over the office, obviously taking it all in. Their desks, the doors at the back of the agency. He was sizing the place up.

King was suddenly very glad that Piper was at Fortunes and Fixes with Mel.

"Did you file a report with the police?" he asked.

"No, no. We came straight to you. We heard things about you."

Though he could hear a faint accent in the woman's voice, King suspected the *good* was intentionally left out of the sentence.

"With missing persons cases it's best to speak to the police first. They need to file a report. And our case load is quite full at the moment," King said. "We aren't taking any more cases just now."

"Don't say that," the woman said. She cocked her head

and smiled. But there were too many teeth in that smile. And when she moved, King was fairly certain he saw the outline of a gun shift under her jacket.

*She has to be packing.* Who the hell would wear a jacket in this heat unless they had something to hide?

"Look at this picture of my friend," she said. "Tell me if you have seen her."

King knew what he would see even before the woman pulled the photo out of her back pocket and slid it across his desk.

It was Lou's photo. Or at least, it was the age-progression photo that he'd seen on the news before the media cycle had —unsurprisingly—swallowed the information whole.

"What's her name?" King asked. "Your friend?"

He pretended to squint at the photo. Then he opened his desk drawer and rummaged. With no small amount of relish, he watched the woman's face grow increasingly irritated as he searched. When he felt he'd dragged this game to the breaking point, he finally said, "I'm sorry, but I guess I forgot to bring my glasses with me. I can't see up close very well. And this is a small picture."

In truth, the picture was crystal clear, but she didn't need to know that.

"Louie Thorne," she said.

Here he had the good sense to look surprised. "Are you a friend of Louie's?"

"No...I mean yes."

King was grateful for this slip because now it gave him a reason to be appropriately suspicious.

He narrowed his eyes. "I'm sorry, but how do you know Louie?"

"We went to school together."

"Which school?" King asked without hesitation, as if he would have been able to answer this himself.

"High school," she said.

"What year did you graduate?"

This question seemed to stump the woman. The man was no longer pretending, however. He stared openly hostile at King, his eyes burning twin holes through him.

"Where is she?" he said. His accent was much thicker than the woman's, and King was willing to bet that this sentence had been quite the feat for him.

"I haven't seen her in years," he replied. "You know about the accident?"

They didn't seem to know what he meant, so King went on.

"Her parents were killed, by the *mafia*." He said this as if it were a real secret to anyone in the room. "Very sad. After that she went to live with her aunt."

"Where is her aunt?"

"Her aunt died of cancer. I saw Louie at the funeral."

This was true. Lou had been the one to make Lucy's final moments so special. She'd carried her to the beach before sunset, had gotten the wood for the fire and the drinks, and even the priest that had performed an impromptu wedding there on the sand with Lucy in King's arms.

It was one of his most beautiful—and heartbreaking— memories.

"I haven't seen her recently though," he said.

The accuracy of this statement depended greatly on one's definition of *recently*. Lou had been understandably busy preparing for the arrival of her daughter. King had not taken her absence personally.

He knew from decades of experience that the closer he stayed to the truth, the easier it was to lie.

"When is the last time you saw her exactly?" The first hint of impatience was showing in the woman's face.

"She doesn't live in New Orleans," he said. "I heard she

had an apartment in St. Louis, so she can't be expected to make the trip down here to see an old man all that often. Kids these days are so busy."

If these goons really were from the mafia, then they could have gotten the address to Lou's apartment the same way they'd gotten his.

Of course, this was the best-case scenario. Because even as they proved to be inept interrogators, King suspected a darker possibility was on the horizon. If they knew that Lou had the ability to go anywhere at any time, then it wasn't that they expected him to provide any useful information about her location.

What they likely wanted was a hostage.

And King didn't like any of the possible ways they might take one.

"You have seen her," the woman said. It wasn't a question.

"Yes, I told you." He tried to run a quick calculation in his mind of when Sampson had visited, how that aligned with Lucy's death. He gave a time that he thought would be plausible even if they checked. "We chatted a bit. I asked her what she did for work, and she said she wasn't really working at the moment. I didn't push her for answers. That's her business. She'd always been quiet, even as a kid, so I just told her a few stories about her old man and we parted ways. That was it."

All of this was plausible.

But still, it didn't seem as though either of them was pleased with his answer.

*Not good, Lucy. Not good.*

Would she come if he was captured? Tortured?

He thought she would, even if he told her not to.

He needed to get rid of these two.

"Look. I'm sorry I can't be of more help to you, but I

need to close up for the day. Maybe you could try social media. Aren't all you kids on social media these days?"

King didn't have an account on a single platform, but it wasn't because of his age. It was because he knew just how trackable a person could be if they put their details on the web like that, for all to see.

The man said something. King didn't know the language, but he recognized the vicious tone.

*Just leave*, he thought. *Leave before this gets ugly*.

He saw her shadow in the corner of his eye before his brain registered who it was, hand on the door, pushing it open.

*No*, his brain screamed. *No*.

"Ma'am, I'm sorry, but we're closing. You'll have to come back at another time."

King had filled his voice with authority and dismissal. As much as he could manage in spite of the sudden spike of fear riding him.

Mel paused in the doorway, her hand on the frame as she looked from King to the two *customers* crowding his little space.

Something passed behind her eyes.

*Run*, King thought. *Run. Don't let them get a good look at you*.

If Mel heard this silent plea, she dismissed it, because instead she put a hand on her hip and, still holding open the door, said, "You don't look closed to me. How come these two get to be in here but you won't speak to me."

Shit.

Mel was going to follow this through.

It was a dangerous game. He could hardly call her on it now.

"If they get to stay past closing time and you listen to *their* case, then I get to stay and you gotta listen to mine too."

Just as King thought she couldn't get any more audacious,

she said, "Or if you won't, I'll be sure to let everyone know about your unfair business practices."

She shouted into the street, pitching her voice, "Because what kind of private investigator won't take new clients and—"

The man and woman pushed past her as if escaping the scene. Mel came into the office and closed the door after her.

"That was reckless," he said. "You don't know—"

"I know exactly who that was," she said.

For a moment he wondered if they were recognizable. Maybe a face from her vision or—

"No, I don't know them like that," Mel said, as if reading his face. "But you don't have to be a genius to know they were bad news. And never, *never*, have you once in all our years of acquaintance called me ma'am as if you didn't know me."

He came around his desk, stopping short of her.

"I was trying to signal that you should leave, get away so they can't see you and—"

"And leave you here to deal with them on your own?" She arched both of her brows. "That's what you'd have me do? Leave my friends high and dry in the clutches of the damned mafia?"

As he stared down into her face, unsure of what he should say, he slowly became aware of her breathing. Of the color rising in her cheeks.

"Don't you ever try to send me away like that again," she said, breaking eye contact first.

"I'm sorry," he said, taking a step back. He was far too close to her, and he knew it.

He rested against the edge of his desk and clutched its edge, which was the opposite of what he wanted to do with his hands.

Mel seemed to busy her hands as well. She reached into her pocket and brought out her cell phone.

"What are you doing?" He didn't want her to call the police. At the very least, they would make it clear to the mafia that he did in fact know who they were.

"Texting Piper," she said. "She said she was going to the park, but if she hasn't yet, I need to warn her."

"Good idea," he said. If they had his work address, they probably had his home address too. And Piper needed to be extra careful coming in and out of the office with those two around. Who was to say they wouldn't figure out about the apartment upstairs and mistake it for King's.

"She's gotta keep her eyes open," Mel said, echoing King's thoughts, while typing furiously on her phone.

Once she'd finally finished her message and her phone made the little swoosh sound that suggested a text had been sent, she returned her attention to him.

"They didn't hurt you?"

The concern in her face made his stomach twist in on itself. "No, they didn't have time for any of that. They just wanted to know where Lou was."

"They didn't even pretend they weren't looking for her? Why did they think she'd be here with you?"

"To figure out whether or not I can be used as bait, probably."

"No." She clasped his hand and gave it a squeeze. "Absolutely not. You will not be anyone's bait, Mr. King. I won't allow it."

The warmth of her hand holding his remained long after she pulled away.

**25**

───────────

T he clouds covered the sun, blessing Piper with a moment of relief from its blistering rays. "Oh thank *god*."

She was still dreaming about an enormous glass of sweet tea that she would drink as soon as she got out of there, but before that could happen, she'd come for a reason.

After leaving Fortunes and Fixes, Piper figured she could use the last of the day's light to visit the park and confirm at least one of her theories.

She had remained convinced that the park was the center-piece of the mystery. All three victims visited it nearly every day leading up to their attacks, and it was the only overlapping location Piper had managed to identify.

Just this damned park.

Reviewing the footage had turned up a few repeats. People who appeared consistently throughout. Either one of them was the killer Piper was looking for, or maybe one of them saw something that might point her in the right direction.

She'd already had six fruitless conversations when she spotted a woman running toward her. She froze, wondering how she was going to respond to this.

But the woman wasn't attacking. She had something shiny in her hands that she held out in front of her like a talisman. Once she was within earshot, she asked, "Is this yours?"

Piper almost said no, automatically. She managed to hold herself back at the last second. She was here to collect evidence, after all. And here was a girl fitting the description of the other three victims—young, pretty, long hair—literally holding up something shiny.

"Let me see," Piper said, extending her hand.

"I found it over by the exit," the girl said, pointing at the fenced-in dog park behind her.

Piper held the piece of metal closer to her face.

It was in the shape of a bone, with a name, address, and phone number engraved neatly into its surface.

Biscuit
1131 Halifax Way
(504) 555-3233

"It's a dog tag," Piper said.

The girl's brows lifted. "That it is. I'm guessing by your face that Biscuit isn't your dog."

She had just turned away when Piper exclaimed, "Oh my god, it's a *tag*!"

The girl picked up her pace, moving away more quickly.

Piper ignored her. She had to make a phone call—several, actually—and now.

It took her a moment to find the right number in her phone, but eventually she did locate the contact info for the first girl who'd reported an attack. Heidi answered on the third ring, the background noise garbling the line.

"Hey, Heidi, this is Piper Genereux with the Crescent City Detective Agency. I have a quick question for you."

"Oh yeah?" She sounded excited, which was not a surprise to Piper. A surprising number of people seemed to relish the possibility of murder and mayhem. "Hit me, girl, what you got?"

"This may be weird, but do you have your address written on your dog's tag?"

"Yeah, I do. I wanted someone to bring her home if she got out. Why?"

Piper's heart sped up. "Did anyone pet your dog or bend close and look at the dog in the days before your attack? Anyone you remember—"

"Yes!" the girl exclaimed. She shouted the way one might cry, *Bingo!* "There was a creepy, scrawny guy. Pale as hell, and he took her picture. I thought it was weird, but I didn't want to be a bitch about it, you know?"

"Thank you, Heidi, that's a big help." Piper hung up without a proper goodbye and immediately began dialing the number of the second girl who was attacked. When she didn't answer, Piper left a message with the same questions.

Willa's sister, Caty, had just answered the phone when victim number two texted a photo of her dog's tag. After zooming in, Piper could see that the address and number were clearly printed on the dog's collar.

"Hello? Hello, is there anyone there?" Caty said impatiently.

"Yes, sorry. Hi. It's Piper. Piper Genereux with the Crescent City Detective Agency. Do you still have Miss Bella Beans with you?"

"Yes, of course. I didn't get rid of my sister's dog," she said. "Why?"

"Can you tell me if the address is printed on the dog's tag?"

*Please please please please.*

After several moments of rustling fabric and Caty's voice calling for the dog, she returned to the phone and said, "It's engraved on a little tag, yeah. Why?"

"That's all I needed to know. Thank you!"

"But—"

"Sorry, that's all I have for right now. I'll be in touch soon with more."

Piper felt awful lying to her like that. She already knew Willa was dead and that her sister deserved to know the truth. But Piper wasn't ready to have that terrible conversation. She really hoped she wouldn't have to be the person to deliver that news at all.

Dani picked up immediately. "Hey, baby. I was—"

"I think I know how he's picking his victims," Piper said. "*Dog tags.* All three victims had their addresses printed on the dog tags and Heidi remembers a guy taking a photo of her dog in the park. Didn't we see a guy..." She gave Dani Heidi's description of the man who'd photographed her dog. "That's what he was doing, right? It looked like he was taking photos of the dogs?"

"Yes, I'll do a quick scrub and see if I can't get a still frame of it. Then I can ask one of my contacts to run it."

"That would be *amazing*, and I would love you *forever*."

"You're already going to love me forever," Dani said, and hung up.

Piper's phone rang again, but it wasn't Dani calling back.

Instead of hello, Bane said, "I've got my eyes on two fuckers now."

"Two fuckers? What are you talking about?"

A pair of moms shot Piper dirty looks.

"I know they're Celesti. They've got that stick-in-their-ass look about them. They think they're slick, but I know everyone in this city and they ain't ours."

Piper had serious doubts when Bane made statements like this. Not only because the girl was too young to possibly know *everyone* in the whole city of New Orleans. Piper was super friendly herself, and she would never say she knew everyone. What about all the tourists? They were in and out all the time.

She was about to say as much when her phone beeped with a text.

"Hold on." She pulled her cell away from her ear and opened the message from Mel.

*Mafia came to the agency. Stay clear for a few hours but get what you need from your apartment before dark, and only if no one is watching the place.*

Piper swore under her breath.

She knew that having the mafia this close to her apartment was going to set Dani off. But that was a reasonable reaction, she told herself, to having her finger cut off by a Russian mob boss after his goons spent the day beating the shit out of her.

Piper pressed the phone to her ear again. "Okay, let's say that you're right about the Celesti. What can we do about it?"

"I'm going to deal with these fuckers, and I want you to share your location with me."

"Bane—"

"Do it! Where there's two, there's more. Not that I can't find you anyway. But this is quicker. And in war we don't fuck around."

The mothers looked ready to come over and lead Piper from the park by her ear. Turning away, she sent her location to Bane, making a mental note that this would be a very temporary thing.

There was a pause, then Bane said, "Good. I'm keeping my eye on you. Get your girlfriend to share her location too."

"I already have it—"

"With *me*."

"I'll ask." Because Piper had no idea if Dani was just going to hand her location over to this chaotic *child*.

Bane hissed into the phone. "Here's my chance to get rid of them."

"What do you mean, *get rid of them?*" Piper said incredulously.

But Bane had already hung up.

Before she could consider her next move, another text from Mel came in.

*King doesn't want you to call Lou. Her presence will only confirm what the bad guys suspect.*

Piper sent a thumbs-down emoji, even though she understood. If a bad guy sent people to New Orleans to check out King, even if it was only to see if Lou still had any connection to him, and then those guys disappeared, that was answer enough, wasn't it? Worse, it was an invitation to send *more* bad guys.

"Wait." She spoke to no one but herself. "Oh *shit*."

The mothers were gathering up their kids now, giving Piper death stares as they led them toward their strollers and started packing them in.

Piper called Bane.

No answer.

Piper texted her.

*Don't kill anyone. If the Celesti disappear then they might think Lou did it and try to hurt us anyway.*

She held her phone for several moments, waiting for a reply.

It didn't come.

Piper wasn't sure how to interpret that.

When two more texts went unanswered, she did the only other thing she could do.

She took a big breath and called Dani. While the phone rang, she considered how she was going to tell her that they had to sneak in and out of their own apartment before dark, without anyone seeing them.

**26**

———

The New Orleans detective had put Konstantine in a difficult position. On one hand, he was grateful that the man had called to let him know that at least two of the Celesti—Konstantine had had no doubt that was who had come—were in New Orleans. This new development confirmed his suspicion that Ettore was trying to track Lou's whereabouts through her late father.

As serious as that was, it wasn't Konstantine's greatest challenge at the moment. It was how to tell Louie that the detective didn't want her to save the day.

If he delivered this news poorly, her restlessness would only worsen, and it was very possible that she would punish *him* for the man's wishes.

He was still struggling to decide how best to give her the news when she burst into their bedroom.

"The Celesti are in New Orleans."

Well, that secret hadn't kept long.

"King told me not to come," she said, her jaw working furiously. "*He* thinks he can tell me where I can go."

Before Konstantine could even say that he'd also received the message, she turned those fiery eyes on him.

"You knew."

Konstantine held his hands up, palms out in surrender. "I only just heard. I didn't have time to tell you."

That was close enough to the truth.

"What does he hope to achieve by keeping me away? Does he think they won't kill him just because I'm not there?" It didn't sound like much of a question.

"I believe," Konstantine dared to suggest, "he thinks that the worst-case scenario is that they see you and confirm your connection. If they can't confirm that, they may just go away and leave them alone. It is the same if I intervene. If I kill any Celesti only because they are in New Orleans and spoke to your father's friend, it will make the detective seem important."

"Because he is," she ground out.

Konstantine rubbed his chin, unsure of what to say next. Eventually he settled on, "He's only trying not to escalate the situation."

"I can go and get them. All of them, and bring them here until this is over."

"You could, if they'd come. But their absence may send the same message. They've already seen the detective. If he disappears, they will wonder why he ran."

"Do you think they know about the others?" Lou eased herself down on the edge of the bed, wincing.

Her pained expression disintegrated his questions. "Are you all right?"

He knew she was considering lying to him.

"*Amore mio.*"

"I'm having contractions. I don't think they're real. But my back hurts."

She'd had contractions a few times in the last two weeks.

Isabella had insisted this was normal. That it was common for the body to practice before the actual birth.

"Are you sure they aren't real?"

"Yes," she said, the lines in her face evening out. "They've already stopped."

Considering that true labor would intensify, not lessen, Konstantine trusted her judgment. He was scared to say it, but he thought the truth was the best course of action now.

"You are in no shape to fight right now," he said. "You told me yourself this morning that you felt you may have over-done it taking Ettore's men last night."

She said nothing to this.

"If you go into another fight, you may trigger your labor. Can't you imagine a scenario in which you are in labor but there is a gun pressed to your friends' heads?"

She still said nothing.

Her silence was starting to scare him. He had the distinct impression that she was not telling him something, and in this moment, she was trying to decide whether or not to speak up.

When she only continued to sit there, her elbows on her knees and her face unreadable, he had to ask.

"*Amore mio?*"

"I can't leave them there. Ettore doesn't get to decide what to do with them. He doesn't get to decide where to apply pressure just to get a response out of *me*."

"This is not about Ettore. Your detective is entitled to his choices," Konstantine said calmly. Secretly he was very grateful for the detective, that he'd thought of Lou's and Elena's safety above his own.

"What about Piper, Dani, and Mel? I could take them now and come back for King later," she said hopefully.

Lou pulled a phone from her pocket, the one he'd gifted her last Christmas. Still, he was surprised to see her use it.

He'd wondered if it was a wasted gift, given how often she failed to carry it when he wanted her to.

He watched her type out a message.

A moment passed and her phone vibrated.

He expected her to leap up, declaring her intention to go and retrieve the women. Konstantine was already deciding in his mind where it would be best to house them during their time in Florence.

Yet, Lou didn't look happy.

"Melandra won't leave him behind," she said.

Lou typed another message and waited. Konstantine noticed that her hand kept going to her back, rubbing it just above her hips.

He scooted forward and began massaging the places she kept returning to.

When the text returned, she looked unhappier still.

"Piper and Dani don't want to leave either. They're all getting rooms in a hotel for the night. They aren't going to meet up in person in case someone sees. They think if I come to the hotel and someone sees me, then it may set them off. They don't know how many Celesti are in the city."

*Too many*, Konstantine thought. He'd set Armando to answering that very question as soon as he'd heard from the detective. He'd reported nearly fifty the last time they'd spoken, but the count was incomplete. New Orleans wasn't a stronghold for the Celesti, but it was a common stopover when trafficking people through Atlanta.

"They are being careful. That's good," he said. "Let them be for now."

He thought she might refuse his touch, knock his hands away and perhaps yell at him out of frustration, but she went soft beneath his hands. She was rubbing her head as if it hurt. When she realized he was looking at her, she said, "I'm fine. It's just a headache."

"*Amore mio*," he said, pressing a thumb into a knot he found just beside her spine. "You forget that I have people in the city."

"If I can't go, what makes you think you can send your people?" she said. "If they see the Ravengers following him around and asking questions, they'll know he's important."

"Or they'll believe we're just curious what the Celesti are doing there. I could even tell my people to ask that very question. It may be our way of throwing them off track. If they take the Celesti and torture them for information regarding their presence in the city, while acting unaware of the detective's existence, it may throw Ettore off his trail."

She lay back against the pillows, pressing her fingers into her temples.

"Rest, *amore mio*," he said, pulling close to her. "I promise, we will find a way to keep your friends safe."


Lou was still awake long after Konstantine's breath had evened out, his chest rising and falling gently beside her. Her mind was racing, unable to find peace. Several issues plagued her at once. First and foremost, her head was killing her. She found it hard to think, and felt as if her pulse raged in her temples rather than her chest.

Secondly, the moment that she'd heard the Celesti had come to King's office—had actually *been* so close to the people she cared about—she'd tried to go to them immediately.

She had *tried*.

Only her power had failed. Again.

When Lou had stormed into the bedroom, feeling as if she could barely keep her skin on, Konstantine had seemed unaware of the strangeness of her entrance. Lou had walked through the front door and up the stairs to their bedroom.

She almost *never* used the front door.

Closets, shadows, dark corners of rooms, sure. But her own front door?

This time she'd had no choice. Her own compass had registered King's fear, which she learned later through texts had risen when Mel had walked into the agency and refused to leave. When Lou had tried to go to him, nothing had happened.

She couldn't help but wonder if the nap had been to blame.

She'd fallen asleep on a patio chaise in the late-afternoon sun. Like a cat, she'd been too warm and comfortable to rise, dozing until the sun sank behind the horizon.

Now the Celesti were in New Orleans and she was stuck here.

Though she felt less stuck now. When she reached for her power this time, she sensed the world thinning as it should. Perhaps because it was late into the night now. And also in New Orleans, the other point in the world connected to her through space and time.

Her friends were asleep. All but King and Mel, whose consciousness she could feel like a hum in her own head. It was possible they were lying awake the same as she was.

But none of them were consumed by fear. None of them were in immediate danger.

She should let them rest.

And she should rest too.

Touching her power as she did now, and knowing it would answer her if she reached for it, that was enough for her own fear to release its hold on her.

Lou would respect her friends' wishes, but if the Celesti made a move—so would she.

That was her place.

Between the Celesti and the people she loved.

## 27

E ttore stood on the jetway in front of his wife and daughter. Behind him, the jet was loaded with the last of his cargo, those essential items he would need for the fight ahead. His entourage was already on board, giving him this final moment alone with his wife.

Florence was ready for him. He'd paid the right officials and put money in the right hands to ensure that Konstantine's church would not be so impenetrable tonight. He could thank Konstantine for the idea. Had he not come to Naples and turned his own city against him, Ettore might not have been so bold.

He supposed *La Strega* could appear now and take him while Sofia and Martina watched, ending his plan before it began. But the day was bright and he had done all he could to divide her attention so that she wouldn't detect his movements. The rest was in God's hands.

"Good luck, Daddy," Martina said, taking his hand and kissing it.

He bent and scooped her up into his arms.

"Be good for your mother while I am away."

"She is always good," Sofia replied. She was looking at him with a strange expression on her face.

"What is it, my love?" he asked her quietly.

"Look me in the eye and tell me why you are doing this."

Ettore bit back against his reactionary anger. "Why do I do anything? For us. For this family. For our future and safety."

"Martina, go to Maria."

"Bye, Daddy." Martina placed a warm, soft kiss on his cheek and then slid from his arms. Ettore watched her skip across the jetway to her nanny, who stood respectfully a few yards away.

"Ettore," Sofia said again, trying to regain his eye contact. "What are you doing?"

"I have to stop her."

"You're going to die."

"You don't have any faith in me."

Her face reddened. "*Ho fiducia in te. Ovviamente.* Who else has been here with you from the beginning?" She gestured at the jet, at their people standing off by the car waiting to take Sofia and Martina back into the city. "Show me one person who has been with you longer."

He couldn't. That was true. Sofia had accepted his offer and promises before he had any right or means to promise her anything.

Still she had stood beside him. When business was good, when it was treacherous, when their future had been bright and when enemies had beset them on all sides—through it all, Sofia had stood with him.

"Don't do this," she said. "She will kill you."

"She will do that anyway," he said. "When I sent Modesto, that was it. It's done."

"I told you not to send Modesto. You should have negotiated with her."

"*Negoziato.*" He had to keep control of his anger here, lest he spoke carelessly.

Modesto had been her brother, and the lie he'd told her to rid himself of the bastard must not come to light. Least of all now, when he was so close to ending this ordeal.

"It's done, Sofia. It's done. I cannot bring Modesto home, and I cannot sit here waiting for her to kill us and take Martina," he said. "Is that what you want?"

She said nothing. He didn't think Sofia was scared for herself, or her daughter. His wife knew *La Strega's* reputation almost as well as he did. How she often spared children and even their mothers, as long as they didn't try to protect their husbands. Perhaps she expected such mercy if it came to that.

"I have to go." He bent and kissed her on the cheek.

She allowed it though her expression remained hard.

When he turned to go, her hand shot out and grabbed his with surprising force. For a moment, he thought she would hit him. Or at the very least make some unreasonable demand.

Instead, she said, "Say it is for Martina, for our family. For the business. Say it again and I will believe you."

"It is," he said. "I swear I am doing this for us."

He knew that look. She wore it whenever one of his dalliances reached her attention, whenever she confronted him about a new affair she'd heard of.

*Tell me it's a lie created by your enemies and I will believe you.*

*It is*, he'd say. But even as she pretended to accept this, there was a deeper knowing behind her eyes.

*And she thinks I'm lying now.*

But what else could he say? That he wanted *La Strega* for himself? That he wanted to own her the way Konstantine owned her. And that if he couldn't have her, he wanted to brutalize her in front of Konstantine's very eyes, with every bone in his body broken so that he was powerless to stop it.

That he wanted to make them both pay—Konstantine and his bitch—for the losses they'd laid at his doorstep. That the risk of his death was but a small wager to place for the possible payoff of his satisfaction knowing that after all of it, he was the one who had survived.

*He* would be the victor.

Sofia's face was hard, her expression distant. "Don't forget to call Martina and wish her goodnight."

"If I'm not busy," he said.

Then, after blowing one last kiss to his daughter, he started up the steps into the jet.

When he took his seat by the window, he caught one final glimpse of Sofia and Martina climbing into the back of the sedan, the driver closing the door after them.

Raffaele sat in the seat opposite him, his cheeks red from the heat.

"I spoke to our people in New Orleans. Everyone is in position. They will take the detective as soon as we let them know we are ready."

"And in Florence?" Ettore asked. He tried to shake this feeling of unease. There had been something in Sofia's final look. As if she'd said goodbye for the last time.

*She truly believes she will never see me again,* he thought. And was that a woman's intuition or wishful thinking on her part?

"They are ready for us. They'll meet is us in Pisa. As soon as we move on Konstantine and the Ravengers, they will attack in New Orleans."

"Good," he said. *Let us see if La Strega can be in two places at once.*

There was always the possibility that she would abandon the detective in New Orleans and join Konstantine in Florence. Ettore hoped she would. He wanted to fight her. He wanted to see how many ways he could inflict pain on her in a single evening.

But he hoped that at least mentally she would be divided. The detective represented her old life. Where she came from, the loss of her father, and the path that loss had set her upon.

Ettore understood how the past could drive a person.

If the detective's murder only caused her to hesitate, nothing more, Ettore thought that opening would be enough to unbalance her and push the needle of victory in his direction.

"Let everyone know that we are on our way," he said, feeling the plane lift into the air. "One way or the other, this ends tonight."

**28**

———————

Mel had wanted to go into King's apartment and get his things for him, but King forbade it.

"You're being ridiculous." She held her cell phone to her ears, speaking to him as if he were far away rather than down the hotel's hallway.

"It's bad enough that you chose this hotel," he said. "You should have stayed at Monteleone with the girls. You're too close to me."

"You think I'm going to leave you here by yourself? What if you need someone?"

Mel opened the hotel room door and peered into the hallway. No one was out there. Taking her room key, she padded down the hall to room 4974 and knocked.

"Someone is at the door," he said.

"Yes, it's me."

"Mel." He swore under his breath.

"Better hurry, or someone is going to find me out here with a dog I'm not supposed to have in this hotel."

The lock clanged. As soon as the door opened, Mel forced her way into the room and closed it behind her, locking it.

Lady went straight to King, tail wagging.

"You shouldn't be here." He stooped to pet the dog.

"The shop is closed today for the festival. I gave all the girls the day off to keep them away and safe. Where else would I be?"

"What about the parade?"

"Dani and Piper are going to be here in an hour to pick me up. We're going to load up all the supplies and then go straight to my booth. Don't worry about me, Mr. King. You're the one who has a target on his back."

Mel had only agreed to sleep away from her bed last night because she had decided that if they had wanted to scare King, it would be likely they would strike his apartment or the shop during the cover of night. It was true that the Quarter rarely slept, but if they came up the fire escape and tried to attack via the balconies, they'd have cover enough.

Plus, if they weren't in their apartments, then Mel's terrible vision wouldn't have a chance to play itself out. At least not there.

"You came straight here after they left you, did you not?"

"Yes," he reluctantly agreed. "But—"

"You're wearing the same clothes I saw you in yesterday. I see the hotel gave you a toothbrush and toothpaste. And you've got your work." She looked from the rumpled bed to the desk that was covered in papers and King's open laptop. "But what about food? Clothes? Coffee?"

"I can buy what I need. This is a temporary problem," he pushed on.

"It is, but we don't know how temporary, do we? I can't close my shop forever. Nor can you close the agency and wear the same outfit for weeks. We need a better plan than hiding in hotels, and until we have one, at the very least, let me get you some clean clothes."

"No," he said, coming to her and stopping just short of where she stood. "I have no idea what their plan is, but it most certainly involves someone watching my place. If they see you go into my apartment for any reason, they will be *very* interested in who you are and how to use you to get what they want. *Me.* You need to stay in public as much as possible today. Let Lou and Konstantine work out how they're going to throw them off my trail. Take your gun with you."

Mel resisted the urge to roll her eyes. "Mr. King. I can't take a loaded Glock to a parade. I don't have a concealed carry permit for that."

"Let's change that as soon as possible," he said, reaching up and pushing a strand of hair away from her face.

She looked up into his eyes, trying to put a word on the feeling she was having now. When she could find none, she simply wrapped her arms around him.

"I don't want anything to happen to you."

He enveloped her. "And I don't want anything to happen to you. So it's in your best interests to stay away from me until the danger passes."

"I don't know how to tell you this, but if you think I'm going to let you face this alone, you're out of your damned mind," she said.

"I promise I'm being careful."

The flash of his blood on her hands filled her mind again.

"You don't know if it's enough. I saw—"

He squeezed her back. "I know what you saw. But it hasn't happened."

"And part of it not happening is you letting me help you."

"Clean underwear is the least of my problems, Mel. Stay away from the apartment. I'll pick up a change of clothes when I leave here. I promise."

"And breakfast."

"And breakfast," he agreed. "Though I wish I could eat it with you."

His tone had turned flirtatious again, and Mel could see far enough past her own fear to realize that she was alone with King in a hotel room, standing in his arms no less, looking up into his face. And he was looking at her with those big blue eyes.

"I would never forgive myself if something happened to you while you were trying to protect me," he said solemnly. "Let me do this my way. Please."

What could she say to that?

She released him, acknowledging the headiness she felt as she did and the notable absence of his heat as she settled onto the edge of the bed.

"Tell me what *your way* is again."

"We stay away from the apartment, agency, and shop. We aren't seen together. We wait until Lou and Konstantine have a chance to remove mob guy's people from the city without making it clear that it's because of me. Konstantine said they just needed time to come up with a plan. A diversion. Or maybe Lou will get impatient and kill everyone anyway. Problem solved."

Was it wrong for Mel to wish for such a thing? She suspected so.

Her bangles rang musically as she fixed her long skirts around her.

"Any idea how long all of that will take?"

"If you're worried about keeping the shop closed—"

"I'm worried about *you*, Robert."

A strange expression crept across his face. "That's the second time you've done that."

"What?"

"Called me something other than Mr. King."

Her face was heating again.

"I like it," he said.

"It's your name, isn't it?" she said.

Her phone went off, sparing her the embarrassment of having to think of something—anything—else to say that would steer them away from the growing intimacy of the moment.

"We're out front," Piper said after Mel greeted her. "We already went by the shop and loaded up everything for the booth."

"Are you sure?" Mel asked. A part of her brain realized she was stalling. She didn't want to leave King alone.

*Keeping him in your sight won't be enough to keep harm from touching him*, her mind chided, even as another part of her insisted that it would.

"We went through your checklist," Piper insisted. "It's all in the back. All we need now is *you*."

"I'll be down in a second."

"Okay. I'm going to call and check on King."

Before Mel could tell her there was no need, that she could see how he was doing with her own two eyes, Piper hung up. A second later, King's cell phone rang.

"Piper," Mel confirmed as he pulled his phone from his pocket.

Instead of hello, King said, "Yes, I'm safe. Yes, I'm taking precautions. Yes, I will let you know if anything changes or I deviate from the plan."

Mel knew she should excuse herself as their talk evolved from reassurances to details of their pending cases.

But still she lingered.

*What are you doing?* she asked. *What the hell are you waiting for?*

The call ended and Mel stood.

"I should go. I should have left before she called."

He took a step toward her, those eyes heavy on hers again. Again the atmosphere of intimacy intensified, and if King had bent to kiss her then, she would not at all have been surprised.

It was like she was watching herself from outside her body. Like it was a different Mel who met King in the middle of the room. A different Mel who reached forward with both hands and took his free one, the one not holding the silent phone.

"Please be careful today," she said, daring to look up into his face.

"I'm always careful," he said. Then, before she could chastise him, he dropped the mischievous tone. "I will. I promise."

"If something happened to you, it would break my heart."

"Then I'll be sure nothing happens," he said. "Because breaking your heart is the last thing I'll ever do."

"Are you sure?" she whispered.

The corner of his lips tugged into a smile, but God help her, those eyes. She couldn't bear the weight of that gaze. She looked away first.

"I'm sure," he said, and ran a thumb over her fingers. "I won't let it happen."

Mel's phone rang again, and she knew she had to go. She had no choice but to release him.

"I will stay out of trouble," he said as she went to the door and opened it. Lady followed on her heels.

"You better," she said.

And with that she was gone.


PIPER THOUGHT MEL LOOKED A LITTLE FLUSH WHEN SHE climbed into the SUV with Lady and her overnight bag in tow. As soon as she buckled up, Piper handed her a coffee and a breakfast sandwich they'd picked up on the way over.

"It's probably cold now because you took too much time coming down," she said.

"Thank you," Mel said, accepting the sandwich. When she offered no explanation about what had taken her so long, Piper turned her attention to the dog, giving her the bacon that they'd picked off of Dani's sandwich when they'd gotten her order wrong.

"We can drop all the stuff off at the booth first, and then take you to the rendezvous with your business ladies. How much time do you have before you have to meet them?"

Mel looked at her phone's clock. "Forty minutes."

"Plenty of time. Do we need to stop anywhere and get you anything? Dani and I had to go out twice last night because we kept forgetting stuff. Who knew it's so annoying, abandoning your apartment in the dead of night."

"That reminds me, Dad accepted my invitation to move the dinner to next Sunday. He offered to come by our place if we were too busy." Dani glanced at Piper before turning on her blinker and easing the SUV into the next lane.

"Oh shit. I forgot about dinner. Did you tell him we aren't in the apartment?"

"I had to. I was worried he was going to stop by and try to surprise us."

"What's our excuse?" Because Piper knew that Dani hadn't told her dad they were presently hiding from the mafia.

"We're getting carpet installed. They told us to stay out of the place for the week. If this goes on longer than that, I'll have to come up with something else."

"What the hell's he gonna think if he comes over and there's no carpet?"

Dani slowed to a stop at a red light and said, "That's a problem for another time."

Piper couldn't help but notice that they had a lot of "problems for another time" piling up for her future self to deal with, and she was not looking forward to it.

*When that day comes*, she thought, *if it comes, I'll just have to remember to be glad that I'm still alive to solve them.*

## 29

Lou stood on the steps of Isabella's clinic, only half acknowledging the conversation between Konstantine and the doctor behind her. Stray pieces of their earlier conversation were pinballing off the walls of Lou's mind.

*Dilating.*

*Any day now.*

*Relax. Take it easy.*

Elena was coming. And early.

Konstantine thanked the doctor, and after they shared one final wave, he came to stand in front of her, rocking forward onto his toes in excitement.

"She's almost here."

He looked as if he were struggling to stay in his skin.

It was cute, she had to admit. She reached up and pushed her hands into his hair.

"Aren't you nervous?" he asked.

Nervous? No. Scared that her power may never return to her, yes.

"I don't suppose you'll reconsider my offer to go away to

an island now, will you? We would be gone perhaps three, four days if Isabella is to be believed."

Lou knew this to be untrue. He would find endless reasons to keep them there. Elena would be vulnerable for years, not days. And far less portable once she was out of Lou's body.

"Sorry, *amore mio*," he said. "I know I said I wouldn't push you."

"It's not that."

"What is it?" he asked.

She searched his face. What would he do if she told him the truth? If she just admitted, here and now, that she didn't have her power. That the connection had felt thin and inaccessible since the night before, that she had reached for it more than once in the moments since and that it hadn't answered her.

"I don't feel like myself," she said. If only because she had to say something, given the intense scrutiny he was subjecting her to.

He considered her face for a moment and said, "I have never had a baby before, but I believe this is normal. Isabella told me that you will feel better in about three months."

Lou almost laughed. "Oh, is that *all?* Just three months?"

The fact that he was trying to soothe her made her decision easy.

She wouldn't tell him. It would only make him worry more. Lou would wait until Elena was born, and if she couldn't use her gift, she would come clean.

*One way or the other, this is about to resolve itself*, she thought. No need to force it.

Even as she thought it, she wondered if she was taking the coward's way out as a way to spare her ego and embarrassment.

What did she think he would do if she were powerless?

Lock her up? Leave her? She didn't believe him capable of either.

"What would you do if Elena had no abilities?" she asked as they began their walk back to the villa.

"What does it matter if she has abilities?" he asked. "I am still her father, aren't I?"

"What if I didn't have abilities?" she asked.

He laughed. "I can't imagine it."

"Try."

She was playing a dangerous game now, circling the truth of her situation.

"If you, Elena, and I were a normal family?"

Her skin pricked at the word "normal," but she didn't interrupt him.

"Perhaps I would not be a Ravenger," he said. "Or maybe I would have to be. You would need more help getting rid of bodies without your gift."

She laughed. She couldn't help it.

"That's your priority? How to keep me in the murder business?"

"I want you to be happy, *amore mio*. That is what makes you happy, isn't it?"

She considered his words long after they stopped for gelato, crossed the Palazzo Vecchio, and watched the tourists amble across the Arno River, their souvenirs in hand.

Once they were alone in the villa, Konstantine pulled her close. "How do you feel?"

"If you're asking whether or not I feel like I'm going into labor, no. Not yet. I have had a few contractions." This was true. "But they seem halfhearted at best."

"Lay down with me," he said.

And she did.

He stroked her hair for a long time, and she allowed this, even though usually it would annoy the hell out of her. As the afternoon light bled into twilight, Octavia jumped up onto the bed, purring. Konstantine made a space for the gray cat in the crook of his arm, murmuring sweet Italian to her.

"How easily I'm demoted," Lou said, amused.

"Never." His tone grew serious. "I will always protect you, *amore mio*. You are the mother of my child. You will always be the most important thing to me. Always."

Her throat was tight, and again she felt the urge to tell him the truth. She simply couldn't believe that he was ready to confront the possibility of her helplessness. What that knowledge might cost them. Would he ever trust her power again if he knew it to be fallible?

She realized at long last what had bothered her.

*I'm not worth protecting.*

She didn't want him to endanger his life, and possibly get himself killed, for the sake of her.

*It's probably just the pregnancy talking. I'm being ridiculous.*

She wanted to tell him what was going on. She just didn't want to start a fight when his concentration needed to be on keeping his people safe from Ettore.

Lou hadn't meant to fall asleep, but the room had grown dark, and with the sounds of Konstantine's soft breathing and the cat purring between them, and the fact that the bed was wonderfully warm and comfortable, all together it had been enough to lull her into sleep.

Upon waking, the last remnant of a dream swam away from her. Where had she been? A dark forest at night, the pines heavy with snow. Piper had been ahead of her some-where in the shadows, calling to her, begging her for help. And Lou had been terrified she wouldn't reach her in time.

When Lou shook off the last of the dream, blinking her eyes open, she knew immediately that she wasn't in her bedroom anymore.

"Oh shit." She sat up, looking around.

She recognized those houseplants. That hook with bathrobes and once-worn jeans. The vanity covered in cosmetics.

She was in Piper's bed—Dani and Piper's bed.

Lou threw back the covers, warring with the twin emotions of aggravation and relief.

On one hand, she was deeply relieved that she'd been able to slip. On the other, she couldn't remember the last time her power had been so uncontrolled that she had slipped in her sleep.

She'd known before dozing that her fear for her friends in New Orleans had been high, and climbing. She just hadn't realized she'd run the risk of slipping to them even after promising she wouldn't.

She heard voices.

Lou slipped from the dark bedroom into the hall that led to the kitchen and living room.

But Dani and Piper were not there.

Lou went to the door that led from the apartment down into the Crescent City Detective Agency and pressed her ear to it.

"There's nothing here. Whatever he's got, he took it with him."

"Keep looking."

A crash rang out.

Someone was trashing the agency.

Lou guessed it could be anyone from a disgruntled client to someone who suspected they'd been watched by the private detective and were hoping to destroy evidence before it was turned over to the police.

She suspected, however, that the two voices belonged to the Celesti and that her compass had brought her here, to this bed of all the friends' it could have chosen, because this was the one closest to danger.

"What's behind those doors?"

Footsteps approached the same moment a contraction washed through her. It was annoying, but not debilitating. Of course, the doctor had said that the inactive part of labor could last for hours.

Lou hoped so. As it would seem that she had something else to take care of first.

She reached for her gift to find it unresponsive again.

So her gift was still not fully her own. The contraction had ended, but Lou felt like her attempt to use her gift only to find it absent was like a contraction of its own, a desperate grasping.

"It's only supplies and shit. There's nothing here. And this one's a toilet."

"What about the third one?"

Lou's heart picked up speed. She had only fifteen seconds to decide how she wanted to play this. As the footsteps vibrated on the stairs leading up to Piper's apartment, Lou reached down and undid the lock.

Then she stepped back into the small alcove on the other side of the door so that the door would block their view of her when they entered.

And enter they did.

It was a man first, tall and slender. The back of his neck was red from the sun and his hairline was damp. The woman's makeup had begun to run for likely the same reasons— because nothing much could stand up to the Louisiana heat in July.

"Who the fuck lives here? It ain't the detective. He's around the corner."

Lou grabbed the woman first, twisted her neck with a satisfying *crack* before she had a chance to cry out. Before she hit the floor, Lou grabbed the man's shoulders at the same time she kneed the nerve in his thigh, dropping him. He managed a small cry before his cervical vertebra snapped, but it was quickly muffled by her hand covering his mouth.

Lou tried to step through the darkness, but again nothing happened. Lou looked down at the two bodies at her feet.

She bent down, feeling the muscles in her back protest, and turned the man over.

Sure enough, beneath his jacket he wore a shoulder holster with two Berettas. Lou's heart lifted.

It was harder to get the holster and pistols off a dead body than she'd expected, realizing now that in all her years, relieving dead bodies of their weapons for the purpose of wearing them herself wasn't a skill she'd often practiced. Maybe she should start.

With some effort she managed to get the holster off the dead guy and slip her own arms into it. The Berettas were fully loaded, with one in the chamber, but she found no extra ammo on the man. Whatever he'd planned to do with these guns, he hadn't expected to exceed the standard sixteen rounds.

The woman was packing too, but Lou didn't have anywhere else to put a pistol. The Berettas she carried were too big to tuck into the waistband of her pants. And given how pregnant she was, it was impractical to reach behind herself to pull a weapon anyway. Her posture was already off from pregnancy, so this was likely the best she was going to be able to do. Now she needed a jacket to hide the guns.

The woman was too slender, her coat too tight for Lou's belly. The man's fit better but came down so far over her hands that it wasn't a practical choice in case she needed to use the guns. Instead, she went to Piper's closet and started looking for something.

Dani had a long fall coat that would have to do. Thick enough to hide the guns but with arms short enough to remain useful.

She looked at the dead bodies at her feet.

Lou needed to find the others. It had been early afternoon when she and Konstantine had lain down in the bed after Elena's wellness check. She checked the time and saw it was only seven in the morning in New Orleans. If she had to wait until dark for her powers to come back, she sure as hell wasn't going to wait in this apartment.

Lou asked her compass if there were more bad guys downstairs. Her straining ears had detected no movement, but perhaps there were more on the street outside.

But her compass, though spinning, didn't alert her to any danger.

So Lou stepped over the two dead bodies, locked the apartment door, and closed it behind her.

The agency was trashed.

That pissed her off, and her first impulse was to right the overturned chairs and start gathering papers into neat stacks before placing them on the desktops. They would have to sort the rest later, but at least it didn't look like two assholes had trashed the place.

Lou went to the window, and sticking to one side in hope of being less visible, she scanned the street.

No one was lurking. No one was smoking or pretending to talk on their cell phone. The street was completely clear.

Lou pulled open the door and stepped out into the morning.

The air had already collected enough heat to feel solid as she stepped into it, even at this early hour. But at least she was correct that no one was standing outside the agency. She tried to lock the door and pull it behind her, but realized it had been busted, the wood around the handle cracked. She wasn't sure what they had used, but King would definitely have to repair the door.

She was forced to settle for closing it behind her.

Relying on her compass, Lou headed in the direction of Mel's shop.

The foot traffic remained nearly nonexistent, which Lou appreciated. Most of her attention was fixated on the strange experience of navigating by foot, with little relegated to scanning the roads for potential hostiles.

Sure, she had used her compass for navigation constantly, but how it had directed her in the past was a very different experience than what she was having now.

When she reached the door of Fortunes and Fixes, she saw that the sign was turned to closed and the door locked. There were no signs of forced entry. She could try to go up the fire escape, but Lou thought, given how very pregnant she was feeling, to do so would be a fool's errand.

She reached for her power again, first sidestepping to the alleyway, where the shadows were thickest, only to find that it still was not responding.

*As long as you come back when it matters*, she thought. Then she revised that prayer to simply, *As long as you come back.*

With no other course of action available to her, she asked her compass to guide her in the direction of her friends and began walking.

**30**

———

King went to the police station first to file a formal complaint. It wasn't that he expected the police to do anything about the mafia stalking him. He simply wanted it on record that he'd made a report, so that if dead bodies turned up, he would be able to say, *See, I made a formal complaint.*

Of course, if Lou did what she did best, there would be no bodies. He had also been able to gain a sense of how well patrolled the parade would be. King didn't like the idea of Mel and the girls out on their own in the crowd. Hopefully there would be too many witnesses for his stalkers to make a move against them, but King thought a little extra police presence couldn't hurt.

He was relieved to see the police barriers go up around the Quarter just as he was leaving the station.

It was after ten in the morning when he made it back to the agency.

The first thing he noticed was the busted lock. He wasn't surprised. He was, however, irritated at the expense, knowing that it would take a few days before the door could be replaced and a new lock installed.

The assholes had gone through what few file folders and unimportant remnants King had left behind, and the neat piles they'd put the documents into hadn't hidden the fact that someone had gone through them.

After checking the supply closet and bathroom for any stow-aways, King worried that someone might be hiding in Piper's apartment. He went up the narrow staircase but found the door locked. He was relieved to discover no signs of forced entry.

What followed were several hours of him trying, unsuc-cessfully, to work.

Once he thought he saw a woman pass by the front of the agency who looked just like Lou. But when he looked again, she was gone, and King was forced to decide that his tired and stressed mind was playing tricks on him. Because why would Lou pass by his office?

Even if she had denied his request to stay away, she could have simply come through the supply closet like usual and directly into the agency, with less chance of being seen.

*I must be more tired than I thought.*

King worked until he heard the chaos of the parade pass through the adjacent street and knew that by now, Mel would be at the booth with the girls. He wanted to see them. Wanted to check on them with his own eyes and felt that in the crush of bodies, he could get away with it.

He packed up his desk, locked everything up tight, and stepped out into the crowd. He still had his toiletries, clothes, and laptop in the backpack thrown over his shoulder.

Still, it wasn't too difficult to navigate the crowd. The flow of foot traffic was with him, and he reached Jackson Square with minimal inconvenience, except, of course, the godawful heat that was baking him alive.

He spotted Mel's booth easily, just east of Jackson Square. She'd set up under the shade of a large Spanish oak tree with moss hanging down around her booth. The girls were both with her, standing in the shade of the white canopy. King passed without stopping, without even looking in that direction for longer than any other passerby, and headed for the queue stretching out of Café du Monde.

He got in line for beignets and coffee.

While he was waiting in line, he caught the first sight of his tail.

A man in a collared t-shirt, his eyes hidden behind dark glasses. He was pretending to talk into his cell phone. The man's lips hadn't moved once in all the time that King had stood there staring back at him.

Once it became clear that King had clocked him, the man turned away, pretending to inspect a rack of postcards. King spotted him again not ten minutes later, his position no less obvious than it was before.

By the time King got his beignets and coffee and took a table on the walkway with a clear view of the girls, the tail had changed his position again. This time he was speaking to a street performer as if they were old friends.

Once King finished his beignets and most of his coffee, he knew it was time to give up his table to the family of four eyeing it desperately. He took only one moment more to pull a notepad from his backpack and scribble a note on it.

Then he rose and stepped into the throng of people. Unsurprisingly, the tail followed.

King stopped at four booths before he got to Mel's. He spoke to each proprietor and took the samples they offered, before moving on.

Piper clocked him first and was about to open her mouth, but fortunately, Dani squeezed her arm at the last minute and her mouth snapped shut.

To Mel, he said, "Are you handing out any free samples, ma'am?"

To Mel's credit, she didn't show a single sign of recognition. She only plastered on her best seller smile and said, "We sure do. Piper, honey, give the man a goody bag."

King accepted the small bag full of trinkets, and as he did, pressed the note he'd scrawled into Piper's palm.

"Thanks," he said, offering them a wide smile, before moving on to the next booth.

He should have expected what happened next.

LOU FOUND THAT HER IRRITABLE MOOD GREW IN proportion to the day's mounting heat. She blamed the walking. She'd walked more today than she had in the last few months combined. She may have been well traveled, but she rarely had to cover so many miles in a single day. First, she'd walked to the hotel in time to see Piper, Mel, and Dani drive off. As she stood on the corner, contemplating what her next move would be, King came out, walking in the opposite direction with a backpack slung over his shoulder.

She'd followed him to the police precinct, keeping an eye open for any Celesti but seeing none. She knew that someone would come, especially once the disappearance of the agency's intruders was noted.

King stayed in the precinct long enough for Lou to buy herself dinner—or at least it would have been dinner had she been in Florence. Instead, it was breakfast, and she ate it at the café, her eyes on the door until King exited the agency just before ten o'clock.

He passed her without looking up, traversing Royal Street in the direction of the agency. Lou let him go. She was more interested in watching the street to see if anyone broke away from the crowd to follow him.

No one did.

Twenty minutes later, Lou rose and retraced her steps up Royal herself. She passed the agency and made it all the way to the alley beside the occult shop again. Like before, her gift denied her, leaving her feet firmly planted on the alleyway's cobblestones.

Slightly more annoyed than she was before, Lou turned back toward the square and passed the agency. This time she dared a peek inside, to find King at his desk working, his brow furrowed in concentration as he sorted through papers.

She chose the dark stoop of a closed shop several doors down that allowed her a view of the agency, looking both ways to make sure she was unseen. But most of the foot traffic remained in the square. She waited.

No one came.

Lou almost moaned with relief when the sun moved behind the clouds and blanketed the Quarter with shadows.

King exited the agency an hour later, and Lou fell into step behind him as he headed toward the crush of bodies clotting the street.

The day might have been hot and miserable, but it seemed people still wanted to see the show.

Lou spotted the tail before King did. Her compass—though useless to her in its usual way—had pulled her attention toward the man almost as soon as she stepped into the square.

He'd been standing beneath the awning of a souvenir shop, talking to two other men who were also clearly packing guns.

At the sight of them, Lou hung back. She did her best to look as much like a normal person as possible. Or at least a miserable person, which wasn't all that hard to fake given the growing pain in her back and the discomfort building in her feet.

She watched the three of them clock King as he entered the square, threw a couple of casual glances in the direction of the booths and walked toward the café across the street.

It wasn't until King's gaze hesitated for a moment too long that Lou spotted Melandra, Piper, and Dani.

She was relieved to see them, her shoulders relaxing against the stone wall of the cathedral at her back.

She hadn't realized how worried she'd been about them until that moment. She was also pleased to see that the Celesti hadn't looked in their direction. It seemed all of their attention remained on King. Staying where she was, she watched two of the men break away and head toward an adjacent corner, just beyond the police barricade. Five minutes later, a car pulled up to the curb and they got in.

Lou pulled herself a little deeper into the shadows. But the car didn't slam on its brakes. Gangsters didn't pile out and rush toward her, guns raised. The car simply pulled away from the curb and disappeared out of sight.

One man remained behind.

After King ate his beignets and drank his coffee, he gave his table over to a family clearly impatient for him to leave it, rose, and started walking down the line of booths.

The closer he got to Mel, Piper, and Dani, the more Lou's unease increased.

But he knew what he was doing. He spoke to them, but there was no recognition or extra friendliness in his face. He didn't linger or make small talk. He simply kept moving.

Thirty seconds after King stopped at the booth, the man walked up to him and pressed a gun into the back of his ribs.

Lou barely saw the glint of gunmetal before he moved his body to hide what he was doing.

Lou jolted forward, ready to attack, and then registered two critical details.

First, the man wasn't going to kill King here on the street in broad daylight.

Secondly, Lou didn't have her power. What the hell was she going to do? Because she couldn't kill anyone in broad daylight either—at least not without causing a real shitshow. And her name and face were already in the news.

She had no choice but to watch the man lead King down a side alley where the car was waiting for them. The back passenger door opened, King was pushed inside, and then the car was gone.

Without a moment's hesitation, Lou hurried back to the booth, went right up to Piper, and said, "They just took King."

Piper gasped. "Oh my god, what are you doing here? I thought you were supposed to stay out of the city."

Mel pushed Piper to the side. "Who took him? His note said he was being followed."

"The Celesti." When these words didn't seem to register, Lou added, "The bad guys. The mafia looking for me."

"Oh shit," Piper and Dani said in unison.

Dani's eyes narrowed. "Are you wearing my coat?"

"Yes, their jackets didn't fit, sorry."

"Whose jackets?" Piper asked.

"The ones on the dead bodies I left in your apartment," Lou replied.

"*What?*" Piper and Dani said in unison.

"We need to go get King or they'll kill him," Mel said. She twisted her fingers nervously. "Do your thing."

"I can't," Lou said.

"What do you mean, you *can't?*" Mel said. "Of course you can. *Go get him.*"

Dani held up her hand. "Tell us what happened, from the beginning, and then we'll figure out what we can do."

"I slipped while I was sleeping. Woke up in your bed." She

pointed at Dani and Piper. "There were mafia in the agency who decided to come up to your apartment—"

"Oh shit," Piper said.

"I killed them, took their guns, your jacket, and have spent the day following King around because I couldn't get my power to take me back to Florence. Then two minutes ago, a man put a gun to King's back and made him get into a car, and I don't know where they're taking him, but my compass says it's not far."

She pointed in a direction.

"The apartment is that way. The agency too," Dani said.

Mel crossed herself. "Lord, it's happening."

Piper threw her a panicked look. "*What's* happening?"

Dani's phone went off. She read the message before saying, "We just confirmed that the man who was getting names off of the dog tags is Marcus Vale. He's got a record. Should we ask the police to go talk to him?"

"Might as well. Our hands are a *little* full at the moment."

"I have to call Konstantine before we find King," Lou said.

"That'll give me time to call the precinct about Vale then." Piper pulled her phone out of her pocket. "One last good deed before we all *die*."

"Don't say that," Mel hissed.

Lou barely registered this exchange as she stepped off to the side with Dani's phone clutched in her hand. Her heart was racing, but she dialed Konstantine's number, which she knew by heart, and listened with bated breath as it rang.

"Ciao."

"It's me," she said.

"Amore mio. What's happened?" His relief was palpable, and she felt terrible knowing she was about to destroy that relief.

"I slipped when I was sleeping."

"Yes, I saw that. Isabella said that you were close to your labor. What if—"

"I can't," she said.

"*Amore mio*, I want to be with you when—"

"No, that's not what I'm saying. Of course I want you with me." She took a deep breath, turning a little more away from the group, as if having her back to them would spare her the embarrassment of this conversation. "I mean I can't come back. My power isn't working."

There was a beat of silence so tense that Lou felt compelled to go on.

"I tried to use it, and it isn't working. I think it's Elena. Or at least, I hope it's her." Lou had missed her aunt a lot in the years since her death, but never more than now, when she wished she could talk to the only other person she'd ever known to share her gift.

"You tried?" he repeated, his disbelief evident.

"Yes," she said. "I tried to use it, but nothing happens."

Was he in shock? Lou wasn't sure how to interpret his silence.

"Has this happened before?" he asked.

She considered lying but said, "Yes. It happened that day I went to the beach with Dani and Piper. And it happened again last night. I wanted to go to King and check on him anyway, but I couldn't."

She wished she could see his face, wished she knew him well enough to know that he had enough self-control to measure his voice. But if she could have seen his face, she would know how badly this blow had landed.

"I'm sorry," she whispered into the phone. "I didn't want you to worry."

"You didn't want me to worry," he parroted, and she definitely detected anger. For some reason, that made her feel better. Anger she was comfortable with. Heartbreak would have been worse.

"If I understand correctly, you have called to tell me you are stranded in New Orleans on the verge of labor, with at least seventy confirmed Celesti nearby. You cannot use your power, I am at least half a day away from you, but I am *not to worry*."

"And they just took King, and we have to save him."

The line went dead.

Lou thought that he'd been so angry that he had hung up on her. That was until Konstantine's anger, which she could still feel if she pointed her compass in his direction, was consumed by shock and fear.

He hadn't hung up. She was sure of it.

Something had happened.

## 31

I'm sorry," Lou whispered into the phone. "I didn't want you to worry."

"You didn't want me to worry," Konstantine repeated.

It wasn't that he was angry, exactly.

He had been desperate for an update since she'd slipped from his arms hours before. It had finally come, and at such a late hour. He only wished it had brought relief, and not more fear for her safety.

But if someone had pressed him to identify the emotion rippling through his body, he would have struggled to name it. Principally, there was fear for her safety. Early in her pregnancy, when she had been captured by the killer Gein, he had come and retrieved her himself. The first thing she had done was leave him and go to Isabella to make sure that Elena was safe.

That was all Konstantine had needed to know about her instincts. That Lou would never jeopardize their daughter's safety, not even for his own feelings. But he had hoped, by coming to her aid then, that an understanding had formed between them. At the very least that she knew, truly *knew*, that she could count on him.

"If I understand correctly, you have called to tell me you are stranded in New Orleans on the verge of labor, with at least seventy confirmed Celesti nearby. You cannot use your power, I am at least half a day away from you, but I am *not to worry.*"

*She kept this from me.*

*She didn't want me to worry.*

*She is still protecting me.*

He had left the apartment and returned to the church once he realized that Lou was not returning and neither was the release of sleep.

And now, as he sat at his desk, the moonlight spilling across the courtyard, he wondered what he could possibly say to her to let her know that he loved her. That she could have simply told him. That it would have been all right.

He supposed it was too much to ask that she—after all of her years on her own—view herself as someone worth protecting. And he himself didn't know how to convey such an idea to her. That what she felt for him, for Elena, was also a feeling that others felt for her.

She had not seen what he had. The faces of her friends, sick with worry. How they had shown up without hesitation, how desperate they were to save her.

Or that was the very part that scared her. That there was some connection to the night she lost her beloved father, at least in Lou's mind.

Her father had saved her life, had protected her, and had paid with his own life.

Maybe for Lou it was that simple. She didn't want anyone else she loved to die for her. And the only way to prevent it was to never ask that they defend her.

"And they just took King, and we have to save him."

He was doing the math in his mind. He could get the jet in the air within the hour. He only needed her to be cautious until he arrived.

But when he opened his mouth to plead with her, an explosion rocked the church. Konstantine was thrown to the ground, his phone breaking on impact. His head hit the stone floor, blurring his vision and making his ears ring.

Konstantine pushed himself to sitting the same time a pair of rough hands grabbed him.

He whirled, ready to strike, but found Stefano looking down at him.

"We have to go," he shouted over the noise. "It's the Celesti. At least two hundred at our door. You'd best call *La Strega*."

Konstantine steadied himself on his feet, then went to the safe against the wall for his gear and weapons.

"How long before she's here?" Stefano said, checking that his own pistol was loaded.

"She can't come," Konstantine said. He fought to slow his heartbeat and clear his mind, but his head hurt.

"What do you mean?" Then Stefano stole a look at Konstantine and swore. "The baby?"

Konstantine didn't correct him.

"Then it is up to me to keep you alive," Stefano said. "Give me that vest. Put yours on too."

Konstantine thought he felt Lou's presence for a moment, and realized that both he and Stefano were likely broadcasting their fear. Konstantine took a deep breath to steady himself.

"Don't pray to her," Konstantine said. "She can't come, and it will only upset her that she can't."

"*Sì, sì,*" Stefano added another gun to the waistband of his pants. "We can manage this. I will call in the others."

*Whether you like it or not, amore mio, I will protect you too.*

"Konstantine!"

Konstantine froze in the act of loading his gun.

"Konstantine! *Mostrati!*"

Stefano left what remained of the partially collapsed office first, stepping into the newly refinished courtyard to find rubble strewn across the floor. Close on his heels, Konstantine searched the darkness for the Celesti. They had the advantage of knowing this maze, each passage as familiar as the back of their hands. The knew which alcoves and corners to use to their advantage. They had killed almost twenty of the Celesti before the passage broke open.

The church doors were flung wide, Ettore Celesti framed beneath its archway.

He'd removed his suit jacket and had thrown it to the ground at his feet. His dress shirt was rolled up to the elbows. He had set fire to the church and stood before him, holding a gun.

Konstantine had a moment to be glad that the hour was late, and it was only he and Stefano here. Even if that did not bode well for him and his friend.

"Konstantine," he said. "*Dov'è lei?*"

"She won't be joining us." He wasn't sure why he'd said it. Only after it had left his mouth did he realize it would have been to their advantage to let Ettore believe that *La Strega* could come at any moment. Let him look over his shoulder for every second of this.

"Is she in labor?" Ettore asked.

"You keep him talking and I'll go around the side and let the others in," Stefano whispered.

Konstantine gave only the smallest acknowledgment. His concentration remained on Ettore.

"It would be mighty convenient for me if she were in labor," Ettore said, taking a step toward him, pistols at the ready in each hand. "In fact, it would be almost as if God smiled upon me."

Stefano began to ease away from him, moving toward the outer wall.

"I had prayed for some time alone with you," Ettore Celesti said, the flames bright behind him. "There are things I need to say to you. Man to man."

Stefano had only made it ten yards before a cluster of the Celesti emerged from the darkness. Ettore raised his gun.

Konstantine fired first.

**32**

---

For Piper, the day had gone from bad to worse. It had been a long day after a pitiful night of little sleep. The heat had gotten to her and she hadn't had nearly enough to eat, about half as much coffee as one needed to deal with this shit, and now, *now*, her best friend was in danger, her mentor kidnapped, and there were not one but *two* dead bodies in her apartment.

She looked at the two bodies, whose necks were twisted in the wrong direction.

"And you can't even *move* them?" she whined.

Lou only blinked at her.

"That's not our biggest problem right now," Dani said.

Piper rubbed her forehead as if that would make her headache go away. "It feels like a big problem."

"But not our biggest," Dani insisted. "And Lou slipped here. That means her gift isn't gone. It just means it's temporarily out of service. Like an elevator."

Lou looked more relieved than anyone by this idea.

"That means we just need to keep the bodies out of sight until she *can* move them. Our more immediate concern is

King. Where did they take him? What are they doing to him?"

Mel turned away, treading a short path in their living room.

But Piper's attention was on Dani. This was dangerous territory. It had been a while since Dani had had a panic attack or even a nightmare about Dmitri Petrov. But that didn't change the fact that a freaking mob boss had kidnapped her, tortured her, and cut off her finger. One of her friends was being held captive by some other mafia assholes.

Lou must have also heard something in Dani's tone because she reached out and grabbed her arm. "We'll get him back."

*A lot could happen before we do*, Piper thought. She didn't need to say it. She knew everyone else in the room thought the same.

"Your compass is still working?" Mel asked Lou.

Lou had taken to pressing a firm hand into the side of her abdomen.

"Yes. I can still find my targets, I just can't go there."

"Is he okay?" Dani asked, her voice an octave higher than usual. "Do you sense any fear or pain?"

"No," Lou said.

Piper knew this to be a lie. She'd asked Lou the same question not fifteen minutes ago, when they'd been walking through the Quarter to the apartment.

*He's in pain but he's not that scared. Whatever they're doing, he's not impressed.*

Piper didn't contradict her now. Especially not with Mel's gaze burning holes in the back of her head.

"They're in his apartment," Mel said. Her tone brooked no argument.

"We don't know that. How'd they get in or—?"

"They're in the apartment," she said again, with conviction. "We have to figure out how to get him back."

"No one can see me," Lou said. "If they see me, the situation will escalate."

Dani stepped over the bodies and went to the fridge to get a bottle of sweet tea. Piper motioned for one as well. Then the four of them were in the living room, drinking their tea as if there weren't two bodies on the floor.

"What if we create a diversion," Mel said. "I'll go to the front door, start asking questions. Maybe I can pretend that his check bounced for rent and demand to speak to him, and then the three of you can sneak onto the balcony."

Lady whined.

"Oh shit, I forgot we put her in the bedroom," Piper said. Lady had been upset about the bodies, and there wasn't really another room to put her in. "Does she factor into this plan?"

"I'll take her with me. I'll go up to King's apartment and make a fuss, you three come up the fire escape and go in through the back. I'll give you my key. I've got a spare to his balcony."

Piper rubbed her brow. "I don't know about Lou climbing the fire escape in her condition."

"I can do it," Lou said.

"Maybe your power will come back soon," Dani said. "Last time she got too much sun, and then the sun set, she cooled off, and it came back."

Piper checked the clock on her phone. "We've got hours before sunset. I don't think we can wait."

Lou flinched. Piper, terrified, thought maybe she'd felt something through her connection with King.

"You okay?" she asked.

"Fine," Lou ground out.

*Geez. Sorry for asking.*

"I can get up the fire escape," Lou said. "But you don't

know what they'll do when they answer the door. They could just shoot you."

"Hopefully Lady will attack first, if it comes to that, and buy me the seconds I need to *not* get shot in the face."

"I think Mel's plan is the best one we have. She goes in the front, we come up the back and get rid of whoever is holding him. How many did you see?"

"Three. Maybe. I can't be sure how many were in the car, but the car wasn't that big."

"We can also call in Bane and the other Ravengers and see what they can do about securing the apartment. She's kinda a swing first, ask questions later person, so I'm terrified she'll make it worse."

"Agreed," Dani said. "We go in first. Secure King. *Then* we call in reinforcements to keep them from coming back."

Lou flinched again.

"Dude, are you sure you're okay?"

"I'm *fine*."

"We can't go up against the mafia without weapons," Dani said. "That's ridiculous."

"You have your pistol, babe." Piper knew this to be true because she'd been really surprised the first time Dani had showed it to her. Lou she was used to carrying guns. But *Dani*.

"I can give Mel one of my pistols," Lou said.

"No need. I have a gun in my apartment. I'll get it before I knock on his door."

"I'll give you one of my pistols," Lou said.

Piper took the gun reluctantly. This was probably the other reason why she couldn't be an agent. She didn't like guns. Even when it came to fighting bad guys, she would rather use her fists than a gun or blade.

"So we have guns and we have a plan. What don't we have that we need?"

"The bathroom," Lou said. "Let me use it, then we can go."

"And I need a shot," Mel said, going to the kitchen and pulling the rum down from the shelf.

"Me too," Dani said.

Piper lined up four shots on the counter.

"You can't pour one for Lou," Dani said. "She's pregnant."

But before Piper could take the second shot for herself, Lou had already reappeared, swept it off the countertop, and downed it.

Piper held up her shot. "If luck be a lady, I hope she's *super* into us tonight."

They clinked their glasses and drank.

**33**

───────────

King had worked for the DEA long enough to know that if the four men holding him hostage were going to blow his brains out, they weren't going to do it in public with so many pairs of eyes on him. And yet, when he'd felt the gun press into the side of his ribs and the gruff voice demanded he get into the car, he'd found himself shoved into the backseat before he could resist.

Now, sandwiched between two men in the back of a Mercedes sedan, he found himself breaking one of his cardinal rules: *never let them take you to a second location.*

The fear that he'd seriously misstepped was only amplified when the Mercedes parked outside of Melandra's Fortunes and Fixes. The men pushed him from the car, demanding that they be led to his apartment.

His mind raced with the possibilities. That they could kill him in his apartment and make it look like a suicide. Or they could shoot him here in the back alley, where they'd parked their Mercedes behind his SUV, and make it look like a robbery gone wrong.

Foot traffic was light. King saw not a soul in sight, and

knew his cries for help wouldn't be heard over the thunderous music of the parade wrapping up only blocks away.

He didn't have a lot of options apart from seeing how this played out.

So he went to the door of Fortunes and Fixes, used his key to open it, hoping that every camera was capturing their faces for later identification, and led them up the stairs to his apartment.

The pain didn't begin until the door was safely closed behind them.

He'd had time to mentally prepare himself for this, at least, knowing that their cooperative tone would only last as long as he played along.

"Call her," a man declared.

Now that they were facing him, King could see that none of them were the same two who'd visited him at the agency. He assumed that they were from the same gang. What had Lou called them? The Celestials? Something like that.

"Call who?"

The man closest hit him in the jaw, and pain bloomed.

Stretching his jaw, King said calmly, "I've put a lot of people in prison. I've pissed off a lot of bad guys. If you think I know who you are or what you want just by looking at you, you're wrong."

"We are the Celesti," one man said proudly. But at least one of the four must have had some intelligence, because he immediately elbowed the man who spoke. So he, at least, knew not to give out identifying details.

That meant there was a chance they hadn't come to kill King. If they had, then it wouldn't matter what they told him. He really hoped the talker hadn't just signed his death warrant.

"We are looking for Louie Thorne," said another. He seemed the most calm of the four. If King had to worry about one of them, this was likely the one. The others seemed unable to stand still, their energy and excitement obviously getting the better of them. This one kept his gaze cold on King's.

Not good.

"Call her," the one with the cold eyes said.

"I can't. I don't have her number."

King's mistake had been in lying. Or at least, he'd told the wrong lie. He should have told an evasive half-truth instead.

But it was too late for that. They opened his phone, using his face to unlock it, and found the number labeled *Lou*.

"Then what the fuck is this?" the one who'd hit him said. They hit him several times for this lie, until King tasted blood in his mouth and was unsure if they'd split his gums or lip.

"A different Lou," he spat, doubling down. "Call it and see for yourself."

He wasn't entirely sure why he was doubling down on this. It was an instinctual move and he had no evidence it would work.

They called the number, and King held his breath.

Lou didn't pick up. And there were no identifiers in her voicemail, only an option to leave a message, which King had often done.

Angry, the man threw King's phone across the room. It struck the wall beside the television and slid out of sight.

*Don't come*, he thought. *I'm okay. Don't come.*

He wasn't sure what Lou's reaction to the call would be. But he had heard from Piper that she could feel when they were scared or hurt, so he did his best to suppress his distress with his will alone.

It helped to think of Mel.

The fact that he was alone in his apartment meant that they'd already altered Mel's vision, hadn't they? If anyone was going to die tonight, it would only be him. Mel would be safe. She would be spared.

Relief at this thought filled him. Then the pistol struck his jaw.

"You better come up with a way to get her here," the one with cold eyes said.

"I don't have a number for her. You saw for yourself. There's no one else in my contacts. How am I supposed to contact her? Email?"

This earned him another ear-ringing strike.

King fought to keep his anger down. This would be the worst time to let it get the better of him. They had the guns, after all. And he was bleeding down the front of his shirt.

King thought back to his training all those years ago, when he'd been the student. His mentor, Richard Black, had been a cold but informative man. A good teacher, if exacting in his approach.

On the subject of torture, he'd said, "Never take it personal. No matter how personal it is. They're just sick fucks who don't know what else to do with all that sickness. More importantly, pray the torture goes on as long as it can. Because when it's over, you're dead. And you don't want to be dead."

King tried to hold on to those words now.

*This is better*, he thought. *Better me than any of the girls.*

King didn't need another woman he loved to die in his arms.

There was also the fact that Lucy's urn was there on the side of the coffee table. He was doing his best not to look, lest the men catch on that it might be of value. But the more the violence escalated, the more his eyes kept sliding to the urn, his thoughts turning to Lucy for comfort.

The man with the cold eyes went over to the urn and picked it up.

"Who is this?" he asked, tapping the side of it with his gun.

"My wife," King said.

The man pressed the end of his gun to the urn. The fear that spiked in King was irrational. It was a container of ash. It wasn't like the man could shoot Lucy. Lucy was dead, he reminded himself. Even if they hurled the ashes off the balcony, nothing would change that.

"How do we contact her?" the man said, tapping the gun against the urn again.

King opened his mouth but no sound came out. He wasn't sure what he wanted to say.

Something sarcastic, like, *My dead wife? Ouija board, I suppose.*

Or something honest: *Please don't destroy that. It's all I have left of her.*

But even as he thought that, he realized it wasn't true. King had Lou, and he had the great-niece he'd yet to meet. Lucy lived on in both of them.

And he'd be damned if he put them in harm's way because of these assholes.

"What are you going to do?" he began. "Kill her again—"

A pounding at his door interrupted him, cutting his words in half.

"Mr. King," Mel called out. "Mr. King, I *know* you're in there, and you ain't paid your rent this month. Don't think I don't know it!"

Lady barked on the other side of the door.

"Shit," he snapped.

Not because he hadn't paid the rent. Of course he had. It was automatically debited from his account on the last day of every month.

"Mr. King. Open up now or I'm coming in with my keys!"

"No," he cried out, ignoring the men with the guns. His

fear was too great to suppress now. Whatever plan Mel had to rescue him—and she must know that something was up to come up with such a ridiculous story—he didn't want her to come into this apartment. "Mel, I'll give you the money later tonight. I promise. You don't need to do that."

"Too bad, Mr. King. I've waited long enough," she said. "I can't let this go on."

There was a weight to those last words, and King had the distinct impression that she wasn't talking about the rent.

She might as well have said, *I'm not leaving you in there alone.*

"Go to the door," the man with the cold eyes said. "Bring her in here."

King realized what he'd done wrong. The man had seen his concern for Mel and figured a live hostage was better than a vase full of ashes.

"No," King said, and dove for the man closest to him, knocking the gun from his hands.

He'd landed a punch before a boot connected with his shoulder, shoving him away.

He tumbled to a stop just beside the balcony door in time to see three figures slip off the fire escape and run across the balcony.

*Oh shit.*

*Oh shit.*

And *oh shit* had been right.

Because that was when all hell broke loose.

**34**

—————

Mel's heart knocked wildly against the base of her throat as she mounted the stairs to the apartments above her shop and crossed to King's door. Then she realized she hadn't gotten the Glock from her apartment as planned and had to double back. Her breathing wasn't any better the second time she arrived at King's door.

*Pull yourself together. You can't mess this up, Melandra.*

Lady had stayed close at her heels, and Mel had been afraid she would bark and give away their position too soon.

But the dog must have sensed that something was wrong. Either in the way that Mel crept or her shaky movements—something must have alerted the dog to the seriousness of the situation. Because it wasn't until Mel had knocked on King's door and called out that she barked.

Mel's phone pinged with a text from Piper.

*Headed up. Talk so they don't hear the fire escape.*

Mel licked her lips and shouted, "Mr. King. Open up now or I'm coming in with my keys!"

"No," he cried out. "Mel, I'll give you the money later tonight. I promise. You don't need to do that."

"Too bad, Mr. King. I've waited long enough," she said. "I can't let this go on."

She thought she heard the approach of steps across the kitchen floor and readied her pistol. If anyone else opened that door besides King, she was going to shoot them right between the eyes.

The locks on the other side of the door began to turn, and Mel knew by the clumsy way they stuck in their chambers that it wasn't King opening the door.

At the last moment, Mel stepped off to one side, raising her gun at the ready.

The door opened, and Lady shot through the gap, snarling.

This surprised the man still holding on to the frame, buying Mel the seconds she needed to raise her Glock and shoot.

The sound of it shocked her.

She'd only fired this gun once before in her entire life, intent on scaring her ex-husband, Terrence. Lou had stepped in front of the bullet at the last minute. Mel had felt horrible about that for ages, blaming herself for almost killing the girl.

That incident had happened out in the open, facing the river.

Shooting someone inside the entryway of an apartment was a different experience altogether.

It wasn't only that the sound was deafening. It was the gruesome sight of a head split open, brains splashing on the wall behind him with such vividness.

The stench was immediate, and Mel turned and threw up on the kitchen floor before she could lift the gun a second time.

The shouting, screams, and dog snarling all rang distant, as if underwater, and Mel had a second to worry she might never hear again. Maybe she had ruptured her eardrums.

Once she'd steadied herself on her feet, she turned in time to see Lou shove a blade under a man's chin and lift him off his feet with the force of her upward thrust. When she threw him to the ground, blood poured from the slash she'd made, soaking King's carpet.

Mel didn't see Piper and Dani, but Lady was tearing into a man's leg while King pummeled him in the face.

"Take it, take it!" Mel shouted, offering him the gun. Her voice sounded strange, but she thought that the ringing was finally subsiding.

King took the Glock and pressed it against the man's temple.

Mel watched the hesitation play across his face. She understood why. King was no executioner. In all their years together, no matter how close they got to death, she'd never seen him take someone's life.

Lou seemed to realize the same because the second after she killed her opponent, she turned and shot King's assailant in the face.

Mel had covered her ears this time.

"Clear," Lou said, and the balcony door opened and Dani and Piper slid into the apartment.

"Where the hell were you?" King asked.

"I told them to wait outside," Lou said.

Mel counted the dead bodies. Four. Good god, Lou had slipped into the apartment and killed three men in a matter of moments. And in her condition no less.

"Call the police," King said. "I'm sure there are more where they came from, and as soon as these assholes don't check in, they might send more. If we have a police presence outside, it might at least slow them down.

"I think we're too late," Dani said. She'd gone to the balcony door, presumably to shut it, but had frozen in place looking at something.

They joined her.

Three cars had rolled to a stop outside the shop. Mel watched as the passengers scrambled out.

"Oh shit," Piper said. "How many people is that? Ten? No, twelve? No, wait—"

"Lou, you're bleeding," Mel said. "Did you get hurt?"

They all turned to Lou, who stood on the balcony, half cloaked in shadows, a strange expression on her face. She touched her stomach and then the front of her pants. Her fingers came away wet.

"Oh my god, did you—" Piper's voice rose in panic.

"No," Lou said. "I wasn't hurt."

She met Mel's eyes.

"I think my water just broke."

**35**

———

Before Lou could process that her pants were soaked not with the blood of her enemies but because her labor was growing ever more imminent, a screeching sound cut through her consciousness.

She leaned forward over the balcony's railing in time to see a car slam into an SUV, blocking off the front of Mel's shop.

Bodies piled from this car too, and Piper gasped.

"Oh my god, that's Bane." She leaned over the railing and shouted, "Bane!"

A girl with twin braids looked up and yelled, "Don't fucking die, Genereux. That's an order."

Then, without waiting for Piper to answer, she swung her baseball bat into the skull of a man trying to exit his Mercedes SUV.

"They've blocked that second wave of cars, but that still leaves us with at least ten on their way up," King said. He checked the ammo in Mel's Glock.

Lou had been stingy with her bullets. She hadn't known how many men they were going to find in the apartment, so she'd killed three of them with a blade. This meant she still had the fully loaded Berettas she'd acquired in Piper and Dani's apartment and the guns left by the four dead men in King's living room.

Lady barked, alerting them to the first arrivals. Lou had a second to raise the Beretta and shoot.

The man coming through King's apartment door lost his skull, his collapsing body hitting the black-and-white tile with a sickening thud.

She also relieved the second, third, and fourth intruders of their skullcaps before an intense contraction ran through her and she dropped to her knees, one hand holding on to the arm of King's couch as if it could keep her in place.

Pain washed over her so strongly that she was only vaguely aware of King stepping past her and taking aim at the Celesti pushing their way into the apartment.

Lou gulped air and raised her pistol.

She squeezed off four more rounds, taking out two more men. Only one bullet went wide, blowing through a cabinet door as another contraction rolled through her.

Someone had their hands on her back.

"Breathe. Take big breaths."

Lou's anger rose. Pain always pissed her off. She yelled, "Get out of the *fucking* doorway."

King, who'd been waiting for the next wave, looked back anxiously.

Lou motioned for him to step aside with the gun.

He conceded.

"Take Lady to the bedroom," Mel said.

Lou didn't know if she was talking to Piper or Dani, but it was Dani who said, "Come on, girl. Come here."

"We need to make sure the doors and windows in the bedroom are locked anyway," Piper said.

"Breathe," Mel said again. "You can do this."

Two more men appeared in the doorway, and Lou shot them both as a contraction began. She squeezed off three rounds that she hadn't needed as she rode the wave of pain. It took conscious effort to force her hand to relax.

"You need to go to the hospital," King said. "We can handle this. Just go."

"She can't," Mel said. And Lou was deeply grateful that she didn't have to waste her breath explaining her situation to King.

Once Mel had finished, he said simply, "Oh. Then I need to call an ambulance."

He searched the room for his cell phone, finding it under the thigh of one of the corpses.

The Celesti had no patience, and that was working out in Lou's favor. They burst in shooting after they could no longer bear to wait in the hallway, screaming at each other.

By Lou's count there were eight dead on the kitchen floor.

"How many more are coming?" she asked through gritted teeth.

"I'll find out," Piper said, before calling out over the balcony, "Bane, how many are in the shop? Can you see?"

If Piper realized that shouting over the balcony's railing into the night while a firefight raged around them wasn't the best of tactics, she didn't care.

A voice shouted back, "Four! I'll get 'em. Hold tight."

Piper stepped back into the living room. "She's totally not going to get them. There are like a hundred people fighting down there. It's wild."

King thanked someone and pocketed his cell phone. "The ambulance is on its way. I don't know how we're going to get you in it, but they're coming. The police just pulled up outside, too."

Lou wanted to take off her pants. Wearing wet, sticky

pants while her stomach convulsed was in her top three worst physical experiences.

"Incoming!" someone screamed.

Lou's compass spun to life. A scream of terror rang through her, coming from that instinctual, survival-driven part of her.

But she couldn't move. The darkness still wasn't obeying her.

The building rocked and glass sprayed across the room.

Lou was thrown against the couch.

Some small explosive had gone off beside the building.

The last four Celesti burst into the room, bullets flying.

King took two bullets to the gut and collapsed. Mel shot forward and caught him, abandoning Lou to wrestle against her contractions on her own.

"Don't," Lou said, but it was too late. Mel was already at his side, shielding him with her body. Lou fired two shots, taking out two of the men, but the third squeezed off a shot that struck Mel in the leg, pulling a scream from her.

Lou was up and moving. She killed the two remaining men swiftly and also stepped into the hallway in time to shoot three more who had come into the shop through the blown-out front door. She picked off another two before Piper screamed, "They're on the fire escape! Lou! They're coming up."

Lou stepped back into the apartment and shoved the door closed, locking it.

"Get the couch against the door," she ordered, and Dani and Piper obediently barricaded the door. "Now put his bed up against the windows in the bedroom, and the four of you go in there and lock the door. Stay in there until I tell you to come out."

"I'll help," Dani said. "I'm not as good of a shot as you, but I can shoot."

"No, I need you to put pressure on their wounds," she said. If only she had her medical kit, she could have started triaging both of them. "And we don't know how long it's going to take for help to arrive."

The first man appeared on the balcony. Lou shot him in the face before he fell back out of sight.

"Go on," she said.

With the four of them—five if Lou counted the dog—locked up in the bedroom with the king-sized mattress serving as a barrier to stray bullets, she could only hope it would buy her the time they needed for help to arrive.

She caught sight of Lucy's urn on its side on the carpet, glass glittering around it like a halo.

Lou bent and picked it up, dusting off the shards, and put it back on the coffee table. She had never been the type, but right now, she felt like a prayer to her dead aunt certainly couldn't hurt.

"Lucy," she whispered. "If you can hear me, we could use a little help."

A second figure came up the fire escape and Lou lifted her pistol.

"Whoa, whoa, whoa. *Strega*, it's me! Uh, I mean Louie. *Lou*. It's just me. Bane. I'm friends with your girl, Genereux, remember? And I work for your man. Assuming he's your man, of course. No assumptions here."

Another contraction twisted Lou's guts as a young girl stepped off the dark balcony and into the light, a baseball bat in her loose grip. Lou remembered meeting her once but couldn't remember where. A contraction rolling in on top of the one she was still having brought her to her knees again, struggling to find air.

The girl bent down. "Oh shit, you're shot. Did you even know you're shot? Make that twice. Can't you feel that? You're leaking like my uncle Vinny's car."

"No." And that was the truth.

"Genereux!" Bane screamed. "She's shot!"

The bedroom door opened and Piper stuck her head out. "Bane?"

"She's *shot*."

"So are they," Piper said. "They're—God, they're not okay."

Bane disappeared into the bedroom and returned a moment later barking orders into her cell phone.

Lou turned in time to see the shadowy figures of two people on the floor, their bodies motionless.

Sirens wailed in the distance, growing closer.

*Hurry*, Lou thought. *Hurry the fuck up.*

## 36

Konstantine turned and spat blood on the floor. Somewhere, a phone was ringing. He could hear it but couldn't see it in the rummage and flames around them. He knew that it must be his people in New Orleans, calling to give him an update on Louie and Elena. But he couldn't spare the attention for that now. He and Stefano had been driven into a dead end.

Stefano's shoulder was dislocated. It hung loosely in his socket, the arm useless. He held his gun in the other hand, ready for whoever came around the corner next.

"I only have two bullets left," Stefano said.

"That's two more than me," Konstantine admitted. His gun had clicked empty in the middle of the last wave. That was why he'd been forced to dispatch the last two men with his bare hands.

Konstantine had called for help, but it had not yet arrived. They needed time.

A hand shot out of the darkness and grabbed him.

For a glorious moment, he hoped it was Lou.

But the face that swam into view snarled before slamming him down on the stone floor.

"There you are. *Sei un stronzo.*"

Ettore Celesti grinned triumphantly down on him.

With a cry, Stefano launched himself at the man, knocking his gun away before he had a chance to bring it up to Konstantine's chin. Ettore hit him hard in the head, and Stefano dropped beside him, unconscious.

Because the gun was out of reach, Ettore had no choice but to wrap his hands around Konstantine's throat and squeeze.

"She's not coming," he said to Konstantine. "She left you to die. Alone."

Konstantine drove his hand up, striking Ettore under the chin, knocking his head back. It was enough to unbalance the man. Konstantine capitalized on this momentum by bucking his hips upward and throwing him off.

He was on his feet before Ettore even finished rolling to a stop. He brought his leather boot down on the man's guts twice before Ettore caught his leg and twisted, pulling Konstantine down.

His head hit the stone floor, his ears ringing.

White-hot pain cut into Konstantine's leg, and he shot up to find that Ettore had thrust a blade into his thigh.

"I missed," the man laughed devilishly, and twisted the knife.

Screaming, Konstantine kicked out, connecting with Ettore's skull before he rolled out of reach. He pulled the blade from his leg and dove, trying to bury it in the man's throat, but was knocked away.

"*Lei non verrà,*" he said. "The woman who gave you everything isn't coming back for you. She knows a lost cause when she sees one. *Che donna intelligente.*"

*Good*, Konstantine thought. He wanted Lou to choose their daughter.

If one of them had to die tonight, Konstantine prayed to the Blessed Virgin that it would be him.

Ettore's pistol went off and a bullet sank into Konstantine's gut.

Maybe the Virgin had heard his prayers.

**37**

———

Lou felt the bullet strike Konstantine the same moment Elena slipped from her body. The silence that followed, both in the hospital room where her daughter refused to cry and through her compass, where she'd lost connection to Konstantine, was the most deafening silence of her life.

Time stretched itself into infinity.

Then Elena cried out. And thousands of miles away, Konstantine took a shallow breath.

In that moment, the full force of Lou's will and determination returned to her.

"I have to go." She placed another kiss on her daughter's trembling cheek.

"Come on. Don't do that," Piper said. "Don't go."

"I don't want to go. But I have to."

*He won't make it if I don't.*

Lou had her heart set on meeting the coming dawn with both Konstantine and Elena safe from harm's way. So she gave her daughter to one of the people she trusted most in the world and slipped from the hospital room.

The relief that overtook her when her power returned, when it obeyed her again as if it had never left her at all, was immeasurable.

Her legs were weak beneath her, and she was bleeding profusely between them, her thighs sticky with it. But she would have to push on to save Konstantine.

When she used her compass to reach for him, she touched his pain loud and clear. He was fighting to mask it. She could sense that too, but now that Elena's power had been disentangled from her own, Lou's senses were heightened.

*Help me pull this off. Please*, she prayed. But she wasn't sure who she was praying to. Her dead father? Lucy? God?

Anyone, she realized.

She'd accept the help from anyone, anything.

When the world reformed around Lou, the darkness breaking open around her, there was Konstantine on the flat of his back, shoved against the stone floor. Ettore was astride him, his hands wrapped around Konstantine's throat.

Without thinking, Lou launched herself forward and struck the other man across the back of his head. This drew fire, but Lou didn't wait. She grabbed hold of Konstantine and slipped.

The burning church melted away, and in its place was the antiseptic stench of the hospital she'd just left.

"*Amore mio.*" He grabbed ahold of her. "*Meno male.*"

Lou helped Konstantine to his feet.

"Stefano," he said.

"I'll get him."

"Wait!"

But Konstantine's words were swallowed by the dark, and a realm of chaos and flame greeted her again.

Stefano's face was bloody, his chest soaked through. He looked all but dead.

Yet his eyes rolled in their sockets when he saw her. "*Strega.* I tried—"

"I know. And he's safe now." She pulled him away from the wall where he'd hidden himself the same moment that Ettore caught her eye. His raised his gun, but Lou pulled Stefano through the dark before he squeezed off a single shot.

Konstantine was still sitting in the dark where she'd left him. He leaned forward, spitting blood onto the floor, clearly trying to catch his breath.

"He needs a doctor," Lou said, placing Stefano beside him. "You both do."

"And you, *amore mio*," Konstantine said. "You're bleeding on the floor."

"I have to go back," she said.

"No, please. *Ti prego, no.*"

"This isn't over until he's dead, and you know it."

A cry cut through the air between them, and Konstantine's head snapped to where it had come from.

"Go meet your daughter," Lou said, kissing him tenderly. "I *will* be back."

**38**

___

Ettore struggled to regain his composure. That bitch hadn't come to fight him. She'd taken Konstantine and left like a coward.

Fury consumed him, and with nowhere to direct it, he fired several shots into the flames.

This did nothing to quell his rage.

"Fucking finish this!" he screamed, spinning a slow circle in the room.

The moments stretched on as disbelief soured in his guts, his face hot from the encroaching fire.

One of his few remaining men appeared at his elbow. "Sir, we need to leave."

"No," Ettore shouted. "No, she will come."

*She has to. She fucking has to.*

"*Ma signore*—"

The man's words were cut short by the bullet slicing through his temple.

Ettore whirled, gun raised.

There she was.

*La Strega.*

Her hair was damp with sweat. The circles beneath her eyes as dark as bruises. And she was soaked in blood from the waist down. Had the crazy bitch given birth then come here to kill him?

Just the idea sparked a laugh from him.

And he found that once he started laughing, he couldn't stop.

"Konstantine was mine," Ettore spat once he was able to suck enough air into his lungs. "You keep taking what's mine. *Sei una puttana pazza.*"

"He was never yours," she said.

She squeezed six rounds out as Ettore ran, diving behind a pillar as a bullet bit into its surface, spitting dust.

He leaned out and squeezed off two shots before the gun clicked, empty. He fell against the pillar, searching his pockets for ammunition.

Before he could reload, a fist slammed into the side of his head.

He stumbled away from the pillar. As soon as he was clear of its protection, the witch fired on him. Eight bullets struck the vest under his shirt with a fierce *thwack thwack thwack.*

When her only gun clicked empty, she threw herself at him, knocking him to the ground with the momentum of her body.

Beneath her, he found it impossible to buck her off. It was as if the gravity had intensified a hundred-fold. She bore the weight of five men, pinning him into the floor, leaving him breathless.

Again and again she pummeled his face, until he got his elbows up to block her. As soon as he did, she slid a blade into the gap above the vest and into his armpit.

Pain consumed him.

Screaming, he bucked her off at last, satisfied to see her hit the stone floor hard.

*She can't breathe.*

He saw her struggling to push herself up onto her hands and knees. She might be *La Strega*, but she was not her best tonight. The blood loss, or perhaps whatever battle she'd survived in New Orleans, had weakened her.

Emboldened, Ettore pulled himself to standing.

"After all this, after all these years, you're going to die just like him," Ettore said, ejecting the empty magazine and searching his pocket for a new one.

"You killed all the Martinellis, Petrov, Yamamoto, Padre Leo's boy—all of them, but you can't kill *me*."

Her eyes were glossy, her hand pressed to her abdomen. She pulled it away and the palm glistened with her blood.

"Here you are making the same stupid mistake as your father. You will fail. Like he failed."

He found the spare magazine and shoved it into place.

"You're going to leave behind a daughter just like he did."

He bent and pressed the loaded gun into the side of Louie Thorne's head.

"All this time, all this fighting, and you've changed *nothing*."

WHEN LOU THORNE HIT THE STONE FLOOR, DIZZINESS overtook her. Despite the intense heat thrown by the flames, she felt cold, shaky.

*I'm losing too much blood.*

She'd thought she had more time to kill Ettore. She knew she wasn't steady on her feet and the exhaustion was catching up fast—but still, she'd been certain she had more time.

When she tried to push herself up to face Ettore, it felt like something tore inside her. A stabbing pain shot through her navel, winding her.

She tried to draw deep breaths, reaching for the Beretta just beyond her grasp.

"All this time, all this fighting, and you've changed nothing," he said. His voice was low, almost seductive.

*All this time, all this fighting, and you've changed nothing.*

That wasn't true.

Everything had changed for Lou in the years since her father's murder.

When her parents died, Lou was a scared little girl who didn't know how to wield the power threatening to consume her. She was so lost, so heartbroken by his absence, that the malignancy of revenge spread through her like wildfire. For years it drove her to hunt and destroy every man responsible for her loss. And when eradicating those fiends hadn't proven enough to subdue the misery eating her alive, she'd started killing anyone and anything that caused harm in the world.

Then came Konstantine. Her friends.

Elena. The light to her darkness.

Every one of them, day by day, transmuted the pain inside her. Every kindness, every act of loyalty, courage, love, and friendship. She hadn't noticed it happening in the moment, but now, looking back, it was unmistakable.

They had changed her.

They had changed her from someone who wanted to burn the world to the ground to someone who had a reason to protect it.

Lou wasn't alone anymore.

She had people worth fighting for.

Because they loved her, *she* had become a person worth fighting for. Or maybe—as her father would have certainly told her—she'd always been worth fighting for.

It wasn't until now that she'd allowed herself to believe it.

And the person who needed to fight for her now was herself.

Ettore held his gun pressed to the side of Lou's head, angling himself so he could look into her eyes.

"You must be very tired," he said. "When my wife, Sofia, gave birth, she slept for days after."

He was looking at her lips. He leaned forward as if to kiss her.

Lou's hand found the gun it had been groping for.

"You can rest now," he whispered, his breath hot on her mouth. "I will be sure to send Konstantine to you very soon. And your daughter. We can't have this cycle repeating itself, can we—"

Louie pulled the trigger.


ETTORE HADN'T SEEN THE WITCH LIFT THE GUN FROM THE floor and point it at his chest. She had looked so defeated, so weak and breathless, that all of his attention had been fixed on her dark eyes.

Just maybe he'd allowed himself to become a little mesmerized by the flames dancing inside them.

But the spell was broken when the force of the bullet knocked him back off his heels. It struck the vest, but that was still enough to overcome his balance. He hit the flat of his back, and before he could get his gun up, she was on him, squeezing two more shots off before he could stop her. One hit his vest, but the second hit him in the neck.

A burst of gunfire erupted around him, and he had a moment to hope that his men would shield him until they could patch this flesh wound.

But their cries told him they were running away, not toward him.

And this was no flesh wound. The blood bubbling up was generous, and he could feel his rapid pulse in his fingers.

She wrenched his vest open, exposing his chest, and

shoved the gun against his heart. He fought her off with his free hand, but it was no use. The room was spinning.

She emptied the Beretta. Every bullet struck home, lodging itself in his chest.

He tried to raise his gun, but she took it from him the way a mother takes a toy from an unruly child.

*Why my chest? Why not my head or—*

"No quick death for me, *Strega?*" His words were too wet. Blood spurted from between his lips. He wasn't even sure she understood him.

Maybe that was why she made no reply. She only knelt down in front of him and looked him dead in the eye.

"You must be very tired," she whispered, a ghost of a smile playing across her lips. "You can rest now."

Surely Ettore was hallucinating. The room was growing darker, and it seemed to cling to her, emanating from her the way light shines from the moon.

Then the church fell away, and he felt the sudden splash of cold, unforgiving water.

*She's going to drown me in her lake. She's going to hold me under until I stop breathing.*

But strangely, the cold waters warmed, and he broke the surface in Lou's arms.

*Where are you taking me?*

He wanted to ask but couldn't find the words. His voice was gone altogether.

So he couldn't ask Louie Thorne anything.

Not about the stench of sulfur choking his nostrils.

Not about the twin moons in the sky.

Not about the death screech of some creature calling out to them across the twilight.

## 39

Robert King wasn't sure what had happened until he opened his eyes and saw the familiar sight of the hospital ceiling above him.

*I gotta stop doing this,* he thought. *I'm too young for all these hospital visits.*

When he tried to sit up, he realized he couldn't because of a weight on his abdomen. He looked down to find a dark head lying on him, two arms draped over him protectively.

Mel's chest rose and fell softly as she slept, a tube running from the crook of her right arm up to an IV bag. It looked as if she'd thrown herself across him and fallen asleep that way.

She couldn't possibly be comfortable.

Unable to resist, he placed a hand over hers. When that didn't disturb her, he ran a thumb over her smooth cheek.

Her eyes fluttered open. For a moment, they remained glassy with dreams. Then she blinked, her expression brightening.

"Oh my god." And just like that she was in his arms, gripping him as if she were never going to let him go. "Thank you, thank you, thank you."

He had no idea who she was thanking, either him or God, he gathered. But he was happy to have this chance to hold her.

"Did you get hurt?" he asked.

"Not like you," she said. "They had to bring you back a couple of times. For a minute I thought you were giving up on me, Mr. King."

"No," he said, and placed a kiss on her hair. "Never."

Something passed over her face then, and the shift was so sudden, King was afraid she was about to tell him some terrible news. That maybe one of the girls didn't make it. Or Lou.

"Did something happen to—" he began nervously.

"No," she assured him. "I told myself that if you woke up, I'd tell you the truth, and I mean to do it."

His heart sped up, and the traitorous monitor announced this fact.

"I love you," she said.

He wasn't sure he'd heard her correctly. He had just woken up from a near-death experience, after all.

"I love you, but I don't know that I can be in a relationship with anyone, not even you." She ran a hand down her face. "I spent so much of my life tangled up in Terry's bullshit, believing that I belonged to him, that I just don't know what it means to be in love with someone. I only know that I don't want to belong to anyone but *me*."

It was true that her husband had left her life for good only two and a half years ago.

"I understand—"

She pressed a gentle hand over his mouth.

"*But*," she said, "I want you with me. I want you *here*. I don't know what will happen. I don't know what we'll become tomorrow or in ten years. All I know is that I want you close.

That became abundantly clear to me when I thought I'd lost you."

His hold on her tightened.

"I'm not going anywhere," he promised.

She softened against him. "Say it again."

"I'm not going anywhere," he said, and squeezed her tighter still. And it was true. What did it matter if Mel took all the time she needed? Or even if she decided that she didn't want to have that kind of relationship in the end? It changed nothing for King. As long as she wanted him around, he would be. "Because I love you too."

She smiled up into his face, her cheeks filled with color. She was more beautiful than ever.

Their moment was ruined when the door opened and Piper stepped into the room holding a giant glass of water.

"Holy shit, you're alive. *Man*," she cried. "You have any idea what you put us through? You flatlined *twice*."

"Tell him," Mel said.

"I just did. I—"

"No," Mel said. "Tell him what you need to tell him. I just did my confession, it's your turn."

"Oh." Piper stiffened. "I mean, he just woke up. I don't know if it's really important—"

"*Tell him.*"

King was certain he'd missed some important conversations while lying in his death bed. But he was equally sure that whatever Piper had to tell him, it wouldn't put a damper on the high he was riding at Mel's confession—*I love you. I want you here.*

Mel pinched her, and Piper blurted, "Ow, I don't want to be an agent!"

King couldn't have been sure what he'd expected to hear, but that wasn't it.

"What?"

Piper sank into the empty chair at his bedside. "I just know that if I go down that path, I'll only be doing it to prove myself. And to make you proud of me. Being an agent won't make me happy. I don't want to do the work people tell me to do or go where they want me to go. I want to work with you and Lou, doing what's important to *me*."

One look at her told him that she was bracing herself for his reaction. King had a moment to wonder what reason he'd given her to believe that he would be disappointed in her for putting her own happiness first.

"You have nothing to prove," he said. "And I'd never want you to do something just to make me happy."

Her shoulders relaxed. "Really? I thought your heart was set on my going to Quantico and doing the whole training like you and Jack did."

That might have been true, but King would no sooner say that now than let someone pull out one of his good teeth. Besides, he knew firsthand that the agent path wasn't for everyone. His own traitorous partner shouldn't have been an agent, for starters.

"You don't need the training," he told her. "You're already a badass."

"Oh man. You know just what to say." Piper burst into tears and threw her arms around him. He patted her back while she sniffed, and when she was done, she said, "I mean, I want *some* training. When I finish my degree, I'm going to do one of those intensive certification courses that specialize in surveillance, digital forensics, interviewing techniques. All the cool stuff."

He was happy to see the relief in her face.

"You don't need to be an agent to do this work. As long as I'm alive, you'll have a job at the Crescent City Detective Agency," he said.

"Which will be forever then," Mel said defiantly. "As I am

abundantly sure we've made it clear that you are not allowed to die. Ever."

And that's how King found himself in a hospital room with two people he loved hugging the hell out of him and feeling like the luckiest man alive.

In a million years, he would never be able to explain how, but in that moment, he'd felt Lucy's presence in the room.

A happy presence. A contented presence.

He pulled his girls—two of them anyway—a little closer.

*Thank you, Lucy. Thank you for keeping us safe.*

Somewhere, a baby cried, and Mel's expression sweetened. "That reminds me. There's someone you need to meet."

**40**

———

*Three months later*

T here he is," Piper whispered from where she stood at Lou's shoulder. "The sicko."

"Do you need me to cause a distraction?" Dani asked. She continued holding the binoculars up to her face, pretending to watch birds in the trees. The three of them stood in the park not because they wanted to take in the majesty of nature but because this was where they'd managed to track Marcus Vale.

"No need," Lou said. She could see her target just fine. She kept her eyes trained on him as he bent down in front of a dog and began petting him.

The woman continued to smile, nervously, clearly forced to make awkward conversation as the young man pulled out his phone and took a picture.

"Un-fucking-believable," Piper said. "Did he learn *nothing?*"

"Maybe he doesn't know that's what gave him away," Dani

offered, stealing a glance. "Or maybe he thinks that he's far enough away from NOLA to get away with it."

Lou thought that was most likely. As she heard it—and she had heard the story no fewer than forty times from the incensed Piper before Lou finally broke down and said they could just take care of him themselves—the police had gone to the home of Marcus Vale to ask him some questions and he'd bolted out the back before they could.

They found an unconscious girl hidden in an unfinished part of his parents' basement. The parents had spent the summer on a cruise, unaware of how their son was using their house in their absence. Finding a girl had been enough to charge him, but he'd managed to evade the authorities since.

"There he goes," Piper said. "Grab him before I choke him out myself."

The guy was hardly Lou's first sexual predator, nor did he have half the combat skills that she was used to defending herself against. For this reason, it required almost no effort on her part to shift through the shadows, appear behind the man, and deal a swift blow to the back of his neck that rendered him unconscious.

He fell to the grass in a heap. The girl he'd been talking to yelped and took off at a run. They watched her go, her dog yipping at her heels.

"That was amazing," Dani said as she bent and zip-tied the man's wrists together, then his legs.

"He went limp like a freaking doll," Piper said. "God, it was beautiful. And it looks like your power is working great. That was so smooth."

"I'm convinced it was just Elena's power interfering." In fact, if Lou wasn't mistaken, she felt stronger and more connected to her power than ever. Still, since her gift had returned to her, she had a newfound appreciation for her ability. The best moment was when they'd brought Matteo,

Gabriella, and the other orphans home to Florence. Lou had basked in the warmth of their elation for days.

"*God*, let's not talk about it," Piper moaned. "Every time I think about our baby having superpowers, my anxiety goes through the *roof*. Let's just get this guy to the station before I spiral."

Before they'd even arrived at the park, Lou had offered to give the killer a one-way ride to La Loon, but Piper had objected. She wanted to provide Willa's family closure by letting them see their daughter's killer behind bars.

"Wanna grab something to eat after?" Dani asked. "I could really go for some Japanese. What about that little ramen place we love in Tokyo?"

Lou was about to agree when a chord of terror shot through her.

Konstantine.

"I can't," she said. She told them of Konstantine's distress call.

"You better drop us off in NOLA and go then," Piper said.

Lou left Dani, Piper, and their catch near the police station before stepping into the shade of an oak tree.

When she emerged from the bedroom closet in their Florentine villa, she found Konstantine pacing the floor.

"*Amore mio*," he cried upon seeing her. His hair was disheveled and his eyes desperate. "You have to find her."

"Find who?"

"Elena. I put her in her crib, and I got into the shower, and when I got out she was gone. *Lei è scomparsa.* Maybe her room was too dark. Maybe she slipped like you do and—"

Lou held up a hand to silence him, and he broke off immediately. Lou threw her net wide, her compass scanning the world for her daughter.

"She hasn't left. She's still here," she said.

"She's not. I swear, I looked everywhere."

Following the pull within her, Lou crossed to the crib and looked down into it. It did appear empty.

Konstantine pointed vigorously at the crib. "I put her *right there*. I swear it."

It *looked* empty, but Lou's compass couldn't be wrong. She extended her hand into the crib.

Her fingers brushed soft cotton, settling on something solid.

"Elena," Lou whispered.

There was a shimmer, and her daughter blinked back into visibility.

Lou couldn't contain her smile. "She never left. She was just hiding."

"*Meno male.*" Konstantine collapsed with relief onto their bed.

Elena's eyes blinked open, and when they alighted on Lou's face, she broke into a grin.

"Naughty girl." Lou lifted her from the crib and held her. "You almost gave your father a heart attack."

Konstantine continued to swear in Italian, his hands covering his face.

Kissing Elena's soft head, Lou said, "You know, I couldn't be trusted not to use my power when I was sleeping either. Not for a long, *long* time. But it's okay. We'll work on that."

"Her gift is invisibility? Not traveling as you do?" Konstantine asked with half curiosity, half desperation.

Lou wasn't sure what to tell him. She wasn't even entirely sure of the truth herself. She had suspicions. That Elena could control the light the way that Lou controlled the darkness. That her ability to become invisible was simply her manipulating the light around her, a variant of her power, which Lou had expected. But would she ever be able to travel via the light the way Lou used shadows? Would she ever have that strange connection to water or La Loon?

Lou didn't know.

"My gifts progressed over time," she told him. "I'm sure hers will grow and change too."

The only thing Lou felt she knew for sure was that Elena would be powerful. Strong.

And Lou was more than happy about that.

Strong and powerful meant safe.

Konstantine rose from the bed and wrapped his arms around them. Into Lou's shoulder, he said, "I don't know if I can handle it, *amore mio*. My heart almost burst."

"Of course you will." Lou wrapped her free arm around him, holding him close. "Together we'll find a way."

# GET YOUR THREE FREE STORIES TODAY

Thank you so much for reading *First Light*. I hope you enjoyed Louie's story. If you'd like more, I have a free, exclusive Lou Thorne story for you. Meet Louie early in her hunting days, when she pursues Benito Martinelli, the son of her enemy. This was the man her father arrested—and the reason her parents were killed months later.

You can only read this story by signing up for my free newsletter. If you would like this story, you can get your copy by visiting ➜ www.korymshrum.com/lounewsletteroffer

I will also send you free stories from the other series that I write. If you've signed up for my newsletter already, no need to sign up again. You should have already received this story from me. Check your email and make sure it wasn't marked as spam! Can't find it? Email me at ➜ kory@korymshrum.com and I'll take care of it.

As to the newsletter itself, I send out 2-3 a month and host a monthly giveaway exclusive to my subscribers. The prizes are usually signed books or other freebies that I think you'll enjoy. I also share information about my current projects, and personal anecdotes (like pictures of my dog). If you want these free stories and access to the exclusive give-aways, you can sign up for the newsletter at ➜ www.korymshrum.com/lounewsletteroffer

# ACKNOWLEDGMENTS

Here we are with our *twelfth* Shadows in the Water book finished and done.

This is where we drop the curtain and share a round of applause.

First off, many thanks to my amazing production team. Hats off to The World's Best Editor: Toby Selwyn. A round of applause The Most Excellent Cover Designer: Christian Bentulan.

And we certainly can't forget my ever-enthusiastic critique group, The Four Horsemen of the Bookocalypse. Katie Pendleton, Angela Roquet, and Monica La Porta. Monica in particular does a great job correcting all the Italian and of making sure I understand Italy's food culture. *Grazie*!

And we can't wrap up these thank-yous without acknowledging my lovely street team. Thank you for reading the books in advance, reporting those lingering typos, and posting honest reviews. Your continued support makes the work worth it.

And last but not least, there's my beautiful wife, Kim, and The Cutest Dog in the World, Maximus Courage—without whose company I'd be too sad to write stories like this one.

Everyone listed above is perfect and can do no wrong. Therefore, any remaining errors in the book are my own.

# ALSO BY KORY M. SHRUM

**Dying for a Living series**

Dying for a Living

Dying by the Hour

Dying for Her: A Companion Novel

Dying Light

Worth Dying For

Dying Breath

Dying Day

**Shadows in the Water series**

Shadows in the Water

Under the Bones

Danse Macabre

Carnival

Devil's Luck

What Comes Around

Overkill

Silver Bullet

Hell House

One Foot in the Grave

Blood Rain

First Light

**Castle Cove series**

Welcome to Castle Cove

Night Tide

## The City 2603 series

The City Below

The City Within

The City Outside

## The Borderland series

Blade Born: A Borderlands Novel

## Standalone Novels

Jack and the Fire Eater

## Short Fiction

Thirst: new and collected stories

Final Cut: stories

## Nonfiction

Who Killed My Mother? a memoir

A Well Cared for Human: self-love strategies for transforming pain
into power

## Poetry

Birds & Other Dreamers

Questions for the Dead

You Can't Keep It

**Learn more about Kory's work at www.korymshrum.com**

# ABOUT THE AUTHOR

USA TODAY bestselling author Kory M. Shrum has published more than thirty books including the bestselling *Shadows in the Water* and *Dying for a Living* series.

She is the host of two podcasts: *Who Killed My Mother?* a true crime podcast about her mother's tragic death, and a second show, *A Well Cared For Human*, which focuses on debunking self-care myths, while offering concrete strategies for improving one's mental health and personal power.

She also publishes poetry under the name K.B. Marie.

When not writing, podcasting, or planning her next adventure, she can usually be found under thick blankets with snacks.

She lives in Michigan with her equally bookish wife, Kim, and their very spoiled rescue dog, Max. Learn more about Kory and all the mischief she gets up to at www.korymshrum.com

www.ingramcontent.com/pod-product-compliance
Lightning Source LLC
Chambersburg PA
CBHW071213210726
48293CB00002B/412